G000253412

'This is a heartbreaking but
portrait of love, betrayal, re
unflinchingly at our societal fa
mistake we make when we fa:

'*Constance* is a novel about possibility – what our world may yet
become and what terror and love can be found by those trying to
survive it. Zigmond's writing transports us effortlessly across time,
dropping us into cities in our past, present and future with ease.
Unsettling and beautiful with a tantalising narrator who readers
will be desperate to pin down.'

'Witty and bleak, uncanny and humane, Zigmond's *Constance* does
not flinch from the truth. This beautiful novel gives us the strength
and pain of being young, the lessons and loss of growing up – and a
prophecy of the future, already inevitable, in which even our losses
will be taken away.'

'A multilayered novel that beautifully observes the complex nature
of longstanding friendships and the giddy immediacy of new love.
Incisively witty yet deeply sensitive to the concerns of our age.'

'Elegant, sharp, heartbreaking and deeply human . . . It dances
on ruined surfaces, falls into hope, flirts with beginnings, denials,
and the indulgence of memory as a fiction. It's a searing exposé of
the mutation of male desire. It questions what is toxic and what
is catalytic in a lifetime, and what can be both . . . Astonishing.'

CONSTANCE

JOSEPH ZIGMOND

THE
INDIGO
PRESS

THE INDIGO PRESS
50 Albemarle Street
London W1S 4BD
www.theindigopress.com

The Indigo Press Publishing Limited Reg. No. 10995574
Registered Office: Wellesley House, Duke of Wellington Avenue
Royal Arsenal, London SE18 6SS

First published in Great Britain in 2023 by The Indigo Press

Joseph Zigmond asserts the moral right to be identified as the author of this
work in accordance with the Copyright, Designs and Patents Act 1988

A CIP catalogue record for this book is available from the British Library

This is a work of fiction. Names, characters, places, and incidents are
products of the author's imagination or are used fictionally and are
not to be construed as real. Any resemblance to actual events, locales,
organisations, or persons, living or dead, is entirely coincidental.

ISBN: 978-1-911648-56-7
eBook ISBN: 978-1-911648-57-4

Cover design © Luke Bird
Art direction by House of Thought
Cover photo © Romann Ramshorn/Millennium Images
Typeset by Tetragon, London
Printed and bound in Great Britain by TJ Books Limited, Padstow

MIX
Paper from
responsible sources
FSC
www.fsc.org
FSC® C013056

*For Charlotte, for your love, imagination,
and an education in being brave.*

I have often had the fancy that there is some one myth for every man, which, if we but knew it, would make us understand all he did and thought.

—W.B. YEATS

By 2064, rising water levels have caused ten years of catastrophe in South-East Asia, India and the Pacific. After crises in China, Brazil, New York, New Orleans, the Nile Delta, Spain, and the Netherlands, the West has responded by shutting international borders, rationing food and limiting almost all vehicle and aviation usage. Citizens are granted finite carbon credits to spend on luxuries like air travel. In the UK, each citizen is entitled to one lifetime return long-haul flight credit via a cap-and-trade scheme. They are entitled to use their credit at any time, or they may sell it back to the government at a high premium.

Most choose the money.

In time, he will remember the foyer as sandstone, but in fact it is pale green plaster, limewashed and cool to the touch. He will forget how he rests his weight against it, in full sight of the staff, and waits for his inhales to supply the demand of his exhales. There's a lag in his vision too, a tremble of his knees, and somehow the certain knowledge he is going to fall. I am gone, he thinks, I have lost myself, I am not myself, I am not. And the humiliating prospect of being helped to his feet is matched only by the fear of not being helped at all. How low he has come.

But his breathing begins to rebalance. The air, mixed clove and vanilla, returns and he knows he won't collapse, he will see it through. I am vertical, he thinks, I am still here, I was always going to be fine. His recovery is quick, accelerated by pride. He walks to the atrium with only a slight hesitation, taking his reader from his bag. He tests his heart rate, breathing, blood sugar; he is an old man, they say. Part of him regards this, even now, as an outright error. As he turns in the corridor, he leans once more against the wall to fish out a tablet or two. It's as much an excuse to rest again as anything else.

The only sight he will later recall, as he reaches the atrium, will be of her. But at the time he is struck by the desolation of the place: the mosaic of broken glass lining the ground, shredded wires like spiders' webs across the corners, a perfect shell hole in the roof where pigeons now roost. A set of revelling Westerners is packing up, either drunk or high on kif, or intoxicated by their power to break the silence of the courtyard. The smell of their food, half eaten, half destroyed. Honeyed fazuelos, ripped to ribbons, which the waiter gathers carefully, licking his fingers between sweeps.

Between their table and hers he manages to subdue rapid breaths, and then there she is. Simply there. An old woman now. Her long hands clasped, the line of her grey fringe fraying slowly in the breeze. The tall glass of water before her seeming to hold all that she is in the heat of these ceasefire days.

1

'Dad, hurry up please.' Kat pressed the horn, which made no sound. She opened my door from the inside and I got in. 'Take your sweet time,' she said, locking the doors again.

'Sorry.'

'Why cut it so fine? You actually want to miss it?'

For the next twenty minutes she drove us through the remaining traffic lights in short bursts.

Dozens of white shoes dangled from the pylon wires. They hung across the road, marking the breeze by day, shining as the stars had done by night. Kat rolled the gearstick while we waited beneath them. A tight formation of old women hurried across in front of us, the slowest squinting at our windscreen. The lights changed. Kat hauled the car around the corner. 'Don't forget to message Mum once in a while,' she said.

'I know.'

'She cares. Don't forget.'

'I won't, don't worry.'

'No. I mean, like, don't forget stuff, Dad. Don't go bloody senile out there.' She steered around a pothole, turning into the station approach. 'You've been lucky so far.'

'I'll bear that in mind.'

She stopped the car. 'And don't forget to come home. I'm only here for another month.'

'I will. Don't worry.' I kissed her cheek.

'Drop me a line when you're on your flight. Just so we know you got through.' She drummed on the wheel. 'Are you even excited?'

'I can't risk the blood pressure.'

She shook her head. 'I guess it's just another trip for you. Like old times?' The beams of another car lit the road before us. 'Dad?'

'Sweetheart?'

'We're used to you being gone. But that doesn't mean you shouldn't come back.' A slight break in her voice. She opened the boot, looked out of the window, waiting for me to leave. 'Don't fuck this up.'

'We'll see each other in a couple of weeks.'

It began to rain. I got out and Kat locked the car, then lowered her window. 'Go round the back to avoid the protests.'

'I know.'

'And Dad…'

'Yes?'

'Please write. For once.'

I walked through the station gate to the platform. The trains were steaming. Their carriages seemed to heave in the lateral rain. We all stood and watched the driver lock himself in with a safe-deposit box which, it was rumoured on the forums, contained a lethal weapon. He was only a boy, with the kind of face that belonged on a roadside shrine to an accident.

A voice announced final boarding. Flutters of movement to the doors. The ghoulish screens of dozens of readers blinking as passengers presented their tickets.

'Can I help you?' a guard said. The patter of the overflowing gutters grew louder.

I handed her my reader.

'You have two minutes. Find your seat.'

I

EMBRACE THE WINTER BLUES, her tag line said. As the tunnel began to vibrate, she grinned through the window, her chlorine-coloured eyes twinkling, delighted by her knitwear.

The train stuttered to a stop. From his corner seat – the best spot, in which you could ride for hours without being noticed – Ali stared into those giant, flat eyes. On the poster someone had slightly misaligned the woman's smile. Her front teeth had fault lines like sugar cubes stacked during a difficult chat.

This was what he did when he was drunk. Other eighteen-year-olds were out being young and free, but Ali rode the Tube, watching people, taking photos, reading his book, staring at the adverts. This was his safe place. He loved the cold winds that preceded the trains, and the warm smell of sooted air they left behind. He could sit and watch for hours, observing the human transfusions. Photographing the crowd scenes, the tiny details – a mouse, a lost scarf – dreaming up dramas to bind them together. But tonight he shifted in his seat this way and that, failing to lose himself in other people. Failing to get into his book as the words huddled together, shivering.

Another train floated in the black tunnel and was gone. Another Winter Blues jumper advert, this time placed beside a poster of a man in red, staring out with brash solicitation. Both models were members of that windswept species whose beautiful faces, he thought, must have more beautiful thoughts. Now a station flickered through the windows, people flashing in and out of his vision.

The doors paused before opening, as if settling on which passengers to choose. I should get my camera out, he thought, and yet did nothing. But then he noticed the doors. Huge letters scratched into them, reading HATE MARIA. One word etched into each door.

Ali was drunk. 'One for the road,' Stov had said, tossing ice cubes like dice into his glass. That one had been a triple. Though it was only 6 p.m., Ali was pretty far gone.

He sat up, looked closer. What had Maria done to make someone so upset? Now HATE and MARIA split and disappeared as the doors opened. It was hard to be sure they had been there at all. Ali blinked.

Somehow those two words were the beginning and end of it all. Even years later, whenever he heard the name Maria he would think of this pair of doors.

At once the carriage was filled with perfect little scenes. He almost summoned the effort to remove the lens cap, but again the booze slackened him in his chair. A string of girls filed on and chatted, tourists pointed on a map, a uniformed Tube worker picked his way through to slump into a seat and hug his rucksack. A near-identical mother and daughter stepped on and exchanged uncomfortable glances as the girls began to sing loudly, sniggering between choruses. And finally, just as the doors were closing, a young couple jumped on. A girl and a boy, his age. The girl was smiling. A private smile, but impossible to ignore – a smile for herself.

Ali opened the book to read the top paragraph once more. He read it twice. Three times. Then he slowly sat up.

He had to look. Had to. He knew he was a cliché, and she was just a face, one of millions. And hadn't he fallen for faces on the train before? Or cherished the screen of hair that hid their features, sparing him the heavy blows of longing? Probably on this carriage, even.

Crushes, Ali knew, were simply the snap decisions of biology, the speculative creation of a perfect whole from a few parts. But still he watched, putting his headphones over his ears as though they could hide him. Was there anything so different about her? He pressed shuffle a few times, and finally a slur of strings poured into his ears. A solo violin circling two cellos as they plucked, searching for its cadence. He hadn't missed the stonewashed green of her eyes, the muscles of her neck, but there was something about the smile. The lips. Ovate, absently bitten, they parted as if they could taste the air, and approved of it. Here, he finally saw charisma for what it was: the conscious possession of confidence.

It fascinated him, immobilized him. Her confidence. It was lightning in a bottle; he knew because he was a bottle with no lightning. He knew only how to recognize it, never how to have it.

He weighed the book in his hands, turned it over and inspected the barcode. Anything not to read. It wasn't clear to him why he was this way. Perhaps because he was an only child. Not the isolation, but the cause – he carried the guilt for his mother's infertility, which had been a consequence of his birth. If, in the immediate aftermath, the relief of his delivery had outweighed the distress over her damage, then that balance slowly changed over the next few years. And by the time he was nine or ten, a grief had taken hold of his parents. A grief for siblings never made.

It wasn't punitive in any way, his parents' resentment, merely present. A discernible lack, borne out under the stress of a failing marriage. Any pet cat or hamster might carry the name of the hopes he had dashed in his wake. Any domestic argument would circle the void he had created, their frustrated voices rising in the absence of a younger infant to protect. They loved him, but he wasn't enough. He simply wasn't the whole plan, never had been. And with no sibling to confide in, he found big brothers in friends who were outsized characters. He read books. He hid on trains. And once in a while he would catch sight of a confidence he would never have.

It almost scared him how exhilarating it was to look; every glimpse was an erosion of willpower. Unlike the rest of their peers, she seemed so genuinely happy that he winced at the promises he would make if she were to turn and talk to him. More beautiful people must have more beautiful thoughts. For him, a crush, the random and absolute ring around the heart, was never so tight as this. He wondered if he would pass out.

The violin settled into a low hum. No longer so hesitant, it grew calm, resigned. The carriage twitched, rhythmless. The boy with her, partially obscured by the handrail, turned his head a few degrees.

It was Simon. Of course it was Simon.

Si hadn't seen him yet, so Ali hid behind the legs of the singing girls, watching the pair: Si and the girl. They were attached in some awful, typical way. Simon, muscular, rectangular, normal, checking his hair in the window, the girl in a long raincoat connected to her heels by a pair of black jeans, a tiny black tattoo visible on an exposed ankle. But at least they were standing apart. That he could bear.

Ali suddenly wished he was sober. He'd spent the afternoon smoking, drinking and watching sitcoms in the basement bedroom of Stov's house. The episodes had each begun and ended and begun again with the same status quo, making it particularly difficult to tell how long they had sat in their stupors.

'It's about the fear of age and death,' Stov had said sometime during the third series. 'They're all in inertia: one episode has no bearing on the next, time never actually goes by, no one gets any older, nothing has any consequence. It's Never-Never Land for adults.'

'I like it,' Ali murmured.

'Living in a world where today has no impact on tomorrow?'

'It's comforting.'

'It's awful, Alastair. No mistakes mean no consequences.' Stov lit a spliff without looking at the flame. He seemed to be intimately associated with the mechanism of his Zippo, fiddling with it so often that his hands carried a faint hint of gasoline. 'No consequences mean no meaning. Mistakes are what make tomorrow worth waiting for. They're the only real thing we ever make. It would be hell living in a sitcom. No, worse: it would be limbo.'

'Limbo? For unbaptized babies?'

'That's purgatory. Limbo is worse.' Stov opened a can. 'Limbo is the land of no consequence. It's an endless fridge full of non-alcoholic beer: always drinking, never drunk. Always pissing, never pissed.' Stov passed the can over. 'Everything ends up right back where it started. And you're stuck with every religious idiot ever born.'

Hours with Stov felt like days. With his grand statements and peculiar analyses, Stov pored over their adolescence absorbed in the minutiae, blind to the bigger picture around him. And then, at some point, he would lean back and make a statement that contained a truth so mysterious it might be months before anyone else in their year understood it. He had been the one to describe porn as 'lonely karaoke' and it had taken until the next school term for the phrase to catch on, which it universally did. At other times his words entered school discourse immediately, for instance when he had told Simon (whose socially insatiable parents were apt to leave him alone for days, occasionally even weeks) that 'Most people grow up. Your parents just grew old.' The silence in the classroom had been deafening.

Led by Simon, it became fashionable to mock Stov for the way he talked, his elocutions and little maxims. Simon had gathered, via his capacity for beer and girls, the elite social group – Lea, who had already done some modelling; Russell the Muscle; and Amos, who was recently doubly bereaved and owned a boat. They all clustered together daily in the school canteen, taking the corner table and enjoying the power of munificent kings. Jovially, Simon would sit surrounded by stolen desserts commandeered from younger students and make jokes for the benefit of the others on their table. Hospitality mattered to him; he shared the spoils with everyone smart enough to draw close and laugh. But to sit near yet not with him was to run the gauntlet of their outstretched legs, and any subsequent dropped trays or stumbles had to be received by their stooges with good cheer, because they all were in this together: there were no such things as victims of jokes, just jokes. Ali and Stov watched this court from the other side of the dining room, in a fragrant spot by the staff toilet.

From the back of the canteen, this group had accused Stov at various times of being 'gay', 'retarded' or a 'dork'. They imitated his bandy-legged walk and asked him if he needed an arse doctor. To their mock-spastic movements he blew kisses, to their limp wrists he rose a steady middle finger. When they broke into his locker, dipped his exercise books in the boys' toilets and returned them ('Just as a joke'), he stifled his rage and reacted only by stretching his lead at the top of every class. But he would also remember Simon's taunts forever.

Simon had been Ali's friend since they were little boys, when – before Simon's parents' particular methods took hold – Simon had been very nice. Astonishingly light-fingered in shops, he had gladly taken all the risk and given his loot generously. He would donate Ali his old Action Men, armed to the teeth. He would challenge Ali to see who could pee against a tree the longest, and when he won, Simon would wheel away in celebration without remembering to pull up his shorts first. Ali and Simon went back further than any other peer he knew, but in the last few years Si had grown into a bristling stranger. They were still friends of old. Of an embarrassing sort. So Ali had never been invited to sit in the cool corner. He and Stov sat alone.

From assembly to geography, changing rooms to the school gate, the personal enmity between Stov and Simon was ever-present. Whenever they squared off, he, Ali, their sole mutual friend, felt the responsibility to bring resolution, but seeing the situation as hopeless, he always avoided it.

So of course it was Simon standing beside this girl on the train. It could never have been anyone else. Ali felt a pang of awkwardness for having just come from Stov's house. The stigma of his association with Stov stuck to his skin like the wrong football shirt.

In this predicament, as in all the previous ones, Ali felt no choice. He had to do nothing. He sat still and avoided the stilted conversation of those who bump into one another on trains.

Grateful for Simon's tendency to study his own reflection, Ali turned away and reopened Stov's dog-eared copy of *The Blind Assassin*. It smelled of petrol. But he couldn't shake the thought of the black-haired girl with the convex mouth. How easily Simon attracted everyone. Simon with his talk. His eye for opportunity. His capacity to impersonate a twenty-something. This he got from his father, his absurdly young parents who acted the same age. They were what, late thirties? He picked at the page's edge. His own parents could have conceived them.

Simon had been brought up on Alice in Chains by people who beat him at PlayStation and believed that tax was outmoded. His father would drink with him, talk girls with him, write songs for them with him. His mother and her friends flirted with him, and gave Simon over to his father for these years of male tutelage.

For this he was roundly admired by his classmates. Parents who were on his side, who would allow him to make his own mistakes provided they could make them too. Incredible luck. It didn't seem strange that his mother called him 'bad boy' and 'hunk', his father called him 'wanker', and they all smoked and swore together. It was sophisticated, everyone agreed. And when the headmaster complained because Simon had made sexual advances to the French teacher, his father argued that the problem was that they hadn't worked. Stov had been right: Simon's parents would never grow up.

Ali shut the book and remembered how his own parents had been his close companions for the first dozen years. But in recent times he had blundered through adolescence alone, a loser – the disquieting lusts, the doubts, the new questions everywhere like some global conspiracy – ignored by his father, not even teased by his mother. He had resented both the maternal attempts to counsel him and the paternal insistence on leaving him alone. And, finally, he blamed himself for the quarrels he provoked between them all. The silences when he entered the room and the meals eaten without eye contact. His parents were nearing the end of their fifties, and the generation gap seemed to be widening. Not for Simon though, who had mates, not parents. Simon came from a font of unspoiled youth so perfectly cool you could swim in it all day and never tire.

Still, he chanced another look at the boy and the girl. It was hard to imagine them well matched, but nor could he predict the damage to be done for a lifetime to come. Simon, lost in his vanity and the girl so self-possessed. And when he looked one final time, they were gone. Ali shut his eyes, relieved, exhausted.

Suddenly, he felt a hand on his shoulder and looked up. Simon was looming over him, grinning.

'Ali, mate, how's it going?'

Ali began to get up and then stopped halfway. Crooked, unmade.

Simon gave him a quizzical look. 'Oi oi.' He squeezed Ali's shoulder affably. Ali blinked two or three times, unable to believe his bad luck. 'Al, this is Cece,' said Simon, quick to show her off. 'Cece, Ali, Ali, Cece.' He nodded. 'Ali?' There was a frown on Simon's brow. 'Mate, you OK?'

Things were moving too fast. Ali revolved in one drunken dimension, the beautiful girl named Cece spun in another field and in a third he noticed how *HATE* and *MARIA* were back together on the doors. Once again, the plight of this unknown pair filled him with sadness, destined as they were for unending reconciliation and fracture. Opening, closing, opening forever. He started to hate Maria too for whatever she had done and was aware, staring at these doors, of his heart breaking for a vandal.

The train gave a murmur.

'Ali?' Again.

'Fine, Si,' he replied. 'I'm fine. Good to see you. How are you?'

'Good, yeah. Can't complain. What you up to?'

'Nothing much.' Ali looked around, as though other words might be written on the interior. 'Where you two going?'

'Plush.'

'Plush,' Ali said, inert. 'Oh, Plush!' he then repeated, faking a worldly smile. And Cece smiled again too. He felt it, like the brush of a single hair on his cheek. She glanced from him to Simon and her mouth opened and paused. Only now did he notice how the skin on either side of her angular nose creased when she smiled, a detail he liked very much.

'It's my fault,' she said, her voice low, broken and pieced back together. 'I just want to know what Plush is like. Everybody's been. You've been, right?'

'Well…' Of course he'd never been. Never been asked, and never been brave enough to ask. And he'd never been particularly desperate to be seen there. Until now.

'Don't spoil it for her, eh?' Simon winked. He was a regular.

'I don't know if I could.' Ali looked her full in the eye and imagined what Plush must be like. 'Have you ever been frisked in a lift in a war zone?'

Simon's smile thinned.

'No?' Cece looked puzzled, and Ali was sure they were about to giggle at his weirdness. He readied himself to make his excuses, but then she laughed – really laughed – and he felt the whole train lurch. A year or so later, he'd come to know what that laugh meant: that she was nervous. But not yet.

So he went on, 'It's one of the places you have to see before you die,' and then added coolly, 'or die before you see, I can't remember which. It's where reputations are won and lost.'

'I'm not sure I want one of those,' Cece said.

'Ali,' Simon interrupted to usher him off, 'isn't this your stop?'

HATE and *MARIA* separated again; people got off.

'Yeah.' Ali moved towards the door and took the handrail, uncertain of his steps. He had no clever line to leave them with.

'Unless you'd like to come?' Cece asked, her voice higher this time. She seemed to have had enough time to take the measure of him, judge him worthy. She had mistaken him, he thought, and he'd be a fool if he waited for her to discover her mistake. 'Come on,' she said.

He squeezed the handrail to steady himself, his knuckles paling to the colour of the bones beneath.

The doors waited, still and calm as though they would remain open always, the safe option home and bed, ready with warm toast and television. An old woman shuffled past him onto the platform just as they began to beep. He looked down the gap between the train and the platform and could not see the bottom.

2

I dream of the night we met on a recurring basis. That night, and the subsequent days, are more vivid to me than any days since. My brain examines the night especially, still looking for the exact inflection point which fixed us on this course. Trying to discover when things started to go wrong.

I dream of Cece. I've spent more time remembering her than knowing her. I dream of her voice that night, calling 'Unless you'd like to come?', of her phoning me to read out favourite lines from her current book. She claimed she could read a book in a day. I dream of the sound of her voice doubling in volume as she appeared at my door, still reading into the phone. 'At the sight of these fascinating trifles which were something new to Lucien, he became aware of a world in which the superfluous is indispensable, and he shuddered at the thought that he needed enormous capital if he was to play his part as a smart bachelor.'

Then, she would close the book and ask what fascinating trifles we each needed and listen carefully to my response, before, without warning or reaction to what was being said, entering my room and undressing us both. 'Balzac to ball sack,' she'd say, dropping and stepping over our underwear as if it were a skipping rope.

And because I give in to the memories, they stay alive. We give each other life.

But then I wake. The problem is waking. The rush to the surface, the bends from going too fast.

*

'What are you doing?' said a voice from somewhere across the aisle. Scottish. The oldest couple in the carriage were chatting away, thinking they were whispering.

'I thought I was going to sneeze,' came the reply.

'Look at the light. Always works.'

'I just tried, it didn't.'

'OK, well, don't think about it and it'll happen. You're probably overthinking it.'

He sneezed loudly and the whole carriage heard.

'You see?'

The carriage briefly glowed as a dozen or so devices lit up. We had passed the threshold into a new county. Readers flashing the terms of the new area all vibrated in sync. People avoided checking them as the carriage went orange and then green, signifying new dean laws coming into effect for each owner. It was rumoured that if you tapped on the option for extra information about the new laws, they automatically listed you. No one knew for sure. The screens died away.

We all went back to our dreams.

Cece took each of them by the arm as they walked away from the station. She and Simon spoke in murmurs which dissolved in the damp air. Wind and rain swirled in the traffic beams. Ali remained the quiet third, tensing and untensing his arm in hers. He marvelled at his own drunkenness, at the grace of buses, at the syrupy roads under the sodium lights. Simon led the way across the road to the club, stepping out with the conviction that nothing would hit him.

Plush was where everyone went for the cheapest booze, the most complicit staff and the most incoherent witnesses. They were marshalled in by men with clipboards in their hands as other patrons were shown out, shivering, exchanging aimless blows or tottering arm in arm onto the grimy avenues off Tottenham Court Road. When they got inside their feet stuck to the wipe-clean floor, and all about them human nature was distilled to its most base, most profound aspects.

No single group seemed to have ownership of the club – not the rude boys, the stoners or the ravers, not the creepy old-schoolers, and certainly not the poshos. Instead, it attracted its own singular cross-section of London youth, the only common denominator being that they all knew that the PROOF OF AGE REQUIRED sign on the door and beside it the MEMBERS ONLY sign (above which someone had scrawled the word 'MASSIVE') were purely symbolic. He had heard it said of Plush that it was 'the best bad club', and also, meaning the same thing, 'the worst bad club', in London. Perhaps the greatest compliment you could pay it, Ali thought, was that there was no way of denigrating Plush without it seeming like praise.

Downstairs, Simon ordered a drink, and then so did Cece, copying his exact order word for word and slapping him on the shoulder. Then they disappeared, or perhaps he himself did, into the deep time of Plush, surrounded only by light and sound. Beats, basslines cut each second down, giving it a certain weight, slicing the minutes into shards of such equal size that by the time Cece appeared at his side to ask him for a cigarette, he hadn't any idea of the hour or why he was still wearing his coat. His relief was probably obvious to her.

'Want to go up?' she asked.

'Sure.'

'How many times have you been here?' Their voices bounced off the breeze blocks as they wound their way up the steps towards the ground level.

'Just once,' he lied. And then, in an act of self-liberation, he added, 'Once is enough.'

Cece walked in front of him, occasionally touching the wall. Others streamed by on the other side, assessing the faces they passed. Shot with pride, he watched them lingering on her, gauging him, back to her, to him, to her eyes, her figure receding. 'And how long have you known Simon?' she asked over her shoulder.

'Since I was five. Our mums were friends. My mum was the estate agent who sold Simon's parents their house.'

'That's nice,' she said. Then she added, 'You close?', but it wasn't really a question. She didn't even turn to look in his direction.

'Quite.' Quite close. 'We haven't seen each other since the end of school,' Ali admitted. He thought involuntarily of their oversized uniforms on the first day of Year Two, the day they'd met. How his pleasure in having tied a tie had been sunk by Simon's subversively fat knot.

'Since when exactly? I'm sorry, I'm asking too many questions, aren't I?'

He smiled at her. Only ones she knew the answers to. It was obvious that, in the pulsating guts of the club, Simon had told her something about school, Stov, or else an equally embarrassing fact about his past.

'Haven't seen him since a party at his house.' He shivered. 'We played the chess drinking game.'

Now Cece turned, looked at him. 'How does that work?'

'I don't remember.'

'So you lost.'

'I think so. I ended up kneeling in the front garden, rainbow-painting the rosebushes.'

'Rainbow-painting?'

'Yes, rainbow-painting, er – I threw up.'

'That's funny.' She paused to look at him, swirling her plastic tumbler.

They were outside now, the street not yet dry. A bouncer directed them along a pavement, divided by a tatty rope marking the end of Plush and the beginning of the outside world.

'Rainbow-painting,' Cece repeated quietly to herself, testing its quality. She'd picked out the term he had tried to show off with, seen how it was certainly pilfered and probably reused here for the first time. Already it seemed she knew what he was like. 'And you've grown apart since then,' she concluded.

'You might say that.'

Her left foot swivelled on its heel and pointed at him. 'And what might *you* say?' She spoke not with malice but with a certain assurance. Perhaps – a sudden doubt hovered – she was enjoying his unconvincing persona, probing the worldliness he was fabricating. Perhaps she was one of those people who was rude to get attention. It didn't occur to him, and never would, that she felt a need to be this way to preserve herself in the world of these London boys. 'I – don't know.' Anxiety filled him. He took another drink and pushed it down. He heard his thoughts distantly, like they were coming from a car radio in passing traffic.

'I'm sorry. I'm being too personal.' Cece shook her head to show she had been impolite, was reining herself in.

'So *I'd* say he cut his losses,' Ali blurted, his diction slurred. He heard it echo on the bricks above.

Cece nodded and showed no other reaction to this minor betrayal of Simon, allowed it to hang between them. They knew things for what they were and could keep a secret without needing to speak it first. A confidential matter now linked them, where previously there had been only mutual curiosity. She leaned back and sipped her drink.

'How do you know Si?' Ali asked at last.

'I don't really.' Then she added, 'We met at a gig. Can't remember who was playing – no one big – but me and a girlfriend were down in London for the weekend and got astronomically wasted. He found me slumped over the bar, trying and failing to get the barman's attention. All I wanted was a glass of water. Simon gave me his lemonade. Then tried to snog me, the cheeky fucker.' She was laughing, but Ali wasn't.

'Are you two – together?'

'What, me and Si? I don't think so.' She gave a snort.

'But you've been seeing each other?' Ali raised a hand in apology. 'Ignore me, sorry.'

'I will.' She shook her head. 'I'm surprised at you. Not that I know you.' Then she added, to close the matter, 'But I hear he fingers a girl like a hoarder looking for his keys.'

Hearing this, Ali snorted a little of his drink, which prompted Cece to send a long laugh into the open space. She imitated his frown as he wondered who exactly this information had come from. And this delighted her again.

The back of the club's exterior was closed off by squat fences and lit with stained fairy lights floating in the breeze. The cataracted bulbs wove around the branches of a small London plane tree in the centre, its roots speckled with cigarette butts and broken plastic cups. Finally remembering why they were there, he took out his cigarettes and offered Cece one. She slid it from the box and cupped it in the palms of her hands, an offering. They smoked as the wind fussed around them, sobering his hot cheeks, tugging at her neatly cut charcoal hair.

'You're a year younger than us then?' he asked.

'Seventeen last month,' she said. 'Why?'

'Nothing. You seem older.'

'You really are drunk.'

'Maybe.' He picked up his drink, forgotten at his feet. 'What did you do for your birthday?'

'Revision,' she said and leaned back against the tree, folding her arms and squinting at the club's tinted windows. Lights oozed through the branches as they swayed, creating liquid constellations which held for a second or two before taking a new shape. 'I don't get to go out much. My dad's like that. He's out of town tonight, so.'

This comment was different in tone. He gazed as she drank, slowing her sips to hide her face. The air changed.

'It's OK, I'm a loser too,' Ali blurted, his honesty surprising him.

'What?'

'No, not a loser. That came out wrong.' He gestured accusingly to his drink. 'Sorry.'

'I'm not a loser.' Her eyes flashed. 'Fun just isn't a choice for me.'

'That's right. That's what I meant.'

'*You're* the nerd. Rainbow-painting the world.'

'Guilty.'

'And you're shit at chess.'

'I am shit at chess.'

'What kind of nerd is shit at chess?'

'This kind.'

Her eyes narrowed even further, comically, so she had to feel blindly in front of her until he placed his drink in her hand, which she emptied into her mouth. 'And what are you doing with your freedom while I'm revising?' she asked.

'A job. In hospitality.' As though that sounded sophisticated. And then, flinching, he said, 'It's not really hospitality. I don't know why I said that either.'

'OK. So what is it?'

'It's a pub.'

'That's cool.'

'I know it isn't.'

'It isn't cool.'

'That's kind.'

'You're welcome.'

Cece fell silent. She finished her cigarette before dabbing it into a little clay pot on the gravel. And however little they both acknowledged it, some significant channel was beginning to connect them. A connection of rapidly increasing power.

A bassline in the earth beneath them broke their reveries. They could feel it against the soles of their shoes. Ali looked down, almost expecting to see it cracking through the street, upending the tree and bursting through the saturnine sky. The relentless pressure to be out, and seen, and drunk, and high, and on it, and out of it, and into it, and off his face, and owning the dance floor for hours and hours and the rest of his youth – this pressure ordered them back inside.

'That's the bell – end of playtime.' Cece offered another smile and a gesture which was either a motion towards the roped pavement or a flick at the wind. 'Shall we?'

'Yes,' he said, disappointed to leave this moment.

They crunched across the leaves towards the lights. 'Simon must be out of the toilet now,' she said. She turned around and faced him, continuing to walk backwards into the light, a silhouette cut from a sheet of night. 'Our friend.'

Cece had a strand of hair on either side of her fringe that curled upwards and bounced when she danced. They hung in front of her face until she occasionally flung them back. By that point Ali knew he was in trouble. When she had left him outside, a light had flickered within him, an electric twitch from his lungs to his groin, the span of his pubescence in a single hormonal dispatch. Nine charged pints of blood moved more strongly, more vividly, acid bright.

This must be more than a crush, more than the wanderings of a lonely mind. It seemed discernibly physical, like discovering a bolt screwed into the side of his head. He flushed, aware how obvious this affliction must be. Projecting from him with all the subtlety of an erection. He stood at the back and drank, intent on ignoring everything as she and Simon wiggled, hugged and chopped the air.

Ali's knees ached and his eyes were dry. Through the window outside, the plane tree moved in the wind, shaking between the sky and the street beneath. He wanted to remove the fairy lights, hung like cheap pearls around the tree's neck. He wanted to load the tree onto a vast lorry and drive far out of the city and retire it in an unnoticed hillside or wood, under some clearing in the canopy, this tree which had witnessed their conversation. He wanted to pat down the moist soil between its roots and admire the dirt beneath his nails. He inspected his fingers, the hand which had brushed Cece's arm as they had descended the stairs and he had walked into her wake of sweat and shampoo and fresh smoke.

From nowhere, an arm appeared round his shoulders, Simon's bunched hand dangling beside his neck. 'Wake up, Ali.'

He smiled. 'I'm awake!' He nodded his head to the palpitations of sound and looked around. Cece wasn't there.

'She's gone to the loo.' Simon pinched him with laddish bonhomie, gripped his shoulder once more to keep one or the other of them upright. He might have imagined it, but Simon's embrace seemed a little stronger this time. 'She's been asking about you.'

Ali stifled his reaction too late – delight escaped across his face. Simon saw it. Ali searched for something to look at, left and right across the découpaged bar, felt the conspicuous darting of his eyes, and so sought out his feet. His trainers were very white, washed by the puddles outside.

Simon's panting was close against his ears. 'Yeah. She's interested.' He shifted his weight, becoming a little unstable, his top half threatening to upend the lower. 'You got any questions? Anything you wanna know?'

Ali shook his head.

Simon next patted Ali on the chest because he was somehow deserving of it, or to show that the situation had changed to one of confidentiality – they were now speaking in their most innate language, man to man, discussing a woman. 'Isn't this how it works, Al – everyone has a question?'

Ali thought about denying it but hadn't the nerve. He looked sideways at Simon's shoes, dark leather, his toes shining in the frenetic light. 'What did she ask?'

'About you?'

'Yes.'

34

'She asked…' Simon grinned and glanced around the room to indicate that he wouldn't normally say this. 'Well, first she asked if you were a bit weird, and if you were always like this and then, well, she asked your name. She'd forgotten it. Don't be upset, pal – she's like that. All over the place.'

Ali didn't think she seemed all over the place. 'So,' he asked casually, 'what's her real name?'

'Touché, Al. It's just Cece.' Simon moved towards him again. 'As in "See see but don't touch touch."' His laughing teeth flashed blue as Ali screwed his eyes shut in embarrassment. Comments like this were the price he paid for being friends with Simon, for the drinks he bought, the people he knew. They shared the kind of sustained gaze that Simon made seem so acceptable, and the thought presented itself to Ali that your friends aren't necessarily the people you'd choose; they're just the ones who got there first.

'No, I mean her full name.'

'Cece.'

'Cece?'

'Ce. Ce.'

'Just Cece? It must be short for something.'

'That's what I thought.'

'And?'

'Cece. She said it's just Cece. Full name. She was like… Actually, let's sit down.' Simon led them to a corner table and loaded himself into a seat.

A new song filled the club, drowning the other noises so completely that they began to move in mime. The room was dominated by a singing voice, solo but duplicated, taunting but hurt. Simon twitched to it as he leaned in and shouted.

'Cece's parents wanted a boy, they were going to call him Cedric.'

'Cedric?'

'I know. It's an eighty-nine-year-old man's name. Anyway, they'd had the scan, where the nurse shows them the baby's tiny beating heart, its tiny fingers and toes,' Simon said, in a baby voice. 'And the nurse goes, "Do you want to know the little baby's sex?" They say "Yeah," and so the nurse points them to the baby's tiny baby dick – just like yours, Al, only bigger.' He tipped the remnants of his drink into his mouth and chewed some ice. 'So they're expecting Cedric, right?'

'OK.'

'And then the baby comes out and they've cleaned it up, and they notice its little dick is so little it's not even there. Cedric's a girl.' A waitress collected his glass. He ignored her. 'So, how did little Cece do that?'

The waitress turned and immediately Simon regarded her – a grayscale vest ending above the small of her back and a tight pair of shorts frosted onto her legs – in a manner so flagrant it was clear he wanted to be caught checking her out and either rebuked or applauded for his excellent eye. He allowed her to collect the final glass before touching her arm, saying 'Excuse me?' and waiting for her to turn. Then he gently finished with a 'Thank you. *Thanks*.' He issued a wink, obliging her to smile.

Simon continued. 'The nurse had mistaken a bit of umbilical cord between the legs for a dick. A big, long, curly dick.' Simon laughed. Even in this noise he was a confident raconteur, occasionally giving extra stress to his *k*'s and *t*'s to hear them bounce like casino chips on the table.

His telling of most stories was well oiled, but this, this one he told like a personal favourite. At the same time, it seemed possible Simon was making the whole thing up. Perhaps the real victim of this story was meant to be none other than credulous Ali.

Ali nodded, and then shook his head. 'You know, Si, I don't need to know –'

'Shhh. Wait. Good part's coming. The fucked-up part, I should say.'

Ali shouldn't have let Simon speak like this behind Cece's back, like a pair of creeps, but he simply nodded again, smiled and played with a two-pence piece.

Simon went on: 'They'd already painted her bedroom blue. Footballs on the walls, cars on the skirting boards, bears, "Cedric" stencilled across the cot. Nothing pink. So they get back from the hospital, they're tired and pissed off, obviously, and just put her in the cot. She sleeps as Cedric for her first week. And then the first month turns into the first year. Until her dad gets round to whitewashing the cot. They raise her as Cedric for all that time. Then finally her dad paints backwards over the *d-r-i-c* first, and, as he's doing it, her mum stops him and says she likes the *c-e* bit.

'So there she is. Baby Ce. And he never gets round to repainting it properly and so the name just sticks. Until her first brother's born. Finally the child they want. And they call him Cedric too! They just duplicated her, how dark is that?'

Simon sat back. Clearly he was expecting a reaction – laughter or amazement. When his smile had faded, or at least been replaced by something weaker, he craned in further and further, their heads getting so close it seemed their thoughts might mingle and Simon would hear Ali's suspicions.

'You should ask her. This is what she told me: she goes, "I was never meant to be a girl at all."' Finally they did touch; he felt the prickle of Simon's close crop as he croaked, 'She wants to be mysterious, you see?' A small asteroid of spittle landed on the coin as he quoted her and brought the palms of his hands down on the table. 'She's a bit nuts,' he concluded, to explain everything.

Again, she didn't seem nuts or even a bit nuts to Ali. And as an almost-friend himself, he wondered what this almost-friendship between Cece and Si was; they seemed like siblings with benefits.

But as they returned to the bar, this question on the tip of his tongue, he stopped. Because there was Stov. Stov was in Plush.

Simon wheeled round to shout in Ali's ear. 'What's that fucker doing here? Did you text him?'

'No. I've got no idea,' Ali lied, never imagining Stov would be interested in seeing, let alone capable of gaining entrance to, a club. This was not his scene. Simon was not his scene. The text Ali had answered had asked if he'd got home OK. Ali's answer had been factual, his invite not genuine. Inviting Stov to congregate with Simon was like trying to extinguish a fire with a pile of books. 'No,' he repeated nervously. But somehow he was back in the middle of this bullshit again, even though they'd all left school. He immediately pulled Stov aside. 'You came?'

Stov shrugged. 'I could tell it was a genuine invite. So I showed up with a genuine wish to be among my peers and "get down".'

'Really?'

'No, Alastair, champ. I was bored. The people-watching here is the best in town. It's the Spanish Steps of northern Europe.'

'You've been before?'

'I have. The real question is, why are *you* here?' Stov was smiling, all eyebrows and satisfaction. Thrilled to see Ali so far out of his comfort zone. 'Don't tell me you like the music.'

'Bumped into Si.' Ali avoided eye contact. 'And this girl, on the Tube.'

Stov tucked a thread of his hair behind an ear. 'I see that,' he said, noticing Ali's eyes on Cece. She was in wild splendour on the dance floor, with Si behind her, a thumb in her belt loop. 'Well, isn't this awkward.' He threw back his head as if to bask in Ali's discomfort.

Cece and Simon were coming over. Simon and Stov exchanged an acknowledgement: Simon's a particularly unsuccessful suppression of total loathing, Stov's a low curtsy.

'What have I missed?' Cece beamed. 'Hi, I'm Cece.'

'Stov.'

'Cool. Are you another regular here?' she asked.

'In no way.'

'It's my debut.'

'Felicitations. You're doing well. Only a few more hours until chucking out time. Will you make it?'

'I totally intend to.'

'If you do, you'll be rewarded with a man urinating on a church door. Possibly a woman too.'

'Actually we tend to go in the vestibule.'

'A very pious crowd,' Stov observed, indicating a group dancing like cats on a litter tray.

'Very much so.' Cece said, giving him the sincerest of looks and then chewing back a smile. Simon stared straight ahead.

No one knew who had started it, but at the root of Simon and Stov's mutual animosity was the standard alpha–geek story. It had climaxed, after two years of squabbling, with Simon goading Stov about his small physique and then Stov the following day handing Simon an upside-down note on which he had scrawled minutely *noʎ uɹɐʍ ʇ,upıp I ʎɐs ʇ,uop* and, before Si had turned it the right way up, smashing the side of a balled fist into Simon's face, knocking him down, bloodying his lips, cracking a tooth.

There had been several witnesses at the bus stop on a sleeting Wednesday morning. By that evening Stov had been expelled, but not before both boys were forced to shake hands in the headmaster's office. Some reciprocal respect was established in these proceedings (because Simon, from policy and pride, had refused to join the witnesses in grassing on Stov, while the sheer efficacy of Stov's sucker punch had won him esteem among their peers). It was only when the parents were called in that things became irreparable. Told of the mutual provocation between their sons,

Stov's mother asked, 'How is it fair then that one is expelled and not the other one?'

The headmaster explained it was because Stov had been physically violent: Simon had stitches in his lip.

Stov's mother turned to Simon's parents, Liam and Carrie. 'And you're happy with this? My son is being *expelled* and yours gets off with nothing?' She motioned to the boys in the corner, united at last in shared resentment of adult interference. 'Even though both of them had been winding each other up for years?'

'That's not our problem. We're not worried about that.' Simon's father spoke for the first time. He was slumped in his chair, his knees spread wide, an attitude of the smartest boy in the bottom set. On his head was a pair of sunglasses presenting a fish-eyed version of the office in skiing gold. He turned to Simon and raised his chin. 'Our problem is you getting floored like that.'

Everyone looked at Simon, whose fingers went to his swelling, purple lip. It was the humiliation. To be censured by his father in front of strangers, his headmaster, even in front of Stov. In the bemusement which followed, everyone realized that Stov's expulsion – which could have been avoided with a conciliatory word from Simon's parents – was impossible to revoke. Simon's man-child father had an obsession with bravado that was, in the circumstances, crazed.

In the next few days Simon, assuming Stov had spread the word of his humiliation, imagined derision all around him. He also assumed the school would learn of his failure to impress his father and so came to loathe Stov all the more. He would have done anything to have been in Stov's place: banished after a first-round knockout, discharged with full peer respect and parental support.

Yet the truth was that Stov had told only one person – their only mutual friend. 'Tell no one, Alastair,' he'd whispered. 'His dad is messed up.' Only the three of them knew, and this was how it had remained. So Simon's added spite towards Stov was groundless. But it was too late.

'Let's get a drink. All of us,' Cece suggested, and all three boys nodded, looking at nothing in particular.

Simon bought the round. Always ready with drinks.

'Thanks,' she said. 'You've got a face like a scratched bite.'

'It's nothing.' Simon put an arm round Cece's waist, and she rested her hand on top of his. 'Old school stuff.'

'Exactly.' Stov produced a smile.

Neither moved, neither would be a schoolboy in front of this woman. Simon and Stov looked at Ali. Ali looked at Cece.

'OK then. Let's do a photo,' Cece said. She motioned for Ali's camera, and handed it to the barman to take one of the four of them. Flanked by Simon and Ali, with Stov standing to Ali's side, she gave them no choice. 'Smile!'

She took the camera back from the barman.

'Perfect,' she said. 'To good times.'

3

Swinging loose, the toilet door at last collided with the wall and woke us with a bang. I didn't move. The carriage shuddered; something in the luggage rack rattled. A blurred world emerged, reassembling itself in grey.

I closed my eyes. Tried to ignore the thrumming, tried to coordinate my breath and heartbeat. I was left with an impression of absence, a blanket pulled away in the night. I was fully awake. Dawn or dusk was bleaching the air.

Another bump.

'This train!' the old man called out.

'I know.'

'I travelled on better trains than this forty years ago.'

'More.'

'You know they're still building super-fast ones in Spain? Five hundred miles an hour.'

'That's an old story, you're getting confused.'

'No? I think it's true.'

'Not for years. No one has that kind of money.'

The aluminium fences streamed by so close I could have reached out to feel them, smoothed them under my fingertips. They looked so flimsy. Feeble compared with this diesel mammoth, this unchallenged straight-line strength. Would they hold us if we derailed? Stop us from hurtling down the bank in a corkscrew of fettered carriages, glass, coffee and mud? Were those sleeping in houses at the bottom safe, or would we burst through their walls and into their world like the wreckage of a great heavenly battle?

I used to imagine what I would do in the event, how I would save myself by locking my legs against the seat in front and sliding down, pressing my back against my own seat so I was immovable and secure, while others who hadn't made plans would be tossed like rag dolls from ceiling to floor.

How much time would a person have before they realized? Half a second to get into position? Less? Assuming the train derailed from the front, perhaps enough to register a sound: the wrenching of a thing from its usual place, the shriek of a new experience from one chassis after the other. Or it might derail at the back, a giant pulling us back by a leash, causing elemental and instant conflicts of force, some parts falling to the rear, some toppling sideways, demanding decisions of physics – which should break and which hold true; who should die, who should die first. The crash fences spraying like grass clippings in its wake.

Would they give me a seat on a later plane if I survived a train crash? They always said there were no later planes, the one you were allocated was the one you got. No second chances, never an exception. But surely in the case of an accident?

The fences spread on and on under the steady glue of the sky. According to my reader, it was a Tuesday.

Ali recalled them all leaving Plush, and how he had talked to fill the stony silences. It wasn't like him, but no one else spoke, so on and on he went. He found himself saying things about the club, the patrons, the lonely tree outside and how it must have wished for death. He then remembered Stov and Cece beginning to bond instantly over favourite Janis Joplin songs, outquoting each other and scoffing at various new covers. After that, Simon had given Cece a piggyback to his house from the bus stop. And then, his arms swollen with muscle, Simon had poured them tequilas. Out of compulsion, the next thing Simon did was plug the camera into his computer to pick and upload the best images. He wasn't going to let the bragging rights of a night at Plush go unused.

After this he showed the boys where to sleep in the living room. Quite how Stov was still there no one seemed to know, but both he and Simon were determined to remain courteous in front of Cece, and so back to Simon's home Stov had come. There was no sign of Simon's parents. Simon then began leading Cece to his bedroom, and they started whispering loudly halfway up the stairs, bickering as they held the banisters. Ali and Stov crept to the open door to watch.

'I want them to sleep with us.' Cece cleaned out her shot glass with a finger.

'What?'

'I want them to sleep with us.'

'What do you mean? In the bed? Four of us?'

'No, don't be stupid! They can go on the floor – like a sleepover.' She touched Simon on the chest. 'You can't leave them down here, it kills the fun. I want everyone to be friends.'

Simon looked bored, and frowned at the notion that Cece could ever have been enthused by sleepovers. He waited for her smile, and when it refused to appear, spoke again. 'The floor isn't very comfy, babe.'

'Oh, they'll be fine. I'm sure you've let friends sleep on it before. No biggie.' She smiled.

Simon gnawed a cuticle then played with it on the end of his tongue. 'Yes, but Stov's not…' He finally cracked, whispering, '… not *my* mate. And Al's more – delicate. He sleeps weirdly, deeply, and he murmurs. There was a school trip to Hadrian's Wall when we couldn't wake him for three hours on the bus.' He shrugged. 'He smoked too much dope when we were younger. It messed with his wiring. Let's just leave them downstairs, OK babe?' He laughed and put his hand on her shoulder.

Cece placed his hand on the banister instead, the smile still on her lips.

Simon swayed. It was rare to see him fail to make light of a situation.

'You said tonight we could do whatever I wanted,' Cece reminded him.

'So you want them to sleep with us,' he said.

'Why shouldn't I?'

'Why should you?'

'Why shouldn't you?'

'Fine.'

'Fine,' she said, her intonation telling Simon that she owned the word and had merely loaned it to him. Her eyes were victorious. She then whispered something, and they both laughed.

After another pause, Stov interrupted, announcing that he

wouldn't stay. There was a party at the house of someone whose mother was a dentist, and they were playing around with all the gear. 'Sounds exquisitely fucking stupid,' he enthused.

Cece gave Stov a hug and told him not to perform any surgery without anaesthetic.

'Of course. I'll give some to the patient too,' he said. And like that he was gone.

At last rid of Stov, a delighted Simon was less concerned about having Ali sleep on his bedroom floor – and Cece still got her sleepover. Simon led his two remaining guests upstairs, Cece to the bed, Ali to the floor, and then Calvin Kleined out to the bathroom.

Alone, Ali and Cece lay at their different heights by the light of an orange lava lamp. She dropped a lazy arm onto the remote control and turned off Simon's music, leaving a layer of calm in the gloom, an exhausted silence. And in it they watched the neighbours' lights pass over Simon's blue blown vinyl wallpaper, listened to the outside, the soaked wind and the aeroplanes, the subdued murmur of their unformed thoughts, before she broke it by asking him why he was friends with Simon and Stov.

'Why?'

'Yes.'

'School. What about you?'

'No, hang on, I mean why both of them? Impossible to be friends with both, no?'

It was a question Ali didn't know how to answer. He couldn't even begin to answer. 'Shared history.'

'With both? You couldn't choose?'

'Should I have to?'

'Tonight it felt like it, yes. You and Stov are cute together, I get that, but you and Simon?' She lowered her voice. 'I'm not trying to be mean – it's just, school is making choices. Are you bad at choosing?'

'No.'

'OK. What's your favourite book?'

'Oh, come on.' Ali couldn't think of a single book. He loved reading, spent entire weekends and holidays alone only with books and magazines, and yet suddenly he felt comprehensively illiterate. 'What's yours?' he said instead.

'Come on, choose!' Cece sat up to rest her head on an elbow. 'Aren't you about to study philosophy at university? Simon told me, and said you're pretty into it too. You don't have a favourite book?'

'I need to think about it.'

'Then you're doing the right course.' She let the silence fill the room around them like floodwater.

'Well,' he said at last, 'what's your answer?'

'My theory is that a "favourite book" is actually a nostalgia for a happy *time*. So I was happiest when I was sixteen, when my dad left me and my brothers in Norwich. He's in the army and had some training thing. We lived at my aunt's for two months that spring, and I loved it. My auntie Jen is so crazy. And I was studying Dante, *La Commedia*, for my exams.'

'No. Good answer, but I meant the other question, about me being friends with both Stov and Si. Why is someone like *you* friends with Simon?'

'Don't you find us compatible?'

'Someone liking Dante *and* Simon? No.'

'Fair enough,' she said, and then whispered, 'I suppose it's two reasons. First is, I enjoy his energy, I guess, the' – she paused to find the word – '*straightforwardness* of it. The fact he wouldn't be impressed by someone who likes poetry. It's like speaking to an animal. I don't even bother. With him I can pretend I'm normal, just like you do.'

'What?'

'Sorry, I'm not trying to be mean. But isn't that what the pub job is about? To be around the regular jocks? Validation from the guys.'

Ali swallowed. 'And the second reason?'

'Oh, simple. I'm trying to wind up my dad. I wanted to find the most arrogant Londoner I could get my hands on and bring him home. Show him what a reasonable fucking daughter I've been till now.'

'What will he say?'

'I'm not sure. That's the experiment. He always told me to do more reconnaissance.'

'So this is, like, fact-finding?'

'Yup.' She then lowered the heel of her foot to show him the tattoo on her ankle. 'It's also why I got this.' It was a small, perfect black circle. Barely bigger than a mole, so discreet it might not exist. He wondered how many people even knew it did exist. It was the kind of tattoo, he thought, that someone who isn't sure gets. The kind he might get.

And so perhaps this Cece wasn't as she came across, but working hard to pass as cool. Copying Simon's order at the bar. A tattoo that wasn't. She had fooled him, for a while.

'I've always had to pretend,' she said. 'And Simon is my ticket to normality. A shortcut.'

'I know what you mean.'

'Of course you do. You did know Dante imagined adolescence as a "meandering forest"?'

'I didn't.'

'GCSE Italian, my friend.'

'Really.' *Really*, though, he wondered, who on earth talked like this?

'Yes.' She added, 'I feel like I'm in a forest sometimes.' She was waiting for him to offer something, the cotton shushing around her when she moved. 'Do you?'

'I suppose. I suppose so, yeah.'

He waited too, his head on the floor, confused, dehydrated. They waited for the other to speak; he prepared a dozen unwitty replies which collapsed under the length of the time passing; and soon, almost out of despair, he fell asleep.

Ali couldn't recall a night so filled with the wanderings of his own mind. He thought he heard Simon at last return and get in beside Cece. Through the gauze of slumber he sensed the shuffling, the muttering, the tactical fidgeting, and even, he thought, a whispered reference to Simon's erection. And every time deeper sleep offered to shut them out, some jealous fraction of himself wanted to remain awake, desperate to know what was going on in the bed above. Agitated and then stupefied, again and again, he succumbed.

The whole night seemed like this – had this permeable quality. Forever sinking lower into itself, pulling him under with a watery weight; and yet always he seemed just one waking, one layer from a lesser version: an ordinary evening, where the colours hadn't offered themselves so generously to the night, where opportunity hadn't cleared a way for him to find his life here, now, only two feet away from this mesmerizing person. Where he had gone home alone on the Tube all those hours ago.

At times he became afraid it might not be true, and he might wake in his own bed, to the cries of next door's new baby, tricked by the persuasion of his dreams. Afraid of this, his last fragments of consciousness had waited to hear Cece confirm that she was real, that this evening hadn't been a dream. He listened for every sound of her legs zipping across the bobbled cotton sheets, her stifled laughter, even giggles perhaps, at the ridiculousness of their situation. Because Cece and he were still connected by that strange channel. Yes, Simon was an obstacle in the middle of it, but their contempt for him flowed around that obstacle, binding them. Someone was clearing their throat. It was Cece; they were conversing secretly in their sleep, so secret they barely knew it themselves.

He drifted, sank into the sounds of his pulse, Simon's clotted breathing. Warm and dizzy, he fell into a vivid new place, somewhere almost pleasant. A dense forest formed itself around him. A meandering wood of fallen foliage, faintly sinister emerald ivies and helicopter seeds spiralling down from high sycamore branches. It was uncertainty, puberty, erections and love; it was the rite of strife, the inheritance of mystery and blindness. Dante's woodland. It was life and love. Why else would it be so overwhelmingly lavish?

'Ali.'

He opened tired eyes, closed them again.

'Ali.'

He was in the black, an unfamiliar black. The darkness at home was different: a sallow gold flooding under the door when his mother returned late from work and left it open to the wavering lamps of traffic outside. The moonlight and her perfumed departure. He felt along the carpet for a glass of water.

She knew she had woken him, and now persisted. He blinked slowly, sipped some water.

'At last, he stirs.'

'No, he doesn't.' He turned over again to doze. So it hadn't been fantasy; good. But then neither, he considered soberly for the first time, was the troubling company in the bed just above. How much time had passed? All at once he was overcome with the wish to be at home, in his own bed, under the dismal protection of his parents' reality. He'd tried being cool tonight, and this floor was where it had landed him. So much for impulse, he decided.

'Ali,' she hissed. 'Ali. Ali, famed hospitality executive! Ali!' She whispered louder. 'Ali!'

He couldn't face her now, it was too strange. What an absurd night it had been. How the light had seemed to follow her around, the furious lines of red and yellow skewering the night in her path, and how she'd made a barman laugh when she ordered. And how she had made the train shudder to a halt and suspend them all in a moment of gravitational pull for the rest of the evening, leaving him still expecting to be sent tottering a few steps, still waiting to make that adjustment back to centre. The whole thing was ridiculous.

Ali didn't want to wake. He wanted to go back to the wood in his dream. The smell of mosses and crushed leaves would be around him. Alcohol and maple sugar and strange, lucid reds. Tiny rain kissed his face, and he smiled and touched it. He was awake. His arm really was wet. He lifted his head and saw Cece perched above the horizon of Simon's hulk, spraying aftershave over the bed.

'Ah. You're awake.' She adjusted her range.

Citric mists descended and formed a dew on his chest. He couldn't think, opening his eyes. 'Why are you? It's the middle of the night,' he said ineffectually. 'Fuck.'

'And you're fragrant.' She lay back, out of sight. 'Are you listening yet?'

He looked at Simon's sleeping form, concrete beside hers. 'Fine. How long have I been asleep?' Droplets of aftershave settled in his mouth, the smell of clementines, acrid clementines.

'I've been considering it. I don't think you're indecisive. I think you're scared.'

'OK then. Great,' Ali muttered. Something bled under his eyelids. His temples stung. He remembered – and now couldn't stop remembering – how he had spent the night reeling from her. Occasionally she had looked at him full beam in a manner not quite flirting, but flirting with the idea of flirting. And now she had woken him to tell him he was a coward. How dare she? What was he doing here, following an out-of-his-league girl as far as another man's floor? No wonder Stov had left. You idiot, you easy idiot, he thought as he rubbed his eyes. Don't react, don't sit up.

He sat up.

'I mean, it's obvious you can choose when you want to. You chose to come out with us tonight.'

'What?' he asked.

'You think ambiguity makes you mysterious.'

Perhaps he'd only been asleep for minutes. Perhaps they were still talking about books and GCSEs and Dante for some reason. But that was impossible: Simon, who hadn't been there before, was audibly – swinishly – sleeping above him. 'Are you joking?'

Perhaps it was encouraging that she was trying to provoke and impress him like this. Or perhaps she was just being who she was with everybody.

'It's a bit ridiculous. It's the kind of thing I'd expect from – well, an idiot. Like him.' She motioned to Simon.

'Shhh,' Ali whispered, and sent a glare of admonition in her direction, useless in the dark. 'Cece, come on – he's sleeping right there.'

'He's not sleeping, he's unconscious.'

'Shhh.'

'Oh please, this guy could sleep through a brick wall.'

'Cece –'

'He'd sleep through his own birth.'

'Just –'

'No interior life, I think the phrase goes. I like him, I do. But I envy him more.'

'Cece.' He lay back again, newly exhausted, newly baffled by each second. 'Try and whisper.'

'OK then.' The sheets rustled, and her toes felt for the floor between his sprawled limbs. Seconds later, she had propped herself up beside him and leaned to whisper in his ear. 'The boy snores too much. Move over.' She took a sip of the water. 'Now come on, what's your favourite book?'

What a stupid thing to do, the way they spoke beside Simon's sleeping body. Like he was a corpse. Like he couldn't hear.

Ali would subsequently try to remember exactly what was said and how loud they had raised their voices. They had talked about school, friends, and what she would do at university – history and Italian, she said, if she could get in.

They talked of not fitting in at school, vomiting before exams, the fear of coursework. How neither of them had realized their schools were posh, that they themselves had been so privileged, they giggled, until their teens. Perhaps even in their late teens, she admitted. Above all, they spoke of loneliness as if it were a shared cousin. How he would seek it in photography, she in writing. She spoke of the rowing boat beside the pond in her godmother's village, a boat in which she would write short stories by day and sleep at night under a jumper. They talked of how neither of them understood, even notionally, what was to be enjoyed about Plush, but as they laughed they realized, suddenly, that Simon's snores had stopped. Ali recalled the look Simon had given him as they had discussed Cece, his eyes quick under three-quarter lids.

As quietly as possible, a little guiltily, Cece returned to Simon's bed, without saying why. Ali watched the mattress collapse and hold its breath as she climbed over beyond his sight line. He slept till daybreak.

Simon mentioned nothing over coffee in the morning. He left the kitchen for a long while to defecate – something which he proudly described as 'absolute chaos' on his return. Yet he made no jokes about the night. Not even in the months that followed. And during these months the downward trajectory of Ali and Simon's acquaintance steepened, and soon they stopped speaking and texting entirely. Simon would withdraw from him, just like Cece, who, apart from accepting a coffee which she didn't drink, hardly spoke that hungover morning. She wasn't rude, but accompanied them both to the Tube station absorbed in a Sherlock Holmes paperback as she walked, without slowing them down or excluding herself entirely. Simon, who was going to work (he had a job at a climbing centre), seemed completely blind to the presence of books. Once on the Underground, Ali wanted to contrive a way of asking for her number, but every way of phrasing the question seemed conspicuous and clumsy. 'It's been fun,' was all he managed through the lattice of commuters.

Before Ali could add any more, Cece got off at Euston on her way to Paddington, and then out of London, back to school or whatever peculiar collective she came from, doing so without hugging or kissing Simon or himself. Just an embarrassed nod. He watched her wander into the crowds, her black hair down the collar of her raincoat, floating, disappearing. And this is how he would have chosen to remember her, if things had gone differently. He wondered if her house was near fields, or tucked away in suburbia, or whether her bedroom looked out onto the ocean so far that you could spot the wind farms on the horizon. She didn't glance back, and he wasn't going to let himself check. The reality to be faced was that she had made no provision for seeing him again. Ali supposed she would forget him and Simon, these two incompatibles. He considered where she went to forget such things, where she went to read her poems, to laugh about Londoners with her real friends.

He walked back to his home – smaller than Simon's, and more full of parents. The tight terracing of the road struck him for the first time as particularly basic and boring. He returned to his job in the Lion the next Monday, which had also diminished to the same limited scale. Cece had left him with a sense of missed opportunity. A hollow beneath him, so deep that whatever he did in the following year visibly subsided into it. The hopeless wish to see her again, to have their night again, became a pure pain of which, as the weeks and months went by, he began to grow fond.

Even decades later, as Ali looked back on their night, when some things were implied and others were inferred, that pain would comfort him. It was his companion, always.

4

The train heaved into an unlit station, doors slid open and shut like respirators; a man sat down opposite. He was short, spectacled, about my age, maybe ten years younger. Sixty-five, perhaps. Most people were around seventy. *The Grave-y Train*, the media called it.

'Do you mind?'

'No, of course.' I moved my coat.

'Sorry to wake you.'

'No trouble.'

'Heathrow?'

'Eventually.'

'If this thing ever gets there.'

'Exactly.'

'You, uh…' He shifted. 'You got on at London, did you?'

'Yes. Yesterday evening.'

London, Brighton, Portsmouth, Southampton, Reading, and then Heathrow. A circle of dormant industrial estates and ring roads.

'Well.' He smiled. 'Worth it in the end.'

'Let's hope so.'

'You wait so long to go, and then the journey seems to take forever.'

I looked around. The carriage was full of huddled figures, conversations hushed in the twilight. The elderly lady had laid out the two passports, two purses and two readers to check and pat again and again as her husband slept. She occasionally spoke out loud, neither quite to herself nor to her husband but to a floating sense of them both. Opposite us down the aisle sat a spindly teenager dressed all in black, and from further behind came the noises of children.

'Younger than I expected,' the man whispered, indicating the family. 'Must have a lot of money.'

I stared at the window, nodded without commitment. Maybe. Or perhaps they didn't have much time. You wait so long, as he had said – and then for some the journey comes too late. 'Everyone has their reasons.'

'True. Even if you go away for no reason, that's still a reason, I suppose.' His chuckle had a morbid echo of phlegm. He unfolded his reader, which sent a haunted yellow up into his face, checked something, put it away and took out a flask and dropped his tone. 'I've got a drop of cadge – it's a home brew, but a good one. If you drink?'

'I won't, but thanks.'

He nodded, put the canister between his knees and watched the greenery for a while. He pocketed his hands and then withdrew them again.

I didn't say anything, suspecting the man wanted us to ritually lament extinct things together.

'You've been there before?'

'Where?'

'Heathrow,' he whispered even lower than before, careful not to cut the quiet.

'Heathrow?' I kept looking away. So he wanted to force the conversation. 'Yes,' I said. 'A few years ago now. You?'

'I went back in the day. It'd be different now, I suppose.' There grew an expected silence. 'We went to Rome,' he said, wistful.

'Wow.'

'It was very beautiful. Then we went to the coast. In 2023.' He looked at me to join the mourning. 'I was, what, twenty-six?

We went on a sort of young lads' holiday, you know.' He lifted the flask again. 'Just a few friends – for the sun and parties. We drank in cafes and went to the coast and partied and snorkelled. And chased the fish.' He paused, considering something. 'Well, we did go round a couple of museums as well, to try, you know. I complained, all the time, got kicked out of one too. Drunk half the time. Thought it was all just bits of broken pottery and paintings of old dead emperors or old dead farmers with their old dead sheep. What did I care? I was in my twenties. Having a few problems. Horrible little shit, I was.'

'We all were, I think.' Swanning around the world, hitting place after place like it could be completed. I thought of the fact that Kat had never travelled, and how now, when I mentioned my time in another country, she was liable to look at me with incomprehension. As a child she had saved my old foreign coins like holy relics.

He swigged with anxious speed. 'I remember when this country was full of that stuff too. Art, history.'

'So sad.'

'Isn't it. Museums, galleries, concert halls.' And then he added, 'And *stadiums*,' with special reverence. 'I was in London the day the Museum of England got hit, I was doing a job in Belsize. You could hear it, the boom. You could smell the burning, the melting, you could hear the collapse of the roof.' I could recall immediately that massive twist of flame shedding its black skin over Russell Square. 'I saw the looting. On TV. My God. And the police shooting them, shooting anything. Can't blame them, I say.'

'Who?' I asked. But he appeared not to hear me.

'Now look at us. Shuttering the museums, selling off monuments. Pawning the nation's art –'

'Not all ours.'

'Well, we knew how to take care of it. Now it's in the hands of God knows who. Unthinkable.'

'Maybe it was our turn.'

'Maybe one day we'll buy them back. Cheers.' He chuckled, drank again. He paused and considered some returning memory. 'I had a colleague there. That day. A guy who worked for me, he got injured. His lungs too, in the smoke. Until then, everything felt like it was happening somewhere else. And we'd rise above it, you know? I loaned him a lump sum, something to support himself with because he didn't have insurance or a pension or anything like it. He died too soon to pay me back. And after that I realized we can't be doing with other people's problems. Other people full stop. It doesn't make us bad people. We just have to take care of ourselves.'

There was no point in replying. I knew the story, had heard dozens like it. We told ourselves we had been reasonable, responsible people until then but had been forced into this attitude. We told ourselves we used to be too good for this world. And we believed it.

'What about you, then? Where did you go before?'

'I…' I stopped. I still hadn't thought of a good reason. But he shouldn't have asked. 'I really have to get some sleep. Sorry.'

'Oh. Sure.' He took another mouthful and I thought of the taste of cold, clean alcohol neutralizing the back of my palette, the sweetness rolling forward to the front of the tongue.

I returned to the window. Before Rome, before the burning, what was it… For a second, my mind floated high, high above us, considering the discoloured train as it threaded through this patchwork of unloved England. What on earth had we done? He and I, this man, bound forever in the judgement of our juniors. Because we had been the face of calamity. Watching the mirror, not the road. The last children. I was no less guilty than him, just more aware.

'I hear,' the man said from his recline, 'they may open the ferry ports while we – I mean you and I, presumably – are away. It would be like the Belgian borders all over again. But worse. Every rowing boat in Europe. A regatta. Just imagine what will pour in.'

'Food. People.'

'Unchecked, mind.'

'I don't remember being checked when I was born here.'

'That was a different world.' He sighed. 'Well, there's still all the bloody pirates roaming the seas. They'll intercept a good few, at least.'

'Yes, there's always the pirates.'

He grinned, having already decided we were of one mind. 'No doubt it's just a rumour. I can't see it myself.'

'If they do open,' I said, 'we may not have to come back at all.'

'May not *have* to?' he repeated quizzically. 'Why wouldn't you want to come back?'

'We don't know what we'll find' – I motioned to the glare of the window – 'out there.'

I V

It was only on the second night of university that anything significant happened. The first night had come and gone with just one, smaller, memorable incident.

After a light frost in the morning there had been a harsh snap by the evening – everyone had said it was the coldest start to the first term in years. Undaunted, the freshers were led through the wind to a bar and fed cheap drinks as the older students assessed their stamina and pliancy.

Ali was nervously enthusiastic; university was an opportunity for kids like him to reset. A fresh start in a new place. But almost at once things weren't right. He spoke to an impressive girl whose drastic cheekbones and wide eyes strayed over his shoulder towards the other contents of the room, gauging if she might do better. Next to her was a guy who smelled of confectionery and laughed with exhausting regularity – especially when nothing seemed to be funny.

Then there was Cleo Torpe, with her expensive vowels and carefully knotted hair and questions about whether Facebook saturated us all with self-expression ('Who is Facebook to normalize poking?' she mused for them both). Sensing his low social status, Cleo left him to circulate with some older boys who'd arrived wearing nothing over their t-shirts. Having ordered drinks in large voices, they held their faces steady while they downed them. And as the night went on they exuded a certainty that, regardless of whether they were easy to like, they were essential to know, repeatedly corroborated by their hailing each other across the room, their shouts like hunting calls. Outside, others could be seen smoking in exhibitions of defiance against the cold, a few even doing press-ups on the pavement to give their muscles an added insolence before re-entering. It was like being at a rich school, just bigger.

Inside, the bar bubbled with acts of desperate cooperation, anxious laughs and hugs. All took solace in the communal awkwardness and in the freshers' customs, the sources of which were as remote as the skills which had built the tabernacle in that old college chapel they had been told to visit.

And, much as young people never believe old age will happen to them, neither did these students believe they would be absorbed into the abstract mass of their predecessors – what the prospectus called 'tradition'. They would be special, because they were themselves.

Through these strangers Ali made for the bar. And it was along the way, strobed through the limbs and vibrating shadows, that he caught sight of her, freeze-framed on the dance floor. She held a pose that seemed to mock the notion of poses while a camera flashed, penetrating the glazed reds and greens with a shock of pure whiteness, and then she reanimated, and, as she was shown the photo by the boy, they laughed and turned back to dance.

Her. She really was there, not a hallucination. Not a lookalike. At his university. A real-world miracle.

Only this was probably the opposite of a miracle. This was a cruelty. This was going to be a three-year, nine-term, daily cruelty. A luminous blotch began to beat faster within him. Not least because Cece was just as lovely as he remembered. Lovelier even than when they had met, because now she seemed familiar.

How long since he had seen her? A year, fourteen months? He envied the man, envied his camera, even his memory card and the photons of the flash which had for that millisecond the exclusive right to dance on her skin.

A figure bumped past him, obscuring Cece, and when she came back into view it was just as the DJ demanded everyone put their hands in the air and she threw up her arms. Ali was transfixed, seized by the sickening realization that someone this wonderful would never recall their meeting. He could already imagine her struggling to remember his name, feigning recognition of his face, clicking her fingers as she pretended. She wasn't the only woman who had occupied his thoughts in the last year – he now had a girlfriend, for one – but Cece was the only one who could materialize in such a random way.

A hand on his shoulder. Some of the others from the accommodation block named The Games were going back. Ali was still holding his money for the bar, but he didn't want to drink, or listen to the rococo laughs of Cleo Torpe and her voluble friends.

Ali had been so excited about university, the first night, this initiation, this chance to reinvent. But gradually he had lost his energy for the struggle: the half conversations, the hours of standing, the efforts to show interest in bright young people and how he was bright and interesting too. And Cece, here, was the final straw. He was stunned into shyness, and in response felt himself descend into an apathy only the vulnerable can affect. Inwardly, he blamed his shortcomings. Blamed Cece for crashing his new life like this. Just as he was getting away from his old world, old school, old self, here was this reminder of them. More than a reminder: a hatch, dropping him back into a time when he was not popular, sure of himself or happy. Only once had he risked asking Si about Cece – her last name, how she was, whether she'd be coming back – but without success. It felt too exposing to try again. She was here now, though, and so were his problems. She had delivered his old baggage to his new home. His deference to Si, his pathetic feelings for Si's old flame. A loser was reborn. He got his coat and stuffed his money back in his pocket.

They all returned to the room of someone called Nell and watched YouTube videos of a goat bleating with a sound so human it seemed a man was trapped inside calling for rescue. When Ali was woken by a text message he was in his own bed, badly needing the toilet, but he chose not to go out of some pathetic fear his nearest neighbour across the corridor would hear his bodily shame. His door creaked, then a floorboard. Seeing through his keyhole a thin layer of light dawning under the door opposite, he went back to bed. That was the first night.

Ali spent most of the next day in a sleep punctuated by the loud risings of his new housemates. It wasn't so much the volume of their conversation, music and cooking as its unlikely clarity. The sound quality through the floor – he found himself thinking as he lay diagonally across the pillow – was amazing. He heard, in the kind of detail he would have thought impossible, every shower taken by the four people on his corridor, and could already predict the point at which the water would turn cold before the yelps began. The world briefly stopped spinning as he heard Cece singing in hers, without interruption when the two minutes of hot water should have run out, meaning either that she had chosen a cold shower to begin with or that she didn't flinch at such a change of circumstance. Both corroborated the image he had of her.

Later, he slipped out to walk by the river, where he photo-graphed the geese huddled against the wind. He drank coffee alone, listening to a voicemail from his girlfriend, Angie. And when she'd signed off with her 'Laterz, lover,' he walked as a person does with a lot on his mind, as a doctor might walk between wards. It seemed a day always waiting to be dusk, and when at last it was, the freshers gathered in town.

That second night they went en masse to HyperMarket to get tanked up on the two-for-one offers. Everybody came. No social separations or hierarchies had yet established themselves; all was to play for, and no one dared not play. Fear of missing out presided over them, and like all autocracies, FOMO had to rule unchallenged before its opposition, JOMO – joy of missing out – could be born.

Ali kept to himself, hid behind his glass, through which the world looked both chaotic and uninteresting. But after one or two pints of this he found himself asking if anyone had seen a girl called Cece. Most thought she wasn't out tonight, though one mentioned a sighting at the bar with another guy. And before he let himself dwell on this, he decided to go find her, face her and see if she did remember him and their night together.

Cece was nowhere in HyperMarket. Ali wandered the club soberly drunk. He was nobody and nothing but his social anxiety. And in these places, he missed Stov. Missed him as an adviser, a counter-energy, missed his other-worldly suspicion of all these people, his inability to feel embarrassed or let anyone deny him a good time.

In a pocket Ali's phone blazed. Voicemail from Angie. Another voicemail from Angie. She would claim he had been avoiding her, and only returning her calls when he knew she wouldn't pick up. He knew this without listening to the voicemails, because it was the truth. It seemed cold, but he had barely considered her since arriving at uni, with everything going on. She was a fact that simply hadn't occurred to him. Back home, in the bygone times of two days ago, Angie had been his life. He wasn't home any more, though, he was here trapped in this social parade, all the while aimlessly shadowing the girl of his dreams.

Around him romances were flourishing, some already on the wane. The night was becoming something familiar, but not pleasant, and he realized now that these experiences would be no different simply because he was a little older and somewhere else. School or university, home or away, he would never know how to want it. After what seemed like hours of feet and waists, he felt drunken nausea rising within him which would either end in vomit or a second wind.

Twenty-three minutes later and, there being still no sign of Cece, he duly vomited behind a car and felt much better. Two calls vibrated inside his coat pocket. He had no energy for someone else, and certainly none for conflict. If he didn't want a girlfriend now he was at university, he would have to come out and admit it, Angie would demand. You can't just drop a person like this. And she would be right. As usual. But it wasn't that he didn't want Angie all of a sudden, it was that he didn't want a girlfriend at all.

From HyperMarket they gathered raggedly in the main dining building. The Boreham Friar dining room, a weary memorial to its own sense of joy, now seemed to him to be in drag. At breakfast, it had been its old austere self, fusty wooden panelling layering all but the columns beneath a balcony for the dons and fellows, uncompromising lights bleaching the Scandinavian furniture that left the contours of the human body unrequited.

But on this night it was striving to be kitsch. Coloured lights shone down on a tatty, exuberant banner that declared WELCOME NEW JUS! (their traditional name as St Julian's students, everyone had felt the need to explain). Glitter balls sparkled in tranquil revolutions. A tinselled bar had been set up in the kitchen, dispensing a free shot as they each entered. Furniture was piled in the corners in tall monuments, leaving tan lines on the floor where it normally stood.

It was a college dance – a bop – but without the music. The freshers stood in their new surroundings either nursing or downing their drinks. Ali was handed a pair of headphones.

Then, a small group in the corner began dancing in the hush. Slowly, almost imperceptibly, the dance spread, and more and more heads bobbed up and down in time. Ali couldn't see them fully but listened to their shouts of excitement, louder and louder.

'I *love* watching it start.' And there she was. Cece, beside him. She had been the first person he'd looked for, he'd prepared lines to tap her on the shoulder with, but none of his contingencies had allowed for her spotting him first. She leaned in. 'It's like watching the sunrise, or something hatching. It's one of those gradual, wondrous things.'

'Yeah.' He strained for indifference, recalling at once how so much of the art of talking to her was in showing no reaction. 'What is?'

'You'll see.' She stood on tiptoes, watching the dancers. 'Perhaps there's something in the water. Or they're all possessed.' As she put a drink into his hand, her pale cyan eyes took him by surprise. He had forgotten just how pale – to look at them was to search for their colour. 'Or I suppose it could be a silent disco,' she said. '*That* would explain the silence.'

'Oh. And the disco.'

'The disco?' she repeated, delighted with this, 'No one says disco. Drink?' she went on, pointing to the glass she'd put in his hand. He sipped. 'How's life?'

'Right now or in general?' Ali said.

'Is there a difference?'

He shrugged.

'Always the philosopher, Ali. Right now, then?'

Boys and girls in blue were handing out more headphones from large buckets.

'Great. Weird. How's life with you?'

'Life with me? We're good, me and life. We're learning to get on. Ups and downs, but now we're making a go of it.' They watched the crowd, and Cece waved back to someone.

Ali waited; waited for her to make sense, waited for her to act like they hadn't spoken in fourteen months, waited to see if she would mention the remarkable coincidence of their arrival at the same uni, the same college, and their nearby rooms. The fact that, when they'd met, she'd said she was applying to other places. Or maybe she still hadn't noticed they were on the same staircase. Which, given that the room plans were on every noticeboard in the college, seemed unlikely. He was attempting nonchalance, but Cece – well, Cece seemed like the kind of person for whom remarkable coincidences were commonplace. Or at least were less interesting to her than the commonplace.

Then Cece said, 'It's nice to see you.' And even added, 'So weird we're both here – but really nice.'

Ali hoped the 'Yes' he said had come out.

'I've forgiven you for last night.'

'Last night?'

'You ignored me,' she said, like this was obvious.

'No I didn't,' he said.

'Avoided me then.' The smile had fallen from her so completely that he wondered if it had only been a trick of the light.

'No, no, I just thought you were busy.'

'Too busy to say hello? Ali, we're living in the same block, you have to acknowledge my existence at some point.'

'I was just caught up.' He tried to be offhand. 'There's a lot going on.'

'My father always said it's impolite to be busy.'

'I didn't mean it impolitely, I swear.'

'You *swear*?'

'Yes.'

'What are you, twelve? Well?'

'Well what?'

'Swear. Go on then.'

'I . . .' He sighed. 'I wasn't *fucking* ignoring you –'

'Very good.' Her smile resurfaced.

He took a sip. 'So fuck off.'

Her eyes widened. '*Very* good.' She drank from a straw. 'Come on!' she said, thrusting a pair of headphones round his neck. 'We've just had our first row. Now we can make up.' She took his arm.

'Hey, Cece.'

'Ali.'

'I've just thought of something.'

That morning he had found a letter in his pigeonhole. An envelope from Stov, stamped in Spanish, containing a small bag of what appeared to be coke and a note in blunted pencil saying: *I want to know if this works. Help a guy out. Be a guinea pig? Let me know. Sx.* Tonight, he didn't pause long to worry about what exactly Stov was getting into, or whether 'this' referred to the drug (which did work) or the attempt to send a couple of grams of it through the post (which had also worked). He'd been concerned over the legal implications for himself as the recipient of Stov's gift, but as Cece began to portion out the drugs, describing herself as an 'occasional refuser', this became moot.

Besides, he'd been offered cocaine a few times before – once by Simon and a couple of times by Stov – and this, he realized too late, wasn't it. But it must have been meph or one of the new pharmacological ones Stov crushed in a pestle and mortar and fed his plants, so it was possibly legal anyway. He wasn't normally enamoured of synthetic drugs' fragile elation, but there was no doubt they had their perks. They unburdened people of their innermost secrets to strangers they admired simply because their eyes glowed in the dark, and made benign curiosity the default reaction to all things. Cece suggested they go easy on it at first and increase the dosage if the night got better. If the night got worse, she said, they'd have to take it all.

5

The engines beneath us accelerated as the train rippled over the surface of a perfectly straight section of track. It had turned colder, and shafts of moonlight pierced the carriage. We were three hours into the journey. Top-heavy minutes fell into one another. The man opposite was in a supine embrace with his armrest, lulled by the bass notes.

The teen was now visible over my companion's shoulder. Their face shone back, gracile but determined. Transit when you're young is about the getting there. But now, in the old body, the travel itself hurts. It aches. The sleep is deeper yet somehow more exhausting. I wondered what the others thought of us, me, the old. Spectres of the past, warnings from the future.

I made my way up the aisle to the toilet. Pissing was like trying to bring to mind an old telephone number. A baby woke as I returned to my seat. The dawn colours were climbing.

The elderly couple were having the conversation again.

'Susanna.'

'What?'

'Are you sure this is our train?'

'Yes, Jack, go to sleep now.' Was it possible I was that old? And yet the hands which rubbed my eyes confirmed it. Their stringed veins and baggy skin.

'Susanna.'

'Why don't you shut him up?' came a third voice. I looked up. A woman, holding a crying child.

'Excuse me?'

This woman stopped beside the elderly couple's seats and shouted in mock slowness, 'Just shut up.'

'There's really no need –' the man interjected.

'Oh, shut up. Some of us are sleeping. Or were.' She held her infant at them in evidence. It gave the required scream.

The wife was cowed. 'We'll be quiet.'

'Look,' the husband said, 'we're all nervous.'

'*You're* nervous?' The other woman leaned in, her face bitter, her inflection hard. 'Hasn't he taken up enough air?' she asked the wife, then shifted the weight of the child in her arms as she bent over to enunciate into his face. She looked desperate, hardened by anger. 'Just shut up and do us all a favour.'

I stood up behind the man. The woman met my gaze; I thought she might spit. But instead she slid past me, chiding her toddler and murmuring, 'Fucking Babyburners. Belong in the ground.'

When she had gone, I sat down, my hands shaking, squeezing my earplugs between my fingers.

Quiet descended again over the carriage. My new companion slept unconcerned with his drinking flask between his knees. He dreamed of Roman girls, of gelato, of days lost forever.

Sometime later I woke. My hands instinctively groped for my bag to check everything was still there. Passport: yes; sunglasses, covered in scratches so familiar the sunlight looked wrong without them: yes; the reader: always, and somewhere on it the barman's photo of Stov, Simon, Cece and me the night we met; and after it the order of service from Simon's funeral. Underneath the photograph of Simon aged twenty-one, stood atop a jeep in some faraway bushland, were the words *University of Fès* scribbled at the bottom. Only days ago I'd carried it to the Department for International Travel. I'd filled out the Justification and sent it for approval. And now I was on my way there, to Fès.

I brought up the order of service on my reader. It was the usual fare: 'To Be a Pilgrim', a psalm, a reading and 'Abide with Me'. Then we had sung 'Morning Has Broken', and memories of Simon's mocking lyrics in a school assembly – 'Morning has broken, vodka should fix it, Blackbird has spoken, fuck me that's strange' – forced me to hide my smile under a grieving hand. Perhaps I would have done better to show it, perhaps some feeling, even humour, might have lent humanity to the proceedings. But the distances between the strange faces told me that, apart from not knowing one another, almost none of these people seemed to have known Simon. There had been no eulogy.

Had that been all Simon had to show for his life? A plain ceremony executed with such humdrum routine by the churchmen and undertakers, so unimaginatively performed and poorly attended it might have been for a nameless corpse, one of those unknown bodies that washed up on the southern coast?

The hymn had crawled on, the organ competing only with its own echo as a few mouthed the final verse: 'Mine is the sunlight, Mine is the morning, Born of the one light, Eden saw play'. Blocks of chords had bounced among the upper register before descending with the cooler air; 'sunlight' on the way down rhymed with 'one light' on the way up. The furniture had creaked when we sat again for the ritual's close: the droning of an electric curtain across the coffin and the silence of those waiting for us to leave.

The exuberance of Simon's youth seemed to belong to distant fantasy. It seemed absurd that he had once been so large in our lives. That others would obediently bring him tips about scandal or ridicule to see how he would spread them or censure them. That tides of opinion would depend on his orbit around the school. That his contagious laugh would, when he told a story, convince you of how sick it was, and how badass you were for getting it. How had he died so alone? What had happened to his life?

It was like my view from this train. Facing backwards, you could watch life race away, but you had no view of what was to come, only what had just passed. And no time to find meaning.

A metallic whine sounded in the darkness, cups and glasses kissing and chiming as a man pushed a tea trolley down the aisle, the dull moonlight bleeding behind the trees.

I could hear again the clink-clink of glasses during the toasts at Simon's wake, back at his parents' house. The illegible, cross-hatched face of his ninety-five-year-old mother, Carrie, who had said 'Thank you all for coming, he is with his father now,' and then sank a glass of red wine with a single gulp in tribute to the men in her life. The perfect circle the few of us had formed a little distance from her, as though her bereavement was contagious. I had stood between her conversation with the priest and a pair of reunited neighbours looking at the pictures on the sideboard: our Year Eleven school picture (which had to be doctored before going on sale to parents because Simon had thrown a V-sign at the camera); Simon in his football strip; Simon popping a bottle of booze on what looked like his four-teenth or fifteenth birthday.

A churchgoer – who had smartly taken on hosting duties, per-haps to avoid introductions – offered me another sausage. Someone had scrounged some wine for the occasion, four bottles of cadge which would have been kept in a shed or attic for an occasion this sombre. The paths to the wine were guarded on each side by loitering single mourners: a man my age who had requisitioned his own bottle, keeping it tucked under an arm, and a very elderly gent whose inspection of the bookcase was interspersed with glances towards Simon's mother, waiting his turn.

I made my way up the stairs to the toilet, the door frame of which still bore the holes of Si's pull-up bar. (This had meant for years that the door would not properly shut, never mind lock, something we had all found amusing.) I hadn't meant to, but I wandered to the entrance of Simon's old room, half expecting to hear the rumblings of his speakers. I looked down the stairs before turning the handle and closing the door behind me.

V

Then more shots and more beers, and now the strangeness of the surroundings became less absurd. Ali had fully deferred today's hangover till tomorrow.

He and Cece carouselled the room introducing themselves to people they'd possibly already met, answering the same three questions again and again – what college, what year, what subject. And as his answers contracted, Cece's expanded into more and more elaborate fictions: increasingly high, she made claims of doing Creationism, or Showbusiness Studies or some other degree, and timed each acquaintance like an auctioneer, abandoning it if her interlocutor failed to show sufficient credulity.

'What subject do you do?' she would ask.

'Earth Sciences.'

'Rocks?'

'Yes.' Then they would ask, 'What about you?'

'Big Philosophy.'

'*Big* Philosophy?'

'Yes.'

'What's that?'

'Three thousand years of men realizing they're unique,' she would say, already walking away.

And every time someone asked how he and Cece knew each other, how their relationship pre-existed if they hadn't been to school together, he watched in pride as they tried to deduce its length and depth. He wondered at this himself – they had met for one weird night and never spoken since. But still he marvelled at the movements of her face as she spoke and the intimacy with which it often addressed his, allowing the others to infer only their own exclusion. He couldn't yet read all her expressions, but perhaps could now detect when her enthusiasm for talking with others had switched to an enthusiasm for simply watching them talk. He had never seen anyone involved in a conversation seem so remote from it. She found everything distracting and nothing interesting, as though she were entertained by such inconsequential tensions and satisfied only that her single constant throughout it all was him.

Was it absurd to think she had matured in the few months since they had met? Or, if not matured, then defined. Not only had her whole girlish countenance become polished, but her ideas, her responses, her whole outlook had, to borrow a word printed on the bottom of the college's beer glasses, vitrified into something firm. Until now it had seemed to him a condition of life that at every point you felt fully grown up – it was certainly the case with him. He knew first-hand the facts of life and sex and, through his grandfather, even death. He'd ticked off the major experiences. Mentally, then, he was pretty much fully formed. This was him.

Ali realized now that Cece was the living, breathing disproval of this theory. She seemed to progress by the hour, to modify with dazzling speed. Not only was this Cece more adult than the first version he had met just over a year ago, but even just tonight her jokes grew subtler, more sardonic (now she denied being a student at all – 'I got offered a Fellowship here last year,' she said at one point, 'because I invented Queer Theory when I was younger'); it was impossible that she would ever cease to embellish.

They returned to the lockers and had another couple of lines.

Only one conversation they had with someone else lasted more than a few minutes. It was with a man whom they hadn't noticed until he'd apprehended Cece, offering her a drink, and then they saw him properly and noticed his age. His eyes were surrounded by lines and his thinned hair had become more an allusion to a quiff than a quiff itself; it made him the oldest man in the room by some fifteen years. He was implausibly old. He tapped his foot nervously and asked them each the three questions.

Answering before Cece plunged once more into the fictional, Ali quickly told the older man: 'We're both here at St Ju's, our rooms are in The Games, we're first years, and we're both in Humanities. Italian and History' – he motioned to Cece – 'and Philosophy for me.'

'Yes, we're humanists,' Cece added with a tiny slur. 'And humanitarians.'

'Right.'

'What about you?'

'And humorists,' Cece clarified.

'Me?' the older man said, 'Ah, Sociology. Behavioural science.'

'Cool.'

'And humans,' Cece finished. 'Obviously.'

'Ha. Yes.'

'And are you new too?'

'He's obviously not *new*, Ali.' Cece laughed at the absurdity.

'Sorry. Ignore her.'

'No, it's fine.' The older man laughed too, gold in his teeth. 'I'm actually here for some research. For my thesis.'

'That's cool,' they agreed. 'Really cool. What kind?'

'It's about observing the nightlife dynamics between new students.'

They looked at one another. Cece frowned and pulled a strap up to her shoulder. 'Unlikely,' she said. It immediately fell back again.

Ali shuffled. 'In what way?' he asked.

'Oh, broadly it's about how they form interpersonal attractions.'

'What's that mean?' Ali asked again with polite confusion. 'I mean in normal terms.'

'Just the criteria which influence young people when they attach. Physical, material, moral, personal values. That sort of thing. I'm here gathering data' – he indicated a notepad in his pocket – 'on the level and causes of live interpersonal attraction between people as they meet.'

Cece was frowning. 'What's your name again?'

'Phil.'

'Phil, do you mean "why do people hook up?"'

'Sort of.'

'And what have you found? What's the secret sauce?'

'I'm not sure yet.'

'Well, here's a starter. For me it's all about the size of their sperm count. You can't be too careful.'

'Ah, very good.' He laughed.

'So what exactly do you do?' Cece asked.

'I ask questions on what the values are that matter most when you haven't met a person before. Are they eligible because of their social skills, interests and activities, personality, social background, cultural background, attitudes, or physical appearance? These all are graded and totalled to determine what the dominant factors are.'

Cece looked at him with poorly contained indignation. She leaned her head slightly to one side. 'That sounds pretty simplistic. Doesn't it exclude, like, basic human chemistry?'

Phil looked around him, eager for an exit from the presence of this particular data. 'Well, there are many subcategories, and –'

'So why haven't you given us the questions?'

'Oh, propinquity.'

'Excuse me?'

'Propinquity. You two obviously already know each other quite well. The subjects have to be strangers. Your likelihood of attaching is proportionally increased by propinquity, which is arguably the strongest factor of all.'

Ali squeezed her arm, but Cece had already inclined her head and hardened her voice. 'Arguably? I thought you said you weren't sure what the dominant factor was?'

Phil looked with anxiety from one to the other. He held up the list, his hands tensing. 'Arguably. Probably.'

As they wove away back through the mob, they learned more about the man. DPhil, as he was known, was a favourite of college life. 'He's harmless,' someone said. 'He's at all the parties every year. No one knows if his thesis is real. In his first year he got drunk and told a girl – a second year –he loved her, which was obviously a bit weird. He's stopped doing that now though.' 'You have to get your photo with him,' said another. 'It's tradition. There's a Facebook page for it.'

By now the floor was packed, the air thicker, the hundreds of shuffling feet louder. 'Him, here at that age. Doing that. Weird,' Cece concluded as they stopped and sunk another tequila. She inspected the lights through the plastic of her glass, a jeweller looking for flaws. 'I don't rate it.'

'Well, his study sounds pretty vague.'

'It's voyeuristic. If it even exists. It's not exactly science.'

'I think he looked sad.'

'He looks divorced.'

'He's way too sad to be divorced.'

'Ali.' Cece gave him a consoling pat on the arm. 'Sounds like we need to talk about your parents.'

More cheering. The crowd was now raucous. She pointed her drink at the scene. A boy, having climbed halfway up a column, was handed an old sports helmet slopping with drink. People began to take off their headphones and cheer, 'Do it! Do it! Do it!' Ali and Cece looked up. The whole floor applauded as the boy drained the helmet and then put it on, roared in triumph and slid to the ground. Cece took Ali's hand to lead them to the middle of the dance floor, tripping through linked limbs in the darkness. Her skin was warm and covered in the softest hairs.

They arrived directly beneath the balcony. The hall swirled with lights which reappeared when they blinked, yet still a hush prevailed. Somebody whooped. 'OHMYGODILOVETHISONE' shouted another in the middle of the crowd. Cece looked at him. 'Ali?' She had to raise her voice but still spoke softly. 'Put on your headphones.' She raised the heavy plastic over his ears.

The outer world muted. Cece mouthed something, and all Ali could hear was the brassy song, the sinewed click and unclick of his jaw in syncopation with his heart. It was like sleep, he thought, or a periscope, or opening your eyes in the bath. He began to test his voice, saying 'Aaaaaah', but couldn't hear it.

Was this what it was like to be deaf? Everyone inaudible to him, he inaudible to himself – yes, this was deafness, and so he assumed deafness would soon become dumbness. 'Aaaaaah,' he said louder. 'Aaaaaah?' And this time he heard. The voice was estranged, coming through the walls.

'Ali?' Cece was staring at him. He closed his mouth. She offered a thumbs up. He returned the gesture.

Ali danced, as he saw other people do. At first with Cece but mostly alone, as they joined various groups, each one linked to the next by mutual friends in crop-circles across the room. He knew if he bowed his head and stared at his feet then he'd appear so occupied by the music, possessed by it even, that others wouldn't pay him any attention.

Ali looked up for Cece, but she had gone. He wondered if she'd dropped him just as she'd dropped every other conversation. And he realized with a spasm of fear that, wherever she had gone, these peers could mean nothing to him without her.

All across the hall, freshers were joining in. He wondered what Stov would say about them. Two hundred students shuffling rhythmically, each content in their own sonic womb. Stov belonged here so much more than he did. He was impressive and intellectual. He was built not only to withstand but to enjoy this crap.

Tiny droplets of perspiration glistened inside the windows, and when Ali looked up, the old dome, overseer of the literary furnishings, seemed to hover, absorbed in a dire judgement that might imminently rain down. Taking off his headphones, he stood in the hot air. Double-tracked voices fell away from his ears, squeaks and murmurs of the hall rushed back in. Cece was back with drinks, watching him. He shouted, 'This is weird.'

'It is. But, you know' – she removed her headphones – 'to state it is to overstate it. And stop that.' She clicked her fingers in front of him. 'You'll stare a hole in that roof soon.'

She had bought them each another tequila. They danced, wandering the sugar-glazed floorboards, and for a while the bop continued as it had always done, the banal mixed with careful acts of rebellion, until, at some unremarkable point, the alcohol hit the drugs and coffee within him, and as he followed her he became aware of a physical elevation to the surface of the sound, and then his mind cutting through the centre of it.

After two, maybe three more songs she returned to his eyeline with a triumphant look. Lifting his headphones, she said, 'You see?'

'Yeah. It's amazing.'

Again she led them deeper through the mellow bursts, through the arms and legs of couples and trios buttressed on the floor. For a breath or two she leaned on him and gave a gentle buckle.

'You OK?' he asked.

At first she didn't reply, and then said, 'Bit homesick. That's all. A bit drunk. Don't worry, I'm not gonna rainbow-paint the hall.'

The mob beside them was growing as they jumped in unison. Her head remained bowed on his shoulder, and in that instant he saw them both from above, as one instinct allowed her to lean tentatively into his shoulder while another almost immediately pulled her back again.

'Next!' She clapped with abrupt energy, as though any further loss of momentum might be terminal for the evening, and slid in with the group.

A wave of arms absorbed them and they jumped too; the song crested and everyone was singing. He hugged someone with an affection so genuine it shocked him. It was the old man Phil. 'Hey,' Ali shouted, 'It's DPhil!' 'DPHIL!' they both continued to cheer, and his final anxieties – about the college, the dome, validation and difference – began to drain away, leaving him light enough to hover in the darkness. With Cece beside him, these people meant something again, and this place was home. The oneness of their experience tonight was almost touchable.

His thoughts returned to Stov, wandering somewhere in South America, waiting for whatever eminence that people expected of him to pass so he could return and enjoy the flatter horizons of failure. Then he thought of his parents, probably reading in silence at the dinner table, faced now with almost no reasons to remain together. Did they realize how he adored them? How his heart shone with thanks for their work to put him here, their boring jobs and semi-urban lives, without which he would not be in an institution like this? Perhaps more boring than the parents of everyone else ('Did your parents come here?' people had already asked), but all the more special for it. He hoped they would be kind to one another. He hoped he would be kind to them.

And then he couldn't avoid thinking of Simon, for years condescending to invite Ali to the parties at his parents' vacated house, and felt, without warning, pity for him. He didn't give Si much thought these days. But being with Cece now amounted to a betrayal of one of his oldest friends. Cece, whose wetted lips created a harmony which only she could hear, the beat yanking their heads up and down, up and down like pump jacks stooping for oil, until their sides stung and they gasped for air – and he loved her for miraculously being there, a love that defined itself as permission to stop thinking about everything else. She danced alone, her neck, her shoulders carrying fragments of light and new shapes, triangles of green and refrigerator blue, replacing each other with phosphorescent calm.

He stepped in and kissed her.

And she tensed.

Her fingers strayed behind his head, pressing her lips firmly against his, and even while she kissed as ardently as he did, her hands now pushed at his chest and she drew back. The air was filled only with their breathing.

She stepped away and hurried through the exit. Without thought he followed, and they stood beside the vast glass wall outside. The song was ending, the domed hall subdued in anticipation of the next track. He leaned in again.

'No.' Her voice low and firm, the darkness folding over her.

'No. Sorry.' So he was mistaken. He was drunk, a drunken, leering idiot. He felt eyes of others on him. His head was swimmingly high. But he was not so far gone that he couldn't review the last two hours in a blink, a mosaic of his errors forming around his feet: her eyes on him when he shouted foolishly, her sisterly embrace, her refuge in him as a friend, not a suitor. A kiss was not the point.

'No?'

84

'No.' Her voice quavering now, just audibly.

'No. OK. Sorry.' Ali held up his palms in apology and stepped back. He lowered his head and waited for her to leave.

In the decades that would pass, he would wonder what might have happened if she had.

But for some reason she didn't.

6

Some part of his room had still held Simon's smell. His ice-lime deodorant rising from the carpet. Almost nothing else remained. His stuff had been thoroughly cleared out, his wallpaper stripped off. It used to be a textured blue paper that felt like puffed rice. I remembered, as a teen, touching it like Braille in the dark when I was tipsy, my hands searching for the light. The wallpaper everyone had.

Only the carpet remembered where his speakers had sat. Where his desk had been. He once forgot about a protein shake left under it for a week, and reported sightings of 'really ripped mutant flies' for our entertainment. The bed. Or rather, the mattress – he said bed frames squeaked too much. The 'sponge', he had unforgettably called it. It was almost all gone, vanished from family history.

In my mind's eye I could see the posters of augmented women pinned to the walls. The noticeboard covered in photos of rampant nights out, football teams and a pouncing lynx. The army green of his bedcovers and the towers of music magazines leaning against the desk. In the corner by the window, though, there remained one final object: his lava lamp, its wire wrapped defensively about it. The slow shapes were long dissolved, and as I picked it up some kind of liquid leaked onto my hands.

A sick, dizzy feeling came over me and my stomach winced twice, three times. Perhaps it was the cocktail sausages. Still holding the lamp, I groped for the window and opened it to breathe.

'I kept this door shut.' Simon's mother, Carrie, was standing in the doorway, leaning on a stick. 'We're not letting people in here.' With her weight hung over one hip, her hand reached up to the light switch. The silhouette of her former careless, adolescent posture blinked in the light. 'The toilet is next door.' She was impassive as she looked at the lamp in my hands.

'Sorry,' I said, replacing it on the floor. 'I just found myself reminiscing.'

'I don't want to know.' She held out her free hand to stop me.

'Of course. Sorry.' I smiled weakly, but her eyes denied me. I shouldn't have intruded. 'I should go downstairs,' I said, just like a little boy. 'Your house holds so many memories.' I felt my own formality. Why was this so hard?

'Well, Simon was extremely popular,' she said.

'Such a loss.'

'Yes,' she replied, somewhat automatically. 'Who are you?'

'Ali.'

'Alex.'

'Ali.'

'Ah, I remember. Ali, from school.'

'That's right. We were…' I looked back at the lamp, a feeling flooding my head again, rising like the lava itself. 'We were all very young.' I leaned on the window frame.

Carrie inclined her head, recognizing me in this light. 'You were also friends with the other boy, weren't you?'

'Other boy?'

'Stov Unwin.' She said the name slowly, deliberately.

'Oh, him.' I closed my eyes, pretending to remember, inhaled air from outside the window as another wave of nausea rose in my stomach. 'Yes. Yes, I was.'

'Stov.' Carrie didn't move her eyes as her head straightened again. And the blazing thought of Stov seemed to reverse the osteoporosis in her back, briefly lengthening it. 'I remember,' she said.

'Hello, hello, just looking for the loo,' boomed a man who had seized a bottle of red and had apparently brought it to the toilet with him. 'Are we going down memory lane? Did I hear the name of Stov?' He had exactly the kind of sunny disposition which would have been welcome at almost any other kind of wake. 'Ali, caught in the middle of that pair, weren't you?'

I had no idea who he was.

'Ali was just going downstairs,' Simon's mother said. 'I need to check on the guests.' She held the door, waiting for me to leave her dead son's room.

I shut the window and trailed behind her as she slowly made her way down, focused on the banister.

'Thank you for coming, Alex. All the best now.' Almost as if I should leave now.

'Thank you, Mrs Penton.' She didn't seem to hear.

I finished my drink, placed it on a shelf and buttoned my jacket. To the sound of flushing, the man emerged from the toilet and pointed at me. 'It *is* Ali Turner, isn't it?'

'Sorry, I'm drawing a blank here. Old age.'

'It's Russell.'

'Of course. Russell. I remember,' I lied. But then perhaps I did dimly recall his voice. Yes, this was Russell the Muscle, now minus the muscle. 'Were you at the service?'

'Er, no. Sadly not.' He waved his reader in explanation. 'Tied up at work.'

'Still working?' I said.

'Oh, you know. The world still just about wants engineers, for now. Even if it's just to advise how to correctly pull things down. You?'

'Retired. But fine, fine. Thanks.' Russell had restored my glass to my hand and filled it.

'Second wake this month for me,' he said. 'What a thing.'

'I'm sorry,' I said. 'Cheers.' We toasted. We drank. We wondered how many others were dead, dispersed. How wrong things had gone. And I thought again that I should leave.

'I saw Stov, you know. Strangest thing.'

'What?'

'It was totally bizarre. In Morocco, of all places.'

'Morocco? No.' Involuntarily I shook my head.

'Why not?' he laughed.

'Stov? Because Stov's in Brazil. Has been for years.' Not that I could remember now where or how long ago I had heard this. A few years ago I'd searched online but had found nothing. What was in Morocco? How come bloody Russell the Muscle knew this and I didn't?

'He's in Fès. I was there – my wife and I took a flight and the Moroccan government offset half the value of the credit for my wife to do some work on an old palace there. And who should be the local notorious Western inebriate but old Stov. You were close back then, weren't you?'

'Best mates. On and off.'

'Funny,' he said to himself. 'Hear from him much?'

'Not so much. Time passes.' Stov hadn't replied to a message for years. A decade. I had tried, desperately. 'But then the memory is useless for that sort of thing,' I lied.

I could in fact remember the message, to the date. His louche voice calling through time. I had received it on my birthday – the first day of February 2048. A nice touch.

Ali, greetings, and happy birthday, if I remember correctly? Thank you for being so much in touch. I do hope things are good back at the ranch. I'm afraid I don't check in much here or correspond with the old universe. You're right, though, I do hear from Cece. She's well. But that's all best left alone.

Sending affection from the offending section.

Sx

A peal of hollow laughter came from the handful of attendants downstairs. The living room door opened and Carrie's voice led someone to the front door, inviting them to come back again.

'I should be going,' I said.

'He's got a woman there, you know. Weird, because I always thought he was gay,' Russell continued, oblivious. 'No kids. Said he's spent half the last forty years either high or teaching literature, or both. He spent the other half in an admin job in the Bolivian army, if you can believe it, and then working for some export company. Said he'd been deported on five continents and still would never come home, even if he could. Now he's some kind of English teacher at the local university. Probably all bollocks.'

'The local university?' I took out my reader to make a note on the order of service.

'Yes, Al-Ak-Ak-Ak-something-something. I can't remember.'

Ali remembered when Simon had said in their politics class that Arabic just sounded like gunfire. Everyone had laughed. Not least Russell.

Carrie sent a glance up the stairs at us as she made her way back into the living room.

'I should go,' I said again.

In the street outside, as the bug's eye of Carrie's bay windows stared at me, I thought, Stov is alive, living with a woman, and I know where he is.

The train had rolled to a standstill – not at a station, just one of those in-between places. The khaki treeline shadows swayed as our eyes adjusted, and for a second, just one second, I could have sworn I could see human silhouettes bolting from trunk to trunk.

One had a familiar stiff peak at the front of its hair, and then it had the walk with the hand across the belt, and then something like Simon's smooth face. It floated past the window before melting into the darkness.

As I blinked, half a dozen flashlights were arcing through the next carriage. Blades of brilliant white cut across certain faces before scything onwards. The officers shouted no warnings before sweeping into our carriage, pausing only to pass scanners along the luggage rack where bags were big enough to conceal a human body. One suitcase, a heavy brown candidate, was thrown with just enough careless strength to the floor to injure or kill any living contents. When nothing happened, its owner – a tall, thin man – moved towards the suitcase offering its key to a police officer who knelt beside it. And, just as easily, the man was knocked to the floor by another officer, his key kicked from his hand. He lay and silently squeezed a broken finger as two more officers destroyed the lock and opened the bag and probed the contents with their torches.

The man opposite me craned to get a view. 'Assistance is futile, as they say,' he whispered.

Within twenty minutes we were all standing beside the tracks, our bags open in front of us. By this point, the police weren't interested in the passengers they could see. One officer rummaged dispassionately through each person's things while the others remained on the train. Peering through the rain at my bag, they took out my heart pills and sleeping pills and inspected them with an apish shake. Would the police still care about these? The possibility fluttered under my lungs as another officer appeared and flashed their light in my face to scan me. Residues of trapped light floated across us and blossomed like algae in the air. They knew I was terrified. But I breathed slowly. The innocent were always calm, even if the calm were not always innocent.

As the officer counted the pills I remembered how once, years ago, a border guard had taken them from me at security somewhere in the Carpathians, and I'd thought I might die from lack of sleep. Back when I didn't know how long I could last without them, I had panicked, bargained the contents of my bag for the little capsules, watch, money, phone, keys, even the ring Kat had given me. Kat, who always used to offer me a trinket from her box of special things before I went away – a foreign coin, one of her mother's old broken earrings or a piece of river glass. She would hand it over, say 'It's precious', and remind me to bring it back. Sometimes she would tell me what power the object possessed, saying 'This makes it sunny', or 'This will protect you from bad dogs'. That border guard took everything, kept the ring, smashed my camera and tossed the sentimental objects away, but I didn't complain; I'd got my pills back.

I held my composure in the glare of the torch. I thought of finding Stov at last, after so many years. I thought of home, where Kat and her mother Madison would be waking. Madison rarely slept through the night, and would sometimes get up to check the house, carrying as a weapon the marble rolling pin inherited from her own mother. When the sun rose she would sit overlooking the garden, cupping a mug of tea that would probably be left undrunk.

In the garden was the warped sweet chestnut she loved, with its glossy hacksawed leaves losing colour each autumn. A tree, said to have been brought from southern Europe by the Romans, that in the afternoon she would observe from the top bedroom in her reading chair, from where she could catch the yellows and browns of Hackney Marshes. The last fifteen years had ripped through her heart.

Every summer, ivy crept across the panes and we would reach out of the windows and pull it down, until a couple of years ago when it had begun to rot from the root.

On the platform, they were preparing to let us go. Inevitably, they had found a stowaway and bundled them off the train in a black hood. 'It was the young feminine boy,' someone muttered, 'and good riddance.' 'No, no, it was an old Asian woman hawking fake tickets,' another said. 'Nonsense,' corrected yet another, the man from the seat opposite me, 'it was a tall man, an identical twin of the suitcase owner, hiding in one of the toilets.' Heads nodded. Twins were said to be unlucky. After all, who needed two?

V I

The bare bulb hung off-centre from the ceiling, and the boxes were strewn across the room, as ready to move out as they were to move in. The bedroom swayed. It was glassy and remote from him, a snowless snow globe. What, he wondered, is a person's character if not their actions? What are decisions but the fingerprints of character? There seemed no way out. Whichever way you looked at it, this was who he was.

'So what's she like then?' Cece asked. 'Your girlfriend.'

When she'd recoiled from the kiss, he'd retaliated, somewhat petulantly, by saying he probably shouldn't be kissing anyone anyway. He was kind of involved. Which meant, though he hadn't advertised it, that he had a girlfriend.

'Yeah, I know. It's your Facebook relationship status, dumbo. I looked you up last night. So. What's she like?'

'Angie? She's tall.'

'And?'

'And – attractive.'

'That's it? What is she, a doll?'

'What else do you want to know?'

The two of them sat on his bed as they smoked the clove cigarettes Stov had sent back from Brazil. Above them, a sock was wrapped over the smoke detector. They had left the bop and been walking around the broad green when Cece had put her head on his shoulder and said if he didn't tell her everything then they couldn't even be friends. So they returned to the warmth of The

Games and up the creaking stairs to his room. Ali was anxious without the all-concealing lights and noise of the dance floor, and could tell she was too. He decided to play some music, although quite which track suited the scene it was impossible to tell.

To his surprise, the room seemed, for a few minutes, to seal them from the events of the evening. This non-space was so neutral and empty that in it only non-actions could occur. Unsure even what to say, they began to kiss in tentative, careful movements. More halting, occasionally mistimed, they lay and kissed until his mouth ached, his adrenaline appeared finally to founder and at last they lay, fazed, in the naked light. He held an exhausted arm around her and counted all the points at which they were touching – their feet together, her thigh on his, her head on his arm, his hand on her side, her brow against his cheek, the countless straight black hairs that ran in rills over his shoulder and smelled so unlike any other thing he could imagine. The softness of their two skins each made softer by the other, soft as diamonds are to each other. He knew when she woke that she would never let him touch her again like this. Maybe because of Simon, maybe because she now knew he was a liar, a teller of feeble white lies.

The longer he held her the more certain it became that this stillness was her parting munificence, so he clutched at every millisecond. And as the minutes passed he accepted how ruined their situation was. He believed in the certainty of love more than ever, but only because he was oblivious to the damage involved and the price still to be paid. An accidental hand brushed his groin when she pulled the duvet around herself, and while she slept he lay mortified by his erection.

But just as he began to fall asleep, she woke, clapped him on the leg and demanded three things: 'Coffee, now. And I want to know what you've been doing for the last year and why we're getting off if you've got a girlfriend. Because I'm not that kind of person. And I need to know if you are.'

He stared, bleary. 'Don't just lie there growing a boner,' she snapped. 'Strong, no milk.'

Ali boiled the kettle and began. He spoke slowly, his throat sore from the smoking and shouting. Other residents stumbled up the stairs intermittently, prompting him to drop to a whisper. He started with the night they had met – on the train, when they had traipsed through Plush with Simon, whose name, when he mentioned it, drew a quick intake of breath from Cece.

He had wanted to contact Cece afterwards but had failed to extract her details from Simon. 'She borrowed my travel card after the club,' he had lied to Simon. 'Do you have her number? I need to get it back. The parents will kill me.'

'No can do, friend,' Simon replied. 'She must have lost her phone or something. I tried it the other day.'

'You don't have it?'

'That's what I'm saying, my dude.'

Then, with a murmur in the background, Simon said, 'Ah shit, I've gotta go. Let me ring you back.' Simon had rung off and never called again.

Ali sipped his coffee and continued to describe the events of the last year or so: he and Stov had travelled looking at universities – prefabs, castles, conference centres or chapels, those that looked like schools or monasteries or miniature Soviet blocs. How they had eventually chosen St Julian's because it offered the highest acceptance rates for above average but below brilliant students – or, in Stov's case, brilliant students with expulsion records. And thus he and Stov had applied together.

He spoke of their many afternoons in pubs spent imagining it: how knowledge would be their playground, and how all they had read about college life – edifying books, bops, girls, drinking games, toga parties, false loves, real loves, sex, sport and all the attendant gossip – would become real. They would be known as those guys who smoked and drank and expanded their minds, the pair of easy-going aesthetes, good-time nerds.

Then Stov had gone travelling. And when he returned, things had changed.

One night, as they had sat in the corner of The Prince's Head, killing an hour before seeing a play in the upstairs theatre, Stov said he'd ditched these plans. He'd decided not to go to university, because more education was no use to him. University wasn't the teaching he needed because he hadn't had enough life to apply it. 'Youth is transient,' Stov added, 'and therefore serious. So serious it shouldn't be wasted on theory. It should be spent, carefully, on fun.'

Of course the other reason, which Stov would never admit, was that St Julian's was never his first choice. Ali suspected that Stov would rather forgo his education rather than take it at a place that was not the absolute best. Was he that stupid?

Looking for flecks of humour in Stov's eyes, Ali had found none, and knew better than to ask – the calumny of asking Stov if he was genuine when he wasn't sure himself only committed him further to it. This was Stov's odd sort of hubris, it was his only intellectual failing: he could resist nothing to prove someone else wrong. Confusing steadfastness with pride, it was what had got Stov expelled, and now, even having achieved top grades under his own steam, it would deny him a degree. Ali knew there was no reasoning with Stov: try to dissuade him and he would dig his trench; ignore or agree with him and he would show you that you should have tried to dissuade him. His statements of intent were always self-fulfilling. They carried the conviction of total singularity. To speak was to act. He was like a member of those tribes whose language had no conditional tense. No sense of would, could or should.

'I think you're referring to the Hopi tribe controversy, though it was discredited as colonial nonsense,' Stov replied, sipping a pint.

'Whatever.'

'Besides, it was thought the tribe had no concept of time, not the conditional tense.'

'Which they did?'

'Which everyone does.'

'Not everyone.'

'I understand time.' Stov ran his palm along the grain of the tabletop. 'That's why I'm not going to waste it trying to learn things that can't be taught.'

'So what will you spend it learning about? Screwing? Drugs?'

'I'm not the one who needs to learn those,' Stov retorted.

They watched the lights of the quiz machine, waited for the plume left by this comment to fade. And if Ali himself often felt the world to be just too vast and complex to be confronted by someone of his own limits, he saw, unassailably, that Stov could abandon himself to it without any effort whatsoever. 'And why not wait? Stov, listen, why not wait?' he heard himself almost begging.

'Because I want to do things *now*. Life is too short to sit in a classroom and be told what life is. I try to convince myself uni is a stepping stone, but then I'll blink and the stepping stone will have become an island. Do you know, fifteen per cent of jobs require a degree in this country, and soon fifty per cent of us will have one? A degree doesn't even get you a job, it just shows you've met minimal expectations. You want to get a degree? Fine. But you may as well go into it eyes open. Gone are the days when education taught people something. The bar of expectation has been moved so low that getting your degree is now a boring characteristic. "Failure" is obviously the more interesting trait.'

For someone who came from little money, had already been expelled from school and had had to sit his A levels alone, his entitlement was bizarre. But it made sense to Stov, which was all that mattered. Was there a chance he would backtrack, given the opportunity? Take the kudos earned by having raised these objections? Never.

They sat in silence. A fucking idiot and a selfish poser, more interested in half-baked principles than honouring their shared dream, Ali thought, and continued to think, until five acts of Shakespeare later, when he had met Angie at the bar and suddenly it mattered so much less.

Ali cleared his throat. 'Then she just started talking to me.'

'Well? Angie. Describe her.' Cece asked, unblinking. 'Properly. What's she like? What's her vibe? Not what she looks like.'

'She's...' He found a word. 'She's... arty.' He expanded, 'An amateur artist. She's the most resourceful person I've ever known. She's never not innovating. Always deciding how to be creative with things.'

Cece waited. Noises in the corridor heralded the return of some of the others. 'Oh, come on. More than that. That's all epithets. Describe her, describe who she *is*.'

Ali sipped his coffee.

Angie. The truth was that it had been all physical, at least at first.

Angie had exquisite limbs. He couldn't say that, of course. But it was the thing he thought about. The way she deployed them onstage, smooth and always moving. Her hair was velvet, close-cut and dipped hot blonde, the colour of wheat. She was half Barbadian, half Jewish German, had brown eyes and high cheekbones. But it was how she carried her limbs that he liked – her long braceleted arms that jangled in the summer heat. He liked to introduce her, watch her extend them and reel people into her embrace. He liked her long body, accentuated by the baggiest of habitual painters' shirts. Most of all he liked photos of her: she always photographed stunningly, her mouth somewhere between a laugh and a moue, her left side (where the arc shaved into her hair finished the line of her Bauhaus limbs, shoulders, neck and jaw) angled towards the camera at a cultivated angle, her whole body a pose of naturalism.

He'd thought her a little absurd at first. But others clearly disagreed, and he soon allowed their opinions to matter to him as much as his own. Being beautiful in pictures was, after all, just as important as beauty in the real world. Vanity had changed the year before, in 2006. And now the significant assessments of events would always occur afterwards – via scrutiny of the digital evidence. Whether someone truly gave themself to the risks and rewards of youth, whether the day had truly been seized, was now judged the day after, online. Apparently experience was no longer something to be enjoyed but to be *proved*. What was once known as reputation was now called Facebook, and they had all signed up within the last twelve months.

Angie's perfection of these skills persuaded him he must be more attracted to her than he knew. Her Facebook wall read like a sponsors' page, her image always pristine, her friends always ecstatic. This website literally counted your friends and published the number. So many (311) couldn't be wrong about Angie. Besides, he convinced himself to adore her because it had seemed so unlikely in the first place that she would let him.

No one else bothered to hide their surprise, or pretend he wasn't an unlikely choice for her, and probably the strangest thing about her. These doubts mostly faded in the libidinous haze of a long summer. She and her smoky-voiced, skinny girlfriends would mention it jokingly, patting his leg as they leaned across and chatted about the virtues of different types of men. He lay with them on the grasses of Greenwich Park or Tooting Common and heard about men who listened, or drove, or smoked dope, or those who built muscle, or loved clothes, or emoted.

They were slightly above him in school years but seemed aeons older. These were mature young women: they had grown out of drugs, befriended their old schoolteachers and explored their sexuality. One had already had a tattoo removed. They were anti-materialistic yet artfully dishevelled, avowedly unsuperficial yet all beautiful beyond coincidence. They spoke possessively of everyone because they were artists and assumed as a basic courtesy that everybody else was too. They toyed with objects they'd chained around their necks – Monopoly totems, bottle tops, diced credit cards or keys – while listing all the kinds of eligible man he was not. The alpha, the artist, the intellectual. Perhaps this is how Angie had claimed him as an artistic endeavour in itself. A raw material.

That night, as he and Stov had sat in the poky theatre above the pub waiting for the play to begin, he had read the programme twice, still incensed by Stov's cancellation of their university plans and this wilful wrecking of their shared future, while Stov chatted freely with the person in the seat beside him. It was, the programme claimed, a 'truncated production' of *Othello* which left just under half the play. Starting with an offstage howling – perhaps of a rape or beating – that was never explained, it was probably quite good, but Ali was too angry to concentrate. And Stov, sensing this, disappeared with his neighbour during the interval.

In the second half, Ali sat in the middle of the three empty seats and let the dense language wash over him. He didn't expect Stov to return, nor did he. Stov had chosen to screw a stranger rather than stay with his friend. Tonight and forever. So Ali was alone at the bar afterwards when the actress playing Bianca stood beside him and asked the barmaid if they had fresh tomato juice, and what time the pub shut, and whether there was an actors' discount.

'What did she say to you exactly?' Cece, who had been walking about the room, finished her coffee and to his surprise got back in bed. Her feet were cool and hard.

'Does it matter?' he mumbled, pathetic in his evasion.

'Can't you remember the first thing she said?'

He could. He always would.

Angie had a habit of asking questions in scattershot rounds, so one, invariably, would find its mark. He had just complimented her on the performance when she said, 'Did you really like it? Not too small a space? How did you find the acoustics? What do you do? Are you creative?' He stammered 'Yes' and then a single 'No' to make sure everything was covered, and when he added that his hobby was taking photographs she fired off another volley: 'Great, what kind of stuff? Portraits? Nature? Do you do fashion? Who are you into? Diane Arbus, Dorothea Lange?' before looking him up and down, analysing his outfit in as much time as it had taken him to choose it, and answering her own question. 'No?' He then muttered that his day job was at a pub, and she stared at him like she was waiting for a punchline. 'Why?'

'For money.'

'Oh. Still, there are more interesting ways of earning.'

'And I get to work nights, which I like.'

'Oh. So you're a night owl.'

'Well – sure, I sleep until the afternoon, but I don't sleep much. It's not tiring.'

'I went nocturnal once, for about a week. I had this awful migraine that wouldn't go, and so I tried some medication but it made me hyper at night. It was so lonely. Although I was very productive. But mostly lonely.' She stopped abruptly and waited for his thoughts.

'Well – I like to read. And you can only do that alone anyway, so.'

'What do you read? What kind of stuff?' And, all uttered in a single inexplicable sentence, 'What about cocktails – can you make any?'

Ali picked one of the questions fanned before him like playing cards. 'I'm OK at a couple. Long Island and Manhattan.'

'Really? Could you make me some?' She smiled.

'Sure.'

'That'd be amazing. I'm doing an exhibition of multimedia at college – a lot of frottage and collage pieces – and we need someone to do drinks.'

'What ho?' Two more members of the play's cast, Emilia and Cassio, interrupted to say they were leaving. They looked at Ali and he nodded to show he recognized the words from the play – something they were pleased with. 'Party at Dani's, you coming?'

'I don't know yet,' Angie replied.

Already abandoned once tonight by Stov, Ali shrugged like he wasn't bothered – because, he told himself, he wasn't.

'Come *on*,' they said.

'How poor are they that have not patience!' Angie said in her stage diction, with a wink to Ali.

'Well, it's your call. Not that I love you not,' Cassio said. He then added, '*Not!*' and they all laughed. Then they each kissed Angie on the mouth and left.

'How long ago was this?' asked Cece. 'You seem to remember it vividly.'

'It's just how I remember it. I can't control what I remember.'

'And what did you – do you – like about her?' Cece's voice steadied itself, her eyes stilled, like some locally anaesthetized patient showing her surgeon she was no panicker.

Ali looked at the sock over the alarm and it occurred to him that their nights together were destined always to become weird.

He couldn't just get drunk with Cece and sing on the night bus or break into a park. No, they were destined to discuss Dante or conduct autopsies of his relationships.

'Apart from the fact she's so fit you can't bring yourself to tell me,' she continued.

'I've said she's pretty attractive, actually. Also, I suppose –'

'What?'

Ali moved over, drew himself away. 'She's – popular. I'd never been in with a popular person like that before.'

The truth was that sometime before meeting Angie, he had found, after their night in Plush, some small solace in the fantasy of impressing Cece – even though she wasn't there. It sounded mad, but in those following weeks he imagined what she would think if she saw him do this or this. Rapidly, he had begun to perform for a mirage of Cece, a child before his imaginary audience. Feeling her presence everywhere, he had bent his identity into shapes she might like: kept pocketfuls of the poetry and idiosyncratic whisky he guessed she would approve of; read great novels; borrowed great films from Stov, who had regarded this transformation in steeple-fingered silence; wandered the South Bank as if it was his cultural Jerusalem; learned to mention B.S. Johnson, to admire Claire Denis, to dislike von Trier's latest work. He had taken photographs of halves of things and learned to develop them in his parents' cellar. He bought a copy of Dante's *La Commedia* and read it.

Not satisfied, soon he was imitating Cece; he copied her private smile, tried speaking with her smart detachment. He wanted her, and so wanted to be her.

He knew all this was pretentious. He was aware of his adolescent intensity, but knowing it made no difference. This was at the apex of this phase, when all things new to him seemed new to the earth itself. No one had ever felt sorrow and obsession this strongly, no one had ever understood these songs and films so completely.

In this appeal to Cece's spirit Ali cultivated a cynical attitude to guard against disappointment. New people in particular were shunned for their failure to distract him from his sense of loss. She had cut from his world an area of her exact measurements, and in her place any new acquaintance was a crude patch.

He felt no choice during all of this, and, anyway, to whom could he talk about it? Not parents, not friends. He mentioned it in an email to Stov, whose whereabouts were temporarily unknown.

Ali couldn't explain, least of all to himself, how much he had changed since meeting Cece, or because of it. He only knew he didn't think of other women. He thought of her so often it was like she was really there. Crazy, his imagination. And yet all he had wanted was for her to see his improved state, to recognize herself in him and give him another chance. But then he was unsure if she wouldn't instead despise his delusions.

Ultimately, he came to realize that all this posturing made no difference to the real Cece, so what was the point of it all? Being alone was being alone, regardless of whether it was aloof. And the emotional gymnastics which had brought him here scared him.

The illusion faded. Bitter, embarrassed by his own company, Ali was lost for days, smoking, masturbating, getting drunk alone in pubs, doing anything to prevent himself from falling into further fantasies. Instead, he decided to test the image he had manufactured. He discovered that it could be useful with girls, as he slept with three in quick succession. It was extraordinary. He mastered a look of bereavement, pressing his fingertips soulfully into candle wax as he spoke in cracked sentences – which came easily when he had little hope of truly trusting these strangers.

One was an older woman (twenty-four, which seemed a different species). They had met in a gallery and she was inappropriately fond of him after only a single night. Her eyes and her unkempt bed attracted and fascinated him with their intimations of experience. She taught him how to take high-exposure photographs of roads at night and survived almost wholly on coffee and peanut butter. She teased him about his patchy stubble and would sleep like the dead after sex.

As a diversion, though, this technique worked only for a while before it became ineffective. First, he hated his forced coldness towards the women in the mornings, and then his solitary panic in the afternoons. Who was this unfeeling Lothario he was trying to be, and how had he ever kidded himself – a skinny, shy boy – that such a transformation was possible? He began to wonder if sex was more like finding an itch, and to what extent enjoining someone else to help was better than just getting it done by himself.

And then he met Angie. By this time, the pretence had almost completely disappeared. When she spray-painted him with questions at the bar, it had been fully two months since Cece had strolled in and out of his life. The dregs of his act had evaporated as Angie spoke, as he realized he was happy to tell the truth to someone who didn't care about his past.

Tired of his antics, of Stov's rejection, of Cece's absence, Ali shed the act and plainly answered Angie's questions. No affectations, no withholding, just answers. And he could tell that Angie kept asking not because she was attracted by the last shreds of his facade – she was not – but because no man had reacted so minimally to her interest. He had reached a point where he was no longer trying, and the less he gave, the more she wanted.

Yes, Iago had motive, he found himself replying, still at the bar. No, he didn't know what it was, nor did it matter. No, he didn't know how many times the term 'devil' was used in the play (twenty-two times, she said), or 'hell' (twelve times). Yes, Othello was saner than Hamlet. No, he didn't know what strawberries symbolized. No, he couldn't speculate.

'Do you even like Shakespeare? Or theatre?'

'I don't know what I like at the moment.'

This was one of the most bizarre things Angie had ever heard. 'I adore Shakespeare,' she stated.

'What other plays should I read?'

'I've read *Othello* and *Hamlet*. Hamlet is like Othello but such a white boy.' Angie dropped a heavy pinch of pepper into the Bloody Marys she had just bought them both. 'You're cute, in a Hamlety, mad agonized teenager kind of way.'

'I'll take it.'

'And I've decided. I'm taking you to my exhibition.'

'OK.' He poked a straw at the heavy red surface. 'I mean, are you sure?'

'I'm always sure.'

In Angie's intense focus, he felt the last of his delusion depart. They got very drunk and arranged to see each other again.

Her energy was infectious. A few weeks later she made him a white necktie with shirt buttons sewn down the middle as though the shirt front were visible through it, which drew genuine compliments. Soon others began requesting them. He liked that about Angie – she was an original. She knew what to wear, how to create things which always contained a safe sprinkling of the peculiar. He felt enhanced by her, even improved by her.

Dating Angie became another passive progression, like doing exams, getting a university place, learning to drive a car. She was another advance towards adulthood, reality, validation. He was finally cool.

7

Heathrow and the smell hit me like a hospital corridor. Pine bleach, carbolic acid and iodoform. The yellow vinegar that smocked cleaners sprayed with bored diligence across the many reflective carpets.

Most of the corridors led nowhere. They connected empty rooms, ran from void to void, each one formerly a shop, restaurant, cafe or newsagent. Branded light boxes still lit them with immaculate, glossy adverts. Ageless models appeared through the gloom like gods, at whose feet children gathered to eat grey yolkless eggs and sleep off the effects of the diesel train. They pointed to the shopfronts and pronounced the strange words. They laughed in delight at the absurd holograms of talking luggage and scowling sports stars. And when once a police officer walked in their direction, they instinctively quietened, allowing parents and siblings to usher them swiftly from the scene. The officer about-turned, disappearing past me into another sunken corridor.

I glimpsed above the officer's collar the blanched skin of a removed tattoo, a patch of white, like foothills on a map. Visible millimetres above his uniform, it might prevent him from rising any further in this profession. Although not technically illegal, body art had become the mark of embattled central Southern gangs, races and racists. Twice Parliament had attempted to ban tattoos, blaming them for being some kind of accessory to the clashes that spread all across the Midlands. Other passengers scuttled from his path, even colleagues.

The sound of jets rose and sucked the noise from the terminal. A windsock convulsed outside. Minutes hung in the air. Clock hands and the rattle of fans fell in and out of time. Crusts of hair and dust, borne on the vectors of vast air conditioning units, looped in floating arcs. Where these shopping halls had once served to kill time, now they stretched it loose: no hope or burgers or hugs, duty-free or last-minute pharmacies, nothing to distract us from our tension.

To the rear of the ground floor, administrators of the Department for International Travel were ushering a small crowd of waiting passengers into the anterooms that flanked their desks. Thin huddles of travellers lowered their heads to listen to their instructions. Readers were scanned, passports uploaded, faces checked, four signatures demanded from every adult. Every so often a sob filled the airport as the sitting figures turned away one person in thirty. Police sat and extended their legs, the tattooed man bringing to his superior the luggage of a detained passenger. The officer addressed the passenger only via their suitcase before waving a hand and returning to their reader. This customer had passed.

Slow eddies of discarded paperwork gathered at the feet of the furniture, to the left of which an old woman had fallen to the ground. She hugged her knees and refused to be moved. A stretcher, apparently kept for this purpose, was carried over to her, and three of the police officers rolled her onto it as a fourth and fifth pointed weapons at her. I thought of my parents, each rolled from their final beds in the terminal care homes. When she was gone the place was left emptier, calmer, as a water level lowers when bodies are removed from it.

'Is there a problem?' I moved to follow them, prompted – haunted – by my failure to protect my parents. 'Excuse me,' I called to the stretcher-bearers. 'Has she got anyone with her? What's happening to her? Excuse me?' but they moved faster than my muscles could unstiffen, and then a hand on my shoulder alerted me to the danger of my protest.

'*Is* there a problem, sir?' asked a tall man in uniform. 'Sir?'

'No, only…' What courage I'd summoned was already failing.

'Don't concern yourself with the status of other customers, sir, that's our job.'

'I'm only asking if she needs a – a witness of some kind?'

'Sit down, sir. We don't want you missing the announcement for' – he scanned my face with the reader in his other hand – 'Fès, Mr Turner.'

I stood still, resisting the force of his hand without moving it. 'Is that a threat of some kind?'

'We don't make threats, sir.' The grip held me. For a second, I thought I'd glimpsed the same removed tattoo scars visible on this man's lower neck.

'Sit,' he said, releasing his hand, and walked away.

I complied and kept myself unnoticed, waiting for the end of the boarding window. I'd never been clear why we might be rejected, or of the rules determining who passed. If it wasn't arbitrary, then the authorities made little attempt to clarify their logic. Opacity was half the deterrent.

Precious seconds ticked down until I saw the opportunity: a short young man, hands shaking, his voice clogged with anger. Everyone looked at him. By the time I had slid into the queue behind him, he was pleading. 'I'll do it a thousand times,' he said, grabbing a piece of paper and scrawling desperate signatures. 'Look!' He held the sheet in front of the clerk before resisting the grip of two police officers. Slowly they pulled him to the left-hand antechamber. I had learned this lesson in Spain. Always queue immediately behind someone who might be rejected.

And that proved correct again.

I handed my reader over, and seconds later I had passed through to the screening hangar. They would let most of us board.

VII

Cece, noiseless for some minutes, clapped unsuccessfully at a moth.

'Shall I stop?' Ali asked.

'No, why would you?'

'OK.'

'So what was it about Angie that made her like *you*?'

'I really don't know.'

The shell he had become excited Angie. He was a whitewashed canvas primed for something new, and his blank answers hinted at some recondite depth. And whereas Cece teased him, and saw through his reticence, Angie overwrote it. With one he had been in awe, with the other past caring. Somehow, disappointment had made him free. Perhaps Angie enjoyed this. In any case, she gradually altered him, taught him how to perform and opine, bought him new things to wear and gave him a new haircut, impressed her tastes upon him as she would on any other material.

What would he be? What was she making of him? What, her friends all asked, could be done with this new Ali boy? They could see the attraction, sure. But he was no artist or creator or collector of objects like Angie and her friends. Photography, though – that could be his thing. They could make of him a man of observation, a selector, an eye: with his abstraction and scepticism this was the person he should have been from the beginning.

She had insisted as a rule that he take his camera everywhere, not just on his solo trips. Now it was a social device too. She encouraged him to photograph everything, the parties, clubs and streets, concerts and trains, and frequently praised the most unremarkable of his results, recognizing something in them that was invisible to him. Soon she was hanging them in the foyers of small cafes and upstairs theatres telling people – she knew everyone – what the photographs meant. Following Angie's lead, her friends purred over the flattest, most indifferent of his photos: the garage doors, wooded fronts, blocks of flats and decorated ceilings devoid of a third dimension, depicting a world that did not go round corners, which he regarded often as artless and bad. They were just surfaces. Or else people liked the images of Angie's friends modelling the clothes she had made, which in practice had only been a case of point-and-shoot in their direction. Her collection was called *Tomorrow Is the Next Day*.

In the brume following a late shift in the pub, Ali would sit before these images while Angie circulated, behaving like it were a real exhibition, greeting friends by placing a palm on one cheek and kissing the other. He had seen in those images Angie's vision of the world, ordering itself wherever she cared to look.

He wasn't alone in being affected like this. What Angie did to him he saw her do to others: how they found themselves exaggerated by the sheer assurance of her pronouncements, defining themselves in relation to her. From her thick mascara to the placement of her every hair, to her belief that it was the duty of everyone to create, Angie moved in certainties.

Ali had fallen for her sense of herself, stark as a negative, which, by contrast, created a more defined impression of him. She had installed him as her plain background. She had cared for input while he was stand-offish; she had added expressivity where he chose scrutiny; she had offered the opportunity and he had taken it, and soon he was so proud to be one half of a cool couple that he forgot about the blurred, deluded period before.

And if he did occasionally recall that time of obsession with Cece, he comforted himself that Angie, unlike Cece, had the virtue of being real.

On Angie's advice he gave up the pub job and worked as an assistant in a design shop. He found himself using new words – a movie was now a *piece*, songs had *texture*, almost anything could be *embryonic*.

He felt enhanced by her. And when she reached for his hand, he felt wanted.

Cece checked her phone and asked, 'Have you told her you love her?' a little too loudly.

'I have.'

He had told Angie after an evening spent in the brisk winds of London Fields, in the warmth of each other's skin on his small bed at the bottom of his parents' house. He had meant it. She had an unnerving way of looking at him, a sustained expectation. 'I love you too,' she had finally said, leaning on an elbow, those tendril arms unusually hesitant, and turned onto her front. And the longer they kissed, the deeper their pledge became, the more he hoped he would escape the memories of that other girl.

Their silence filled with all sorts of things. From the quad, they could hear someone shushing another person extravagantly. 'SHHHH,' they giggled. 'People are sleeeeeeeeping.' He and Cece listened to a songbird somewhere beyond. It chirped as they sat waiting for the partygoers to leave. Through the window Ali saw the little dark lines crinkle above the treetops as more birds hopped in the disturbance.

'Sounds pretty flawless, this Angie gig.' Cece could no longer hide the upset in her eyes.

But Ali didn't dare stop in case he tried to touch her. 'That's what I thought,' he said. 'But –'

'There's a but.'

'There is.' And he heard the guilt in his own voice. 'Yes.'

Something was wrong. Something which slid beneath his shoulder blades in the night. Unanswerable, unaskable questions, such as: did Angie's smile exist in a natural state, or was it just a cover? Did she have a sense of humour at all? And what did the line he'd repeatedly seen her use – taking off her clear, non-prescription glasses to show it was a moment of insight and saying, 'I think art is useful because you can walk away from it' – really mean? Why were her unlaced boots always the only dirty thing about her? Was it because she wanted you to know she had more important things to dwell on? And what if she had not been so excellent to look at? This was the question that nagged him above all. Would her peers have flocked to her work then?

Increasingly he wondered whether her precocious accomplishments owed less to talent than to looks. If true, it was perhaps a fact of life – looks counted, undeniably, for so much. But then it followed that his own new-found popularity also owed less to his own qualities than to her appearance.

And it dawned on him that perhaps the people he was drawn to were a particular type: Stov, Cece, Angie – all effervescent characters who had in common a declarative presence and an ability to meet Ali further than halfway in every conversation. They were better than him, he knew that. And the correlation between the two women was appallingly simple. He had wanted Angie to be Cece, and had almost willed this into truth.

Somewhere inside he was searching for different brands of the same person. And he only started to notice these similarities when what truly distinguished them also began to emerge. Both had a gregariousness. Both were attractive. But where Cece was sincere in most things, Angie believed in nothing. Everything she liked, or disliked, or lied about, had been measured with the yardstick of peer consensus. Angie, who overtly rejected maths in any context of utility, had memorized the first one hundred digits of pi in order to recite them with offhand brilliance. She claimed not to know what colour her eyes were, insisting they were grey when they were objectively brown. She would maintain she didn't know who Tom Cruise was, making it a flag of her independent spirit. She spoke constantly of Art with a capital A, as though it were a war in which one could be awarded citations for levels of mindless courage. No part of her could not be customized in the service of popularity.

He had a weakness for charismatic people who he saw were no more than entitled, insecure and arrogant. And just before that apprehension passed, he started to grasp why he needed to be in their shadows.

What followed this was a realization that all his teenaged judgements of Angie were unfair. She had been attracted to his apparent lack of agenda, while he had wanted her as a substitute for another woman. And in this, he saw tonight, no person could ever succeed. It was shitty of him to be with her because he couldn't have someone else. And if youth was his excuse, then it made his actions more grievous: Angie was herself a tender girl at heart, and he had abused her insecurity.

When he had finished speaking, Cece sat against the bedstead and looked to the door.

'And do you?' she asked. 'Still? Love her?'

'No.'

'Did you ever?'

'I thought so.'

'And when did you know you'd stopped? Two hours ago? Just in time to jump the next available girl?'

'The other night, I think. When I saw you again.'

'How nice.' Cece tutted. 'I make people realize how little they like each other.'

The apologetic ticks of a clock buried in a box. He looked for clues in Cece's reaction. Should he try to explain further? Tell her how many hours he had searched for her on Facebook, how many strangers he had described her to before giving up? How he had read *La Commedia* in case he ever saw her again? Could he call to his defence the yearnings, the devotions which the thought of Cece had immediately provoked? The conviction that since becoming aware of her existence he would always want to be near her? These would be laughable at best, sinister at worst. The fact was, however uncertain he felt about Angie, he had never expected to see Cece again, never mind see her here. As she knotted and unknotted a bow around her dress, beams of light haloed her profile, illuminating the faint hairs curling at the top of her neck. He loved her hair, again and again, every time it changed, which was all the time.

'The crazy thing is, I think you really believe these things,' she said at last, got up and walked to the door.

'Are you going?'

'For a walk.' Her voice was pinched, and she wouldn't turn to show him her face. 'Plus, it's only fair to give your erection a rest.' She undid the latch, said, 'Goodnight, Ali,' and went away.

Ali rewarded himself with a cigarette, his fingers trembling with the rush that a large act of selfishness can induce. He had unburdened his insecurities onto someone else, and more than this he had effectively discarded Angie without telling her. He was dazed with guilty relief, almost delighted it had happened; that Cece had asked so directly and he had answered so instinctively. His eyes were heavy and he considered how he'd told the story, and how some details he'd omitted now seemed suddenly important.

Random but perhaps significant, they included things like Angie's faint, musical Bajan accent; or her serious rapture when she found baby segments of oranges tucked within larger ones; or the time they had made love behind a London fairground and celestially vaulted (where you lay and looked at the night and floated into its endless space) and discussed what songs they would like to die to, and kissed until first light.

At points, he'd told Cece every detail he could think of, other times only a summary. Some weeks later he would read in the library about the Russian distinction between the 'fabula' (the raw facts of an event) and the 'syuzhet' (the way a version of those facts is told). And in the months and years that followed, he would consider his syuzhet as he had told it to Cece, and which parts of the fabula he had selected, cut, reordered or mistook to construct it.

For now, though, the randomness of his self-censorship was oddly pleasing, because, like many young men, he was able to convince himself of the potential a higher pattern present in the gaps between his decisions.

This resignation calmed him. He'd done the mature thing in agreeing to tell Cece, hadn't he? The telling itself, well, it mattered less. That she had walked away was no great surprise. It was probable that she would ignore him for weeks to come, and plausible that she might even find Angie and tell her of his snakery.

The only thing he really regretted was her exit, but something – either cowardice or fatalism – told him there was no use in running after her. With fumy fingers he dragged his contact lenses out of his eyes and dropped them into the ashtray, resting as they dried into two hard shells.

A knock at the door. A glorious, double knock on the door.

She hadn't been gone long, perhaps the perfect amount of time – just long enough to level out but not so long as to punish him. She was always going to come back.

It was Nell, the hippy from upstairs. Nell, genial even as she watched the satisfaction, then chagrin pass across his features.

'Hey, how's it going?'

'Good.'

'Cool. We're playing night frisbee on the green if you want to join?'

'Mmm?'

'On the quad. Frisbee. It's great. It's got lights on it and everything.'

'Ah,' came his own glazed voice again. 'I thought it was a UFO.'

'A UFO?' Nell gave a puzzled look. 'No, UFOs wouldn't come to this town.' She walked in. 'There's nothing to do. Everything's too square.'

'Are we allowed on the quad?'

'Who cares?' Nell then took a seat. And before he knew it, she was talking about what sinister things quads were. 'It's important we reject their rules,' she said. 'The exclusivity of space is a basic evil, the "Do not walk on the grass" signs, so that we can all enjoy not being able to enjoy walking on it. I always think the kind of people who designed quads must have been – you know – sexually repressed. It's something about the straight lines. You know, something there comes from the same twisted mindset that confuses abstinence with constancy, you know? Or, like, self-harm with self-healing. As if facing something every day we want but can't have improves us! I mean, man, life is better than that! Right?'

He thought about Cece, wandering the edge of these grasses beneath his window every day for the next three years. Three solid years of pain. Nell interpreted this as an expression of agreement.

'It's all upper-class bling anyway. Lawns were, like, just designed as status symbols to show other people you could afford to keep land without building or growing anything on it. Uncultivated possession of land is the first symbol of capitalist sadism: I am more important and powerful because I have this.'

He nodded, but what he meant was *Please stop talking.*

'A status symbol that shows people you can afford things they can't. That's what I see when I look at this place: ownership of capital, and ownership of nature. The assumption we can control the environment and other people. So much of modern economics is just the same sadistic bullshit –'

'Wait, wait.' He looked at her properly for the first time. Nell was a good person – he'd heard her sing early Dylan in the shower and address her plants by their Latin names. She dried teabags on her windowsill and he'd heard that she had once been arrested for occupying a tree.

'What?' Nell asked.

'Nothing. How did we get on to this?'

'Frisbee. I'm just talking crap. The point is, you should come out.'

'I'm a bit drunk.'

'Perfect.' Nell got up and offered her hand. 'Get a jumper.'

'No, thing is, I'm waiting for…' He looked at his watch. Was she coming? Probably not. And so what if Cece did return to find him gone? Wasn't there something to be said for playing hard to get? 'OK, fine. But just tell me.'

'What?'

'Is frisbee a euphemism?'

'Yes.'

'For what?'

Nell allowed herself a duplicitous smile. 'Weed and frisbee.'

8

The aircraft gave a cold whine as it banked away, tipping its wings to the shrinking blocks of Heathrow.

The tannoy addressed us: 'Ladies and gentlemen, I'm now obliged to read you the conditions of your flight, so please do listen carefully.

'*With this flight credit, His Majesty's Government of the United Kingdom and Northern Ireland undertakes to grant you safe passage for transfer to a single destination state within member, outermost regions or outside the territories of the IUS (the International Union of Signatories) as agreed in the Borders Agreement of the Treaty on Commonwealth Union (2025) and the Treaty on the Functioning of the Commonwealth Union (2025). In accordance with the Global Treaty for Comprehensive Extradition (2026), His Majesty's Government will then undertake your return within no more than forty days of the date of departure, unless you are legally confirmed to remain in permanent residence within the destination state. If on the date set by the Department for International Travel you do not present yourself for return at the relevant port, airport or embassy, your safe return to the United Kingdom and Northern Ireland is not guaranteed by His Majesty's Government. This travel is granted in accordance with the personal Justification as submitted by all recipients and approved by the Department for International Travel. This travel is granted in good faith, and no person or persons will be granted later additional return travel provision under any circumstances.*

'*Additional credits can be bought through the Department for International Travel Exchange at a price arranged by the Commonwealth*

Commission. No person or persons may under any circumstances attempt to attach foreign persons to their flight credit or redesignate their flight credit to any other name. No person or persons may under any circumstances travel from their destination state to another state (other than the United Kingdom and Northern Ireland). Such attempts are considered criminal acts in all states and His Majesty's Government will not undertake to grant safe passage or protection to any person or persons who attempt to do so.

'What that means, ladies and gentlemen, is if you do not arrive on time for your return flight, we cannot guarantee you'll get home again – so please ensure all necessary arrangements are made. Further information is in the Traveller's Advice on the screens in front of you.

'I should say also that much of North Africa is, as you'll know, legally a completely independent region, so please ensure your situation is understood by your accommodation staff, guides, et cetera. Different countries, including the Kingdom of Morocco, have their own versions of Sanction 4, so don't assume they'll understand what your situations are, or where you're going back to.

'If this is your first time travelling internationally or in an aircraft and you have any questions, please check your Advice Screen, or ask an air steward...'

The captain dispatched his speech to his small audience levelly, reading the legal print with a lightness belied by the solemnity of his informal asides. The stewards, clad in different blues, wandered the aisle between passengers, offering screens, scratched and old with ghostly buttons, which I declined.

Edges of London passed through the window. One breached green belt, and now another, and another. It sprawled on and on, decayed housing built for a different future.

Five minutes later, an insect emerged from the baggage rack and buzzed at the window. It paused and folded, then climbed again. Making half attempts at the window it then rested on the lip of the blind, wings occasionally catching the full glance of the morning sun, separating colours onto the mottled plastic.

The plane was cold, I had forgotten just how cold they could be. And the last time I flew I wasn't old. I wrapped the nylon blanket around my legs. When I woke, the insect still just about buzzed from limp armrests to peeling safety manuals and finally to the discoloured floor. How fast planes lose their looks – at the same pace as people, perhaps. After fifty, sixty years, redundant wiring led nowhere, racks were stuffed with old manuals, broken seats lay prostrated.

A vibration in my bag; my reader glowed with messages. Some from old friends – retired reporters also hankering to travel. Some from protest groups who had somehow spammed me with condemnations for the flight that hadn't yet landed.

One from Kat, poetic as ever, said:

So I haven't heard from you, even though you promised. Will you ever write, I wonder? It must be strange for you to travel again. Perhaps you do appreciate the privilege.

When you come back I'd like to talk, not that it makes any difference to you. Two reasons:

I'm taking my flight early; I don't see the point in waiting.

Also, Mum met someone. I'd like to tell you more. It's going to be good for her. You'll be relieved I know.

k

I read it, twice. She'd sent it in the middle of the night; was she sleeping? I tapped her picture, let her guarded smile fill the screen.

'Excuse me? Sir?' The attendant raised and slowed her voice. 'Can you hear me?'

'I'm not deaf.'

She slowed her voice again, chiding me. 'You can't have devices switched on until the in-flight light has come on. Sir? Could you put it away?'

I pretended to comply. But when the attendant had walked away it illuminated again. 'GO BACK?' asked one of the buttons. Yes please, was the answer. Just a little.

I read Kat's message again. So Madison had met a guy. I was pleased. It had been years since Anatoliy had died, and she hadn't had anyone. Except me, in a way. She and I had never been more than consignatories, no matter what Kat's obsession with the definition of our marriage had been.

'Sir, please put that away.' The attendant raised her voice from the front of the cabin.

This time, I did. I didn't raise doubts about whether a fifteen-year-old reader could upset a two-engine jet aircraft that had made ten thousand trips. That when aircraft crashed these days it was never by mechanical fault, whatever the news said. Instead I thought of Kat. My little Kat. I couldn't write to her now, I just couldn't. I would tell her everything when I got back.

I shut down the device. But as the hours passed and we entered different national airspaces, the newsbar flashed in the side panel with various regional propaganda. Two rescue ships had been damaged in the Mediterranean, one struck in the rudder and able only to operate in precarious circles, the other defending it with only one functioning cannon. There were reports that multiple boats, carrying over eight hundred people, had landed off the coast of Gibraltar: the worst breakthrough in the Mediterranean for almost a year.

The corner of the screen blinked dumbly with images of the refugee enclave of Melilla in northern Morocco, where children and adults raised their rafts to their shoulders in reaction and carried them to the shores like coffins to a burial.

VIII

Seven black silhouettes were spread across the massive quad playing frisbee in the darkness. Nell tried to explain the physics to him as they stumbled over the green, chasing the rainbows left by the LEDs on the frisbee. Nell had seemed at first to be just one of those modern stoners who came for the music, stayed for the drugs and gave minimal thought to the environmental stuff beyond questioning their parents' second car and learning a few rants from the internet about single-use plastic.

But Nell was more than that. Icily lucid on the science behind everything from ecology to astrophysics, she spoke matter-of-factly about the different velocities moving over and under the frisbee's shape, the lower pressure of the airflow beneath giving it trance-like lift and the higher pressure above producing downward drag and therefore her capacity to steer it. Instead of simply being a pothead, Nell wanted to grow up to be a rocket scientist and marry her passion with her pantheism by exploring the universe.

She went on, chatting about how the frisbee seemed to paint colour behind it in mid-air due to the phenomenon called persistence of vision, how the speed of it exceeded the eye's sixteen frames per second, prompting the brain to apprehend the image just long enough to perceive a completed picture, even though it had filled in the gaps itself, and although he made noises of comprehension and approval, Ali had by this time stopped listening.

One of the silent figures bent a crooked throw round the large grandfather oak in the top third of the quad. For some reason, he couldn't stop wondering if he had done Angie an injustice. They had been happy with one another in many ways, after all. But when he had been unhappy, it had been acute, worse than he could admit even to Stov. He began to console himself with memories of dysfunction that might excuse his behaviour this evening.

Memories of how, occasionally, when out with her friends, he had felt a crater open between himself and Angie. If he made her laugh, for example. Normally, Angie didn't laugh at things he said. So when she did laugh properly – a lovely, natural, lyrical, triple-filtered laugh – it was the exception that proved the rule. She didn't expect him to amuse her.

Or the way she somehow held back when they smoked a joint together, never giving herself to the drug more than was coolly dignified. She wasn't introverted, she was withholding.

Or the way she bristled then fell silent if ever she were no longer the most beautiful person in the room, a contingency she had so rarely encountered that no ready response seemed to have developed in her. Or her 'go-thither' eyes, which met his when he interrupted a conversation with her girlfriends. Or her unctuous manner with nightclub owners. Or her use of 'if you will'. Or the sex, a wrestle of courtesies, ending with a mutual refusal to climax first. Those were the times he felt no closer to her than to a stranger.

Ali wondered then if he had ever really been moved by her. Or had he felt warmth where there was only brilliance?

A black figure, prominent against the hall lights, picked the frisbee from the wet grass and whisked it beyond his and Nell's vicinity. The disc hovered over the empty straight of the green before a silhouette plucked it from the air.

The disc came to Nell and she threw it again. 'You're quiet, man.'

'Yeah, sorry.'

'You can't work the dark silent type look in the dark, you know.' Her throw fell wide, nearly executing some hydrangeas. 'She won't notice.'

'Who?'

'Her.' One of the profiles was retrieving it from the flower beds that lined the hall. 'No, that's Ravi.' Nell rotated him by the shoulders in the direction of the other corner. 'Cece, she's over there.'

Nell was clearly so wise to Ali's intense focus on Cece, despite his efforts at discretion, that he almost squirmed. But he was too excited to care. There was a person somewhere in the shadows outside the library, there must have been – he realized – at least two others to complete the shape around which the frisbee made its circuit. The shadow that was Ravi threw a perfect curve out to the shadow that must have been Cece. It stopped where Cece was, a metre off the ground. 'She's good.'

'Yes,' Nell said. 'All OK between you?'

'Yes, we're just catching up. We knew each other a bit before.'

'Cool.'

'It's a pretty big coincidence. Ending up at the same college.'

Nell thought about this, and her thinking face looked like the stifling of a sneeze. She curled a finger before her mouth and then concluded, 'Well, think about it. Only seven per cent of the national population go to private schools. And yet a private school student has a twenty-nine per cent chance of getting in, which is double the average. Around forty-five per cent of the people here are private school. How many students do we have – three thousand? Four thousand?'

'I guess.'

'Let's say three thousand for now?'

'For now?'

'So that's one thousand, three hundred and fifty private school kids. How many private schools are there? Two hundred and fifty?

That's an average of five kids per private school. And bear in mind Cece has been to a lot of them.'

'Really?'

'Let's say she's been to ten schools. She knows a lot of people here.'

'*Ten?*'

'That's at least fifty-four people in this university she was at school with. So, in this little privilege farm: not *so* unlikely. And then there's the special thing about Cece herself.'

'Which is?'

'Cece talks to strangers. So in the pool of public school students, Cece knows more than most. She's the outlier.'

'How come she went to all these schools?'

'I don't know. But the fact she knows us isn't so improbable.'

The frisbee sliced towards Ali, dipping at the last second to head height.

'She *is* good.' Nell looked out to the figure.

For a while their throws zipped along the wind, twinkling from hand to hand as though cast by wands.

'So,' Nell said, 'are you going on the march tomorrow?'

By now Ali had no idea what they were talking about. This evening seemed to be pulsing out its final beats of sense. Were they still talking about Cece? God, he thought, I'm too tired.

'I don't think so.'

'Well, try. We've made our own drugs.'

'OK.'

It was on that night Ravi's right arm was broken. Their frisbee circuit – a hexagon – had become a pentagon when Ravi had returned to his room to get a jacket and, while there, had tried to close his window. The old loose counterweight frame first resisted and finally gave, crashing down onto its sill, shattering both of its panes, the momentum sending Ravi into the night sky and onto the paved walkway two floors below, cracking his head, breaking an arm and two ribs.

Soon rumours had started that blood had sprayed over the flower beds, so much so that one of the neighbours who found him, a medical student no less, had passed out. The other had seen Ravi, his arm sickeningly disjointed, trying to get up again and again, obstinately holding onto his blood-soaked jacket. Small crowds were gathering around the benches and smaller quads, well-lubricated revellers united in concern, suddenly aware of how sober they could be if there was a serious attitude to be taken. They moved out of the way as an ambulance trundled over planks laid out on the grass by the porters, the first vehicle to do so in a hundred years, or so they said.

After the commotion, Ali spotted Cece, static, leaning against the oak, silently watching Nell roll another joint.

'Hey man,' Nell said, and hugged him, like they'd been greeting this way all their lives. 'Rough times,' she said, then wandered off.

'How was your walk?'

'Nell caught me,' Cece said, 'made me play frisbee.'

'I know. Me too.'

It wasn't clear if she'd heard, or if her concentration was in the branches above her, sifting through the evening's events.

They shared the silence. It was a clean, dark night, polished and vast. Cece plucked some blades of grass and squandered them on the breeze. 'I should go to bed.'

'Yes.'

Smatterings of other conversations became audible in the dark, plaits of smoke rising into the sky.

'I'm sorry –'

'Yeah, terrible for Ravi, isn't it.'

'Terrible. Poor Ravi.'

'Yeah.'

It was impossible not to overhear the others still gossiping in the walkways on the route back to Ali's room. Everyone was trying to remember if they had met Ravi during the first three days, and, if possible, claim a personal connection with him. They found him easier to pity if they could convince others to notice them by proxy, and although the party atmosphere had gone, no one minded giving up drunken abandon for the thrill of being near a live drama.

'We sat opposite each other at dinner. We were going to go on the march tomorrow.'

'I helped him unpack his dad's car – who's gonna call his family?'

'We were dancing earlier and you could tell he's a really nice guy. So horrible.'

Already photos were being tagged online and a cultish reconstruction of the evening was under way, in which all Ravi's movements before the accident could be traced. He saw among them a photo of Cece taken from the dance floor, with Ravi bowed obscurely in the background. The next few minutes led him on a trail of images of the week. He clicked on Cece's face, then Angie's, then his own, all these images just floating out there, alive but infinite, distant as stars.

Before Ali went to bed he watched the ambulance taxi back over the quad, its urgent blue lights reminding him of the colours of the dance floor of only two hours before, a déjà vu that only showed how little order there seemed left in the evening, only his incessant thoughts.

He left his room and ascended the stairs to Cece's door, where he raised his hand to knock. And then he just stood there, frozen like a living statue for about a minute, his knuckles an inch from the paint.

9

Then all at once the screech of tyres and the wind quelling the wings. The loose-hinged tables and curled linoleum throbbing as though the whole plane were alive. The tremble and then the passing of fear. The miracle and the boredom. Already the others began to shuffle towards the exit and stand at the door, silently protesting against its obstinacy. We stepped out of the aircraft and into the thick air, a wall of light in front and above us. The banister on the stairway was warm.

Attendants passed us our refrigerated luggage and one of them, no more than a boy, picked up mine with an officious swagger and led us across the tarmac. No big deal. No checks on the passengers at all. We couldn't believe it. Not that there was no security: the runway lots and vehicle entrances teemed with soldiers guarding the fuel tanks. They stood in the shade of their cannons and gazed hard at the horizon, the one road leading to and from the airport.

When I asked if he was a real porter the boy spoke no English, and when I asked him to return the bag he miraculously developed some. A couple of the other passengers threw him looks, but the boy wasn't trying to rob me, or at least not yet. He vanished into the mobbed street, promising to fetch a taxi as I prepared his tip from my wad of food sachets, creased like palms.

As I waited, an aged hologram mouthed welcomes on a loop. A policeman rested on the heel of his handgun and checked his reader. The airport was mostly a shell, about two-thirds of the area behind the manned cordon having been gutted long ago. Sunlight and sounds from the shuttered windows spilled into the ransacked gaps. Two tiny drones buzzed around the rafters. On a wall beside an empty shelf was a paper sign in French and Arabic, with an English translation beneath: *The defibrillator has been removed for maintenance. We apologize for any inconvenience.*

The policeman asked to see my Justification credit. I handed over the reader and he stood inspecting the stamp codes. He brought up a map of my travel history and raised an eyebrow.

The boy returned, grinning. 'No taxi.'

'And my bag?'

'On bus, here.' He plucked my passport from the policeman's hands and took me outside to the road and its instant clatter, its smears of unrefined petrol on baked stone. The bus to Fès glittered as I paid him, and we set off with a jounce, leaving him sitting on a bollard, his legs dangling in the brown shade.

An hour later, where the smooth stretch of the toll highway broke into gravel, we stopped at the terminal. A half-dozen bus drivers in sunglasses sat in an arc under shabby cafe umbrellas, patiently waiting for the Westerners to stop ignoring them and enquire about prices.

Most said they couldn't take me near the medina, but finally an older man agreed to go as far as he could at the end of his shift, and would drop me at Place R'cif if possible.

'From American?' he asked in the rear-view mirror. Since I was the only one in the vehicle, it was essentially a taxi.

'No, from England.'

'No?' Eyebrows appeared above his sunglasses. 'Here for business, kif?'

'Kif?'

'Kif business? Rif?' He pointed his arm out the window towards the mountains on the distant side of the valley.

'No. To visit a friend.'

'OK, OK.' He gave me a knowing smile as the empty road twinkled across his lenses.

He took us through the Ville Nouvelle and its clusters of tiered hotel blocks, which had abandoned their obsession with symmetry and total whiteness.

Later a police car filled the mirrors and the driver grumbled something. He slowed as it overtook, its driver evaluating us before turning off at the next junction.

'Where Fès el-Bali where?'

'The university.'

'University? Al-Karaouine?'

'I think so.'

'Al-Karaouine University, yes. Oldest university. Very old.'

'That'll be it. Let's go there.'

He dropped me near the mosque by a gate to the medina, and gave me directions to walk to the back. I paid him more than I could afford, and he asked how I was getting back to the airport. I said I wasn't sure. He shook my hand and left.

The streets dilated and narrowed around the mosque's vast bulwarks, occasionally promising open spaces only to thin to tiny alleys no wider than my armspan. The bag gouged my shoulder as I followed his directions through the arid colours – orange cubes under terracotta roofs, as though a wave of ruddy earth had swept through the town and dried in the sun. To slow my heavy breathing I rested a hand against a wall. The quicklime in the air tasted of long-forgotten foreign summers.

A cluster of children gathered around me, gabbling. The few girls pawed at my arms and ran away giggling to circle at the edges of the group while the boys asked in French if I needed a guide. They grew more confident as they slowed me down, so I picked the youngest to ask how far it was to the university. She stopped in her tracks, thought, and pointed just to the end of the street and said '*Là*' in a milky voice, causing the others to exclaim in disappointment at her honesty and the loss of a bigger tip. I put a meal sachet in her hand which she squeezed and then examined, paused, and looked up at me. A person from some other world.

I X

'And many of you will be familiar with St Julian's through Morwenna Steele, whose most famous song, "No Matter", was first sung in this hall.' The principal read the lyrics aloud:

'All change, please, all change.
Remember your things, remember your coat,
Please take your shopping, and your oldest wish –
That thing you wanted, you even promised it.
Have you forgotten your word? Your so-called bond?
The dreams you had, they've all but gone.
How the grey matter turns to black.
Your changes changed but you stayed the same.
(It's all lost luggage on empty trains.)
No matter, no matter.
All change, please, all change.'

Ali didn't recognize the words. Or perhaps they did ring a bell: hadn't his mother listened to Morwenna Steele on holidays? Or perhaps one of her songs had been used in a perfume advert.

'She first sang the song in this room when I was an undergraduate. Of course, it sounded quite different then. So I'd like to talk today about that word, *change*.' The principal paused, closing the book of Steele's lyrics. 'By the way, can everyone hear at the back? Good. I don't like microphones.' He surveyed, unseeing, the hungover faces before him.

It was the day after the night of the bop, the night of Ravi's accident. The night Cece had shaken his universe. Was she here?

He couldn't see her. It was possible she had never intended to come, but he also wondered what her absence might mean.

'I'd like to talk about change,' Principal Faulk continued. 'There's that bad joke you'll have heard a dozen times: "How many academics does it take to change a light bulb?" "Change? Change? Who said anything about CHANGE?"'

Some of the students laughed, others shifted in their new-found lecture posture. Two boys got the giggles either side of a girl who checked her phone about every forty seconds, her thoughts elsewhere.

Perhaps Cece simply hadn't wanted to see him. Perhaps she was complaining to the dean about him now, asking to be moved to a room away from Ali Turner, and the bizarre narrative he had constructed following their one and only meeting in London more than a year ago.

The principal paused. He turned over his sheet of paper, placed a finger on the lectern and continued: 'But things do change here, and we like that. So the question you should be asking today is what kind of change you are interested in, realistically, at your age. Well, there are types of change. There is change in the world, progress, you might call it – social, scientific, and so on. You may be thinking you're not interested in that sort of thing yet, you're interested in what's going to change for you right now, and understandably so. What do the next few years have to offer you in terms of personal change – as a student, as a mind, as a person? What new knowledge will you gain, what friends will you make, what new music will you listen to, what wisdom will you pick up?

'I could tell you that here you will find new things, you will shed old things, you will refind old things. I could tell you that here you will learn to think for yourselves. These are clichés read aloud by welcoming principals and presidents and provosts in university inductions up and down the country, but what do they really mean?'

Ali imagined Cece's packed bags sitting in the porters'. The porter calling her a taxi as the senior tutor gave her an embrace of solidarity, assuring her the college would explain to the father she was returning to so early and so grieved. Absorbed in the glossy drama of the first couple of nights, how careless of her feelings had he been? It was a question of degrees, he knew that. But he kept imagining Cece always moving away from him towards the bedroom door, wary that he posed an emotional danger.

'Well, I always say,' said the principal, clasping his hands at this opportunity to say again what he always said, 'that you should think of knowledge as an island in a vast sea of ignorance.' He drew an oval island on the whiteboard behind him. 'The more you change, and learn, the bigger the island of knowledge grows. Think then how this affects the sea around it. As your island grows, so does its circumference, and it is now exposed to more of the sea of ignorance. The island has eaten away at a little of the sea, but, more importantly, it is now in touch with more of the sea – you are now aware of much more that you *don't* understand. As knowledge grows, so proportionally does the knowledge of our ignorance, and therefore what we might discover. Every territorial gain of knowledge produces a thousand more touchpoints with new ignorance. Seek answers, and you create new questions.'

Principal Faulk smiled as he wandered from the lectern, perhaps remembering a phrase he had delivered in a previous year.

Calm, Ali told himself, *calm* – Cece would have asserted herself if she'd wanted to. And yet what little he understood of her had been redefined in that odd minute among all the drunkenness, when she had seemed to slump into him on the dance floor. That second, her confidence, the camouflage of what he sensed to be an ever-present vigilance, had slipped. She was not the needling interrogator of their first conversation, nor the serial dropout of however many schools Nell had counted. And he wanted to know what lay beneath.

'I learned, when I was an undergraduate,' the principal went on, 'that the term "to learn" itself partly comes from the Old English word *læst*, meaning "the sole of the foot". The sole of the *foot*. Think of your feet, soft and sensitive at first, then toughened and calloused but still soft and tender in areas. Learning, then, is walking the track. It comes from a mindset which equated thought with action, the tough sole of the feet and the tough soul of the man. There was serious belief in the Middle Ages that words had a real power and, if correctly iterated in prayer or spell, could affect reality. And perhaps' – he slowed in order to show that he was getting to a good bit – 'this is a useful definition of education. Words can affect reality.'

With his white foam of hair and wide shapeless gown, the principal resembled a cresting wave on which he carried the flotsam of a pair of Buddy Holly glasses. Occasionally, as his corkscrewed tie got in the way of his arms, or his hands became lost in his gown, he seemed lost and fragile.

'But all of us, whatever we study, can recognize that learning in this sense is getting out there, walking a path, getting the blisters, the splinters, the dirt, and experiencing the world for ourselves. Learning is not merely static, mental and private, it is in motion, communal and public. It is hard knocks. It is *mutual*. Even the word "understanding" itself literally means to stand in the midst of, to place ourselves physically in a landscape of knowledge. To educate ourselves then is thus to involve ourselves physically in the world. To walk the island, to explore not only what is unknown but what is already known. Just because things have already been discovered, it does not mean they are not worth returning to.'

Perhaps she'd had a bad trip. Perhaps it had been the drugs. Stov's powdered plant food. A latent reaction. Was she still in bed, coming down? Or sleeping in her own vomit? Was she dead? And it would be his fault. Manslaughter at least. The sentence and shame would be one thing, but accidentally killing Cece after all this yearning was another. Ali got a hold of himself.

Principal Faulk went on, 'Our species has convinced itself on numerous occasions that we have faced a "final frontier": God's reason, Alaska, the brain, space. But in our haste to unearth the new, we can miss the value of the old. I'm talking about other people's problems, other species, other politics, other ideas, other attitudes to change, their hunger, their jobs.'

Ali breathed deeply again. Cece wasn't there because she didn't want to be lectured by an old man, not because she was dead.

'Don't simply look outwards to expand the island frontiers – look also inland, and you will find much to change.'

This last cadence was delivered in a way that suggested the end of the speech, until the reverie was broken by a quick-fire triplet of the principal's coughs.

After the induction they were all taken to the Freshers' Fair. On the way, a brilliant torrent of rain reinforced their collective sense of excitement, and as they stepped into the massive hall it was filled with an appropriately hot, damp energy.

It was everything everyone had said it would be – a crash course in student preoccupations, a bazaar of more free, valueless stuff than you could possibly carry. As he browsed the stalls, he failed to sign up to any because he was paralysed by choice. He didn't know who it was he wanted to be, who he was or who he was going to become. He didn't know what he found appealing, nor indeed what would appeal to other people. The room demanded he decide, and he wasn't ready.

Absorbed in the throng and wary of joining the wrong type of club (was Poetry Club too conceited? Who were the Assassins? What was Real Tennis?), he therefore joined none. Indecision was easier. He saw other students walking the aisles, selecting hobbies like clothes from a rack. They were kids, ignorant of their limits, which this market would lead them to discover.

Finally he was attracted to the Environment and Politics Society stall by the guileless grin of Nell, and, finding his hand hovering over a petition urging *RADICAL ACTION AT GLENEAGLES*, he almost decided to commit to signing. Surely this was straight-forward, and good, and uncontroversial. It was also where he first saw his own signature already on the page, staring back at him like his face in a puddle: *Ali Turner.*

It was odd, not least because he hadn't written it. But immediately he liked it – it was the mark of a steady mind and hand, a signee of important petitions, and he could tell it was Cece's version of him. He just knew. It had her magic.

The more he looked through the petitions on the table, the more he found this well-made, straight-backed signature. *Ali Turner*, a critic of Western reluctance to send aid to Palestine; *Ali Turner*, a determined supporter of Make Poverty History; *Ali Turner*, a petitioner for proper desalination plants in Iraq.

He was pleased. Cece had made choices for him. And, as his leaping heart was aware, she was talking to him.

She had begun, he could see, by volunteering him for the Conservative Society. Very funny. And then Cheerleading had apparently seemed a natural counterpoint. Roller Hockey was next, for reasons he supposed even she could not explain, and after that, with the Samaritans, the floodgates had clearly opened, and soon he saw his name signed to Beekeeping, the Minimalism Society, Queer Society, Street Spirit Society, the Ancients Society, the Modernism Society, Feminists, Masculists, the Liberal Democrats

Student Club, the Fishing and Shooting Association, the Animal Protection Society, Mechanics, Ottomans, Champagne and Cake (men bring the champagne, women make the cake), Morris Dancing, Psy Trance, eight college choirs, three bands and an administrative post in the University Union.

When he found her, she was sitting beneath a ten-foot portrait of a prince, holding all her leaflets, smiling with enough satisfaction for them both.

'Hello,' he said.

'Yes?'

'Which other societies have you been signing me up to?'

'That would be telling. They'll fill your inbox soon enough. Which is your favourite new hobby?' she asked.

'I seem to be very committed to Nell's petitions.'

'Yes, well, they're important. Are you going on the march? It's in ten minutes. It's to save the universe. You're signed up for it.'

'I've seen.' And then he said proudly, 'So are you.'

'Am I now?'

'Yep.'

'Well then.'

'So what's it actually about, this march?'

'I thought you knew.' She handed him the leaflet. 'I can't be expected to care about every society I sign you up to.'

He looked at it. 'Or we could go somewhere?'

'Yes.' She stood. 'All right.'

So they returned to The Games and slept together.

10

A congregation of smoking men sat beneath the green of the university roofs. Topping one was an ornamental finial shaped like a sting, under which the thick, open doors and a pair of intricate curved arches channelled a noiseless breeze. A wide, glinting courtyard spinning with flourishes of dots spread its shade over me, first blue then green, squares then circles, pulling me towards the three fountains at its centre. All around them, tricks of geometry seemed to create steps and pools in the ground before becoming solid by the time I crossed. One window in the upper floor looked down onto the courtyard.

I wandered through the white symmetries until a man with a radio stopped me and held out his hand for a pass. He was animated and confused at my intrusion. I said that I didn't have a pass and attempted to explain. But I realized he didn't understand my English or my French, and after looking around he hurried me on and on, through gilded arabesque corridors and under horseshoe-shaped cloisters to a closed room. With a brisk speech he fetched another man from within. This man was much older – his beard was flecked with grey and the hair beneath his *taqiyah* was thinly white – but he moved with a young impatience, and in his hands he held a beautiful leather-bound book that he tucked under an arm when he shook my hand. He calmly reassured the gatekeeper and turned to me, his English reedy, stating, 'You should not be here. You have come for research? Photographs?' looking to me and then to the gatekeeper for confirmation. The gatekeeper stared.

'No, no – I'm looking for a teacher here.'

'A teacher? Of Al-Karaouine?' His English rose with scepticism.

'Yes. Dr Unwin?'

He noticed the bag in my hand. 'No, no one like that.'

'No? Are you sure? Perhaps you could check?'

'Sir, we are only scripture scholars – this is a school of religion.'

'But he –'

'Your friend, the doctor, he is a teacher of Islam?' He unpicked the arms of his reading glasses and put them on – a sign for me to leave – and opened his book.

'I don't think so.'

'So you see.' He extended his arm towards the doorway in a polite but firm gesture. There was nothing else to say; the lines of his face expressed adequate sympathy but told of larger concerns awaiting his attention in the next room. 'I must ask you to go. You should not have been here. You are the first in – oh, many years.' He glanced up at the ceiling as he paused, as though the weight of centuries past rested on the beams. 'We don't have many visitors any more, you would not have been able to wander through here before. Please.'

As he spoke, the shock, the enormous futility of my journey, poured through my knees. The use of my last flight. The money. The fact that Russell must have lied to me, or got it wrong, or Stov had left Fès. Whatever the case, he wasn't here. I had felt so sure this time. But still I wouldn't see him, or the woman who was with him. It was so damaging it felt almost like relief, because I could go back to England knowing I had at least tried. I picked up the bag and walked to the door. Maybe Stov wasn't even alive any more.

'Perhaps…' I turned as the old man shut his book, thought for a second and asked, 'What is the name of your friend?'

'Dr Unwin. Stovah Unwin.'

'Ah *Stov*.' He turned the book over in his hands. 'I just thought. Stov. Yes, that is different.' He spoke quietly to his colleague, mentioning Stov's name, prompting the gatekeeper to smirk knowingly and approach to pick up my bag. The old man instructed him not to and they had another brief exchange in which the gatekeeper seemed to object to my presence but deferred to his senior. He left my bag, and the room, shaking his head.

'So you do know him, Stov?'

'Yes. Fajir Stov, he calls himself – it is his joke. It means "the sinner". He has come to us, it is true. Many times. But he does not teach here, you have got that very wrong. He has not been inside, as you are now.'

'I'm sorry, I didn't realize. This whole thing is a mess.'

He smiled slightly. 'Aziz wants you to leave, and he is right. But, well, you have come in already and the harm is done. So please, let us walk.'

We went through to a colonnade.

'So you are his friend.'

'Yes, since we were children.'

'In England?'

'Yes.'

He was leading me back through the outer buildings. 'He wanted to enter the university and we did not permit it. We only allow people here who worship Allah. So you should not be here, and not Stov, even though he said he had come to God.'

'Stov said that? He said "come to God"?'

The man nodded. Arches appeared regularly and then irregularly, filled with sequestered light and air, each chamber holding its breath for a thousand years. The private majesty of the ceilings, the patterns of flowers, fractal and infinite, mesmeric colours perfectly conceived and carefully made – had Stov been converted by this? If any building could captivate a person, this place might,

I thought, as blotches formed on the walls and the floor became unsteady. The old man gripped my arm. 'You are unwell?'

'No, fine.'

'Perhaps we go outside.'

In a courtyard the tiles and unpainted plasterwork blazed with white light; jasmine and hollyhocks decorated the air, tantalizing the bees. Perhaps it was my light-headedness, but there seemed to be too much space between all these things.

'Sit, please. Your friend was stopped at the gates of the mosque years ago.' He turned his face up to the sun. 'Stov asked for the dean, that is me, and showed his qualifications. He was very confident man. He asked me if Al-Karaouine needed a teacher. I said we are a religious university, so we do not need this kind of university teacher.

'But he had the smell of alcohol and kif in him. And no true Muslim comes to mosque like this. And we don't give entry to men who are not Muslims.' He turned. 'You are not here for kif, I think?'

'That's right.'

'I thought not. So we sent him away, and again we did not see him for a while. But he comes back to the mosque – he is always polite, he always says salaam and calls us all Father even though he knows this is not right. "Father, Father," he would say, "one day you will take me." Other times he is clean and smart and gives *baraka* – his money – to the boys and the beggars.'

Bird calls sounded behind his speech as I imagined Stov the religious penitent, then the drunk, and finally the fool. It was hardly believable. Above the courtyard, a thin stream of smoke crossed the sky's otherwise absolutely blue complexion.

The dean stood and clapped the dust from his hands. 'At last I gave your friend the name of the newer universities. I said to him, they might enter you there. He is now at Al Akhawayn, I think.'

'Al Akhawayn?'

'Yes, Al Akhawayn. We are Al-Karaouine. It is not far from Fès. It is a new university and they will do well for him there. From what I saw he seems like a clever man and he has learned much to teach. He is a Western man, and they like a Western man. But your friend, he is not a man for religion.'

'No.'

'But he is a man of peace, and joy. He has the will to be good. Whatever else. I like Stov. Mr Fajir Stov.' He walked us the short distance of corridors back to the gate where I had begun. 'It is good that he gives money to the beggars. I heard he gave much. So many have come from their villages to bus stations and the public squares. The slums outside the medina are full.' The dean limped under the burden of my bag. 'I would like to ask a question,' he said, panting a little. 'It is not often we get English any more. Some French and Chinese, and Americans of course.' He paused for breath. 'You are from London?'

'Yes.'

'Very nice. I have not spoken to a Londoner for so long. I lived there. For one half year, when I was young boy. Before the – what do you say? – "continental conflict".'

'Where in London were you?'

'Old Street – you know?' His voice had a slight tremor.

'Very well.'

'I was there. For my cousin's family. They sold…' He made the movements of a video game controller. 'Big electronics. Big televisions.' He smiled. 'You were there?'

'Yes.'

'The world has changed. Very much.'

'Yes.'

'When I was a boy I said, "I want to live in London." Then, in London, I wanted to come back to Morocco. In England it felt like the government, the people, they wanted to help the world, with laws to reverse the damage. But like you say' – he shook my hand and gave it a cordial, statesmanlike pat – '"if wishes were dishes, then beggars would feast". Laws are not facts – that is why we have free will.'

I waited on the paving slabs, their centres eroded by the footfalls of a thousand sandals. I retrieved my reader from my bag and charged it in the brilliant light of the court. The green roofs shone in the sun and above them small flocks of birds wrinkled the sky. This was real. Stov had outdone himself: offering himself to an orthodox university, charming the priests. It was either a bad joke or a real attempt at conversion. The former would be an achievement even for Stov, and the latter some achievement for God.

The old man was right. It wasn't the old Stov's kind of university, it was more of a monastery, an appendage of the enormous mosque, poised like a crustacean over the town. Exactly the kind of place Stov had always avoided. But perhaps he had changed, I thought, as a group of young men skirted the other side of the quadrant, their reed mats under their arms.

But it was also the most peaceful space I had been in for many years. More peaceful than any college, park or church. Unchanged in all these days of destruction, oblivious to the droughts and wars, the abandoned plazas, rotting palms and vacant highways beyond. Contained in this bright, simple radiance was what anyone would stay for: the total erasure of all other things. Everywhere, even in the shaded corners where nothing stood, was a stronger afterglow, a building's calm in its own permanence.

The old man left me there and beckoned for the gatekeeper. 'Wait here. We will find your friend, where he lives.' He limped away through the arches. Back to his shelter. A refuge from time.

X

Nell's march had crossed their path between Stone Street and Tyde Lane on the way back: a porous stream of Pantone umbrellas undeterred by the police and puddles. Between the megaphones at the front and curious tourists at the back, Ali and Cece had joined in and slipped away again when they passed the turn-off to St Ju's.

Then they'd gone via the library, which was completely empty because everyone was at the fair, and as Cece climbed the ladder to sit on the flat top of a bookcase, he wandered the floor perusing the cellophaned hardbacks. After he told her he had broken up with Angie on the phone that morning – in a quiet, pained exchange riddled with clichés – Cece was silent.

'Oh, so this is why you've been ignoring my calls?' Angie had said down the line. 'That's cowardly now, isn't it?'

'I'm sorry,' he'd said.

'Only say that if you are, please.'

'I am.'

'Then why are you doing this?'

He had also known what Stov would have said (*Do it. Mistakes are the imperative of happiness, Ali*), and all in all he felt entirely unqualified, and lacking in theories about the world – what Stov called 'panchrestons' – to be the person living his own life. All he knew was that he was slightly stunned by how painful he'd found the break-up. At the final severance he'd rediscovered the pulse of his affection for Angie. Both he and she were more distressed than expected, and, unhelpfully late, he'd considered for the first time what a long and mutually supportive relationship they had conducted relative to their youth. 'Perhaps we can be friends,' he'd said.

'Perhaps.'

And he heard the beginning of an escaped sob as Angie hung up the phone. She really liked me, he thought. Apparently he had done a fine job convincing himself otherwise.

Sitting at the foot of the stepladder, he proceeded to mumble to Cece some half-truths, or halves of truths which, paired with the correct other halves, might have been whole, as he clumsily tried to find out what she thought of it all. 'So that's that,' he said.

Cece took a hairband from around her wrist and set it on the shelf. She stared out of the window, holding her breath. Light from the street trickled in at oblique angles. The smell of churned wet leaves. 'It's OK to be sad,' she said, sitting up. 'I'm going back to The Games.' She descended the ladder and walked past him. 'Coming?'

Then they were in her bed, and he was amazed by how much of her seemed unfamiliar, that the time spent imagining her had not acquainted him with her radical softness; the rhythm of her rising, collapsing hips; the doleful murmurs, asking him not to stop, that he could elicit from one so normally affirmative when he paused his hands; the desire to touch her neck, to curl her straight hair behind her ears, to hold her fingers.

He didn't remember much more about it afterwards, didn't try to reconstruct this afternoon for many years. And when he did, it returned to him all in one breath. How he had found himself focussing on her posters (a Joni Mitchell album and a Man Ray portrait which would be stolen by a French student called Gifford during a hall party weeks later) while she balanced a thumb on his collarbone and he kissed the curve of her breasts as he was trying not to come. And his realization that if she had decided in the library (or maybe at the Freshers' Fair) that they would fuck now to save him from further infatuation, then perhaps this was why she had laughed so readily at the moments of awkwardness that normally went carefully ignored in bed – fiddling with socks and condoms. But it hadn't worked because, as she poured lower onto him, her naked surface tensing in front of the light, he began to rise above all the anxieties of the place, the pool tables and the library, the gardens and roofs of The Games. And beyond them St Ju's itself, the Fair, the dusk, the morass of a peopled world, all destined to be burned up by the sun anyway. All he wanted to say was *I have known you now, I will know you always*.

The coincidence of their both coming to St Julian's was at the heart of it. There simply was no explanation as to why they were both here other than luck, which had corroborated all his instincts: they were meant to be together at college, living together, and such things did not happen for no reason. Happenstance like this was rare and Cece had been behaving as if it were too gauche to be worthy of comment, which made him feel like he was slightly mad. Coincidence was what made their sex unique. And coincidence would provoke their first argument, minutes later.

As he rolled away, dizzy, exultant, a cramp in his hip, he knew her nonchalance would continue. He wasn't stupid, nor unaware that young people were often, like him, conditioned by hormones, hopes and illusions, determined to fulfil their expectations of romance at university. But the way he saw it, his overlapping with Cece was an inevitable part of his becoming whoever it was he would become. To call it fate sounded ridiculous, but however you wanted to describe it, when you subtracted the parts of their mutual demographic, friends, interests and education, there was still some untold residue. Surely even she would have to admit that something more had brought them this close, their hot and tangled limbs here. Deep down she also felt it, he was sure.

'I don't feel it.' She shrugged. 'This is sex.'

'Just sex?'

'Don't say it like that. Not "just".' Cece slid a leg over the top of the duvet and let it cool, her tattoo even more innocuous than he remembered. 'Sex is a lot.' She indicated beyond their cotton den to life outside the window. 'When you get sex, you're getting the truest, closest part of some people. Don't look at me like that either, I'm not being mean,' she said. Her general suspicion of the relationship between lust and love she called 'the procreation instinct', and with little sense of the occasion, or perhaps – and this only occurred to him later – an entirely considered one, she explained, 'Sex isn't just the genesis of life, the sort of one-time spark, or father of life, but also its mother, the long-term keeper. And perhaps it's healthy to learn and accept this? Because if sex is life, then perhaps it's *all* life. Perhaps sex is the only thing that exists.' She said this as if it had been practised in advance, or was quoted.

A carillon of bells, a soft edge of cast iron muffled by the heavy evening air, drifted above the town.

'There's more to life than sex,' Ali said.

'Ah,' Cece enthused. 'But I would say the two are precisely equal, no more, no less. Life comes from sex. Sex brings us to life.' She stopped to listen to a tide of careless, inane laughter which rose from the quad and dribbled into pledges to renew the jubilation at dinner.

They lay without a noise. Calm light drizzled on Cece's skin, making it pink and sullen.

'Shit,' she said. 'It's started.' She leaped from the bed and turned on the radio, which began to speak of patches of rain, sharp frost and a dry morning in Hampshire and the Isle of Wight. She lay again and listened, eyes shut, still.

Afterwards Ali asked, 'Is that where you're from then?'

'Yes.'

'Do you need to know the weather there?'

'I always listen, with my youngest brother.' She turned her body. 'I don't need to tell you why.'

He took the hint. 'I assumed you came from Buckingham Palace.'

'Why?' She sat up to sit on her heels. 'What, you think *I'm* posh?'

He nodded. 'Or just strange.'

'Well, that's one way of looking at things.' She rested her head on her clasped hands.

'What's that meant to mean?'

'Well, maybe I'm not the only naive one here. You act like you've never been outside the Circle Line.'

He ignored her, got up, picked one of her towels from a shelf and wrapped it around his waist. 'So what's your proper name?'

'What do you mean?'

'"Cece". What's it short for?'

'It stands for my entire being – isn't that enough?'

'I mean what's the abbreviation? No one seems to know.'

'Who's "no one"?'

Ali lay beside her again, a hand on her hip. 'Well, Simon says it's because you're pretending to be a big mystery,' he said.

Her leg retracted with a jolt. 'Don't.' She pulled the covers over herself and looked at him with the kind of belligerence only possible from a few inches away. This expression lapsed into a casual interest in the colour of her hair when held to the light. He failed to say he didn't think she was a myste-rious act, because he was afraid he might admit more: that she was the most genuine, real person he'd encountered thus far on earth.

But perhaps her reaction was to something else. As he extended a hand and stroked her in semi-serious appeals for clemency, he wondered if Cece still had feelings for Simon. He traced a finger from the shallow depression behind her knee until his knuckles grazed the small of her back, smooth and still damp like the walls of a cave. His hands, led by a homing instinct, traced her waist and now her ribs, and he hauled them in to fill the gaps of his own shape and kissed, so gently, the point where her neck met her hair.

That particular awkwardness having passed, he got up again and, hyped by his nakedness, went to the toilet at the end of their corridor, fired a stream into the middle of the bowl and wondered if girls got the same gratification from a well-needed piss.

While he considered the many things about girls he simply didn't understand, he began to hear a kind of brittle beat coming from her end of the corridor. As he returned, the sound of curtains being roughly drawn forwards and backwards along their pole was interrupted by a deep sigh of frustration. Things slammed against walls and even the door, chequering the light as he looked through Cece's keyhole. Furious cries were partially stifled by a sleeve held to her mouth as she paced towards her mirror and stopped. She gazed, her head lowering in staggered degrees, at either herself or some other object contained within the reflection of her wardrobe mirror. At last she sat with her back to him and leaned to one side, an unimaginable cocoon of distress forming itself around her.

Still outside, he was unsure whether to disturb this. For the second time that week, his knuckles hovered over her plywood door.

Slowly knocking and opening it, he saw the contents of the room strewn on the floor, her recently unpacked things toppled sideways, her lamps, chair and bedside table lying as though the place had been turned ninety degrees. Posters, books and stationery were splayed at various distances from their proper places. Cece, cross-legged in the middle of it, was banging a make-up case on the floor with one hand and, with a straw in the other, trying to skewer a carton of juice. She inhaled the liquid, calming herself with each deliberate gulp.

His mouth hung open. 'What happened?'

Her voice was raised before he'd even finished asking. 'You're all so full of *shit*!'

'What?'

'You and Simon. Like little boys. Little bastard shits. No wonder Stov's appalled.'

'What are you talking about? What did *I* say?'

She mocked his voice: "'Simon says you're pretending to be a big mystery." Does he now? *Simon*, what a great guy! Let's all quote *Simon*, the great sage and hero of our day! Stov was right.' Her arms moved wildly, independently. He had no notion of where this had come from or why it was escalating so suddenly. What was there to get angry about?

'What's Stov got to do with all this?'

'We Facebook message each other. I've become fond of him. Look, we have more in common than I ever will with you or Simon. He's the only one who's honest.'

'Why? What's this about?' Ali sat down beside her on the grooved carpet.

'I won't be questioned.'

'But you're so defensive —'

'I'm *not* defensive.'

He shrugged, palms upwards.

'I don't care,' she said. 'I don't fucking care any more.' Cece threw the empty carton into the corner where the bin had been.

Simon had warned him: the hot ones were always crazy. 'I don't get you.'

Her voice was curt now. 'You don't *get* to get me.' She began to restore scattered pennies to her purse. 'Ignorance is bliss, trust me.'

'Really? You don't need to treat me like that. I'm not a kid.'

'You're nineteen. You're a kid.'

'So are you.'

'No.' She shook her head.

After a minute he began to clear away the mess. In the absence of anything else, to break the tension, he tried to articulate the problem. 'You're impossible to know. You're so confident.'

'Don't, Ali.'

'You're so damn waterproof I can't get through.'

'Ali –'

'You don't see yourself. No doubt, fear. Nothing. Nothing comes near you. That's what you're like. It's like trying to befriend a fucking tiger.'

Ready to shout back, she hesitated and frowned. 'Did you say a tiger?'

'Yes.'

'A *tiger?*' The tip of her tongue hovered thoughtfully over her lip.

'Yes.'

'Or a lion?'

'I suppose.'

'Or a bear!'

'Well, whatever, yeah.'

'That's it!' She laughed. 'That's great. A tiger. Raar!'

'What? What is?'

'Raar! What an idea!' she said, erupting in laughter, and every time her laughter subsided and she had the breath, she roared 'MEEOOOW!'

And then as soon as it had started it stopped, and an earnestness overcame her. She propped her head on a nearby pillow and leaned against the wall, shading her eyes like they had enjoyed a picnic and conversation had only just turned to more serious matters. Flat light often spilled in at this time, thickening if someone in the clock tower opened their window, bouncing it onto the cream paint of her room, and he could count the seconds by the motes of rising dust.

'And you were?'

'I was what?' he asked.

'Frightened by this tiger. When we met?' She was still. 'The beast of self-consciousness?'

'I suppose.'

'That's because you're vain.' She laughed. 'And you know, vanity is just shame but better dressed.'

He had to smile at that. The storm had passed. For a while, they lay turned away from each other on either side of the little bed. The mattress, long ago drained of its buoyancy, sagged in the middle. With agonizing slowness they both rolled back to the middle. Their backs now touched, and his heart lit up. 'Cece?'

'*Ali?*' she replied in a so-serious voice.

'When did you and Stov start messaging?'

'Oh…' She cocked her head in calculation. 'Probably, I don't know, beginning of the year?'

'Huh. How come?'

'Are you jealous?'

'I'm not your boyfriend, how could I be?'

She ran a hand down his arm. 'We just talk.'

'Do you talk a lot?'

'A fair bit. He's a good friend. Why?'

'Just wondering. He doesn't message me so much these days. That would explain it, I guess.'

'Because?'
'Doesn't matter.'

After they made love again, she turned the pillow and bashed it, sending up plumes of old feathers. He considered the sunlight trapped between the window and its reflection on the wall, and he thought the good weather would hold.

11

The gatekeeper was striding back, a reader wrapped around his arm, his attitude entirely different. He even deigned to speak some English and smiled with genuine warmth. 'To your friend,' he said and led me down a twist of road to a taxi at the bottom of a street, spoke to the driver and shut the door behind me.

'I can't afford this,' I told the gatekeeper, showing him my reader.

'No pay. You go. For Stov!' He chuckled and stepped back into the vastness of the mosque. 'To find him.'

By now the town was waking.

The cafes would once have been brimming, the shopkeepers haggling, the tourists bringing mess and money to the city, intercepted by guides, funnelled by children. Instead, men sat and watched the birds prick an unfinished sky, women skinned oranges, leaving piles of peel at their feet, while kids chased each other around tall stacks of chairs which leaned together as though in idle gossip. Dogs slunk down the middle of the cobbled roads, and alleys resonated with the hooves of unseen donkeys. Old women sat in the shade and slept. Broken balustrades hung from white balconies.

Soon our arc around the edge of the medina came to an end. Like most return journeys, coming back was half the length of arriving.

'Here,' the taxi driver said.

'There?'

'*Non. Ici.*'

Looking about, there didn't seem much to support the idea of 'here'.

The driver pulled up beside a large crumbling exterior masking a series of old riads. He took my bag, left it beside a doorway and drove off in haste. There were no windows to peer through, no names on the doors, no one at either end of the winding street. I lay a hand on the flaked paint then knocked. No answer. By now the sun craned over the town; when, a minute or so later, the silhouette of a woman appeared in answer, it was impossible to pick out her face in its delirious glare.

'*Oui?*'

It was not a face I knew.

'*Pardon. J'espérais trouver un ami.*'

'*Qui s'appelle comment?*'

'Stov. Unwin.'

The woman stepped onto the pavement. 'You are here for Stov?'

'Yes, sorry, do you know where he is today?'

'What is your name?'

My voice sounded tired.

'Ah, you are Ali?' She looked me up and down. 'Come inside. Stov will be home this evening. I am Nadia.'

I followed her in. Perhaps forty-five, feasibly younger, she was an unbroken column of a person with earnest eyes.

'You are so welcome here,' she said. They lived on the ground floor in a set of high-walled wide rooms mapped with mould. Nadia waved me to a settee. 'Stov will be very surprised, very happy.' She sat on a chair in the shape of an ampersand.

I sat with an involuntary sigh.

'You are tired – please.' She got up immediately, found me a pillow and walked to the kitchen doorway. 'You should sleep now. The heat can be so hard. We can talk later, I am going to read.

I will remain in the courtyard.' After bringing in a tray of sweet tea she closed the door gently behind her.

I was left to the chipped woodcarvings and paintings eviscerated by damp. Nadia wasn't what I had been expecting. Were she and Stov a couple? Struggling for money or not, their things all looked either priceless or valueless – an ancient brass door which bore the scars of forgotten conflicts was fixed to a wall that was pasted with newspaper; a chandelier of cutlery hung from the ceiling; a crate on the floor acted as a side table, and on it the pages of old paperbacks, bruised red with contraband wine, curled in the heat beside puddled candles. An ornate blind studded like armour partly hid stacks of papers and files. Photos of Nadia lay everywhere, loose, in frames and stuck around the base of an old piece of polished metalwork, a large shallow pot propped on the shelf like a mirror.

After some tea, which was hot and sweet with apple sugar, I thought how she'd animated when I mentioned Stov. The metallic jangle on her wrist as it reached eagerly into the sunlight and took my bag, sending long etchings of her onto the cobbled street. I thought of how she looked like Kat when she sat, patiently curious about my presence.

Increasingly everyone looked like someone I knew; the children gazing through the wire fences at the jumbo jets and those peppering the spare streets of Fès. Even some buildings here resembled places from other countries. At one point I was certain I'd seen Simon again, cropped and bulky, holding a blue boot bag over his shoulder, as he walked with beefy indolence through the medina. Illusion was the final consolation of age – the presumption of being surrounded with proof of one's relevance.

Love is dreaming. Even self-love.

I took some pills. One for my heart, one for sleep.

Fingers of steam from the pot grasped upwards. The cutlery slowly oscillated above, two forks meeting in dull chimes that lulled me to sleep.

When I woke, my face was ridged and moist against worn velveteen. Ancient plumbing rattled somewhere in the building and a slapping sound, like the beating of a sheet, drummed itself out. It was morning.

I got up and found Nadia in the courtyard, standing on a chair, pulling vines from the facade. She was alone. I tried not to look disappointed. 'Hello again.'

An arm motioned me to sit. 'Do you feel much better?' In stilted English, she sounded each syllable with care.

'Thank you. Much.'

'Have some breakfast.' In the morning quiet I could locate her accent – it was sixteenth-arrondissement, educated. A long time since I had heard this Parisian voice.

'Thanks.' There was fruit, honey, bread and butter. Nadia came down, wiped her brow with her gardening gloves. She didn't eat but sat, stirring the honey jar.

'What time is it?'

'About eight. You slept for a long while.'

'The night too? So it's tomorrow?'

'It is tomorrow already.' She smiled. 'I thought you would wake with the prayer, but no. My mother would call you a bed for flies.'

'I sometimes sleep too much. It isn't good for me.' How many pills had I taken? I never could remember.

'Better than not enough.'

'You'd think so. I'll have to set an alarm.'

'Tomorrow I will send in the stray dogs.'

'All at once?'

'Yes. They feel safer that way.' She reached for another vine, dry leaves falling from her shoulders onto the ground. 'We as well have the cat here. This cat scares the dogs, but it does not come inside because Stov scares the cat.' She pulled her chair in and poured some tea. 'He chases them all and bangs pots. He is a little boy.' She blew on it, her expression never less than serious. 'He is not here, yet – Stov.'

'No?'

'No. Soon.'

'Ah. OK.'

'I'm sorry, Ali,' she said, like it was a humiliation.

'It's OK.'

'You must of course stay here.'

'Thank you, it's all right. I'm so pleased he – and you – are here. I'll just wander round today.'

'I could show you around?'

'No, no, you must be busy. I can't take up your time.'

'You can wash dishes?'

'Yes.'

She spread her arms wide. 'Then I have time – it would be very fine for me.'

'Are you sure?'

'Yes!' A brown brindled dog with a fight-bitten tail galloped into the courtyard and nuzzled her leg. She dropped a crust to the floor for it and stood. 'Let us go as soon as you are done.' She placed a few things in the backpack on the chair next to her – a purse, keys, sunglasses and, if I wasn't mistaken, a penknife, slipped into the front pocket.

XI

Ali paused; he thought he heard a voice, soft and light, muffled through the plastic walls of the shower room next door. He hesitated again at a creak in the corridor, so faint and dubious that it seemed like a signal for him to stop and see the absurdity of his frozen self.

All was quiet.

He relaxed and looked at the words – *9.30 p.m. Street Spirit Society with Cece* – and, hearing the click of the latch and a patter of feet, hastily turned the page.

Had he physically jumped? Hopefully not. Something pulsed behind his eyes and he was aware of the crisp sensations in the building – the blend of bleach and fried food; crockery clashing in the kitchen; five or six sound systems playing, mongrelling into subgenres where they met in the corridors – all these things simultaneously emerging from just beneath his consciousness to blend indistinguishably before falling back into singular strands of others' lives.

It was week two of uni.

Yes, he was nervous, but he allowed himself to blame it on the very real surprise of someone bursting into his room – doubly surprising because he'd just stopped expecting it. There should be a word for this, he thought, for encountering the newly unexpected. Which language would have it? German, Greek?

There she was, behind him, stretching silently in his arm-chair – the same acrylic armchair they had in every room that caught on everyone's clothes and bobbled them, like one side of

Velcro reaching for its partner. Slumped on it, she exhaled with satisfaction. He willed himself to recover some control, to linger over the diary, even delay his upward glance that extra second as he managed his important social calendar.

Seconds passed. Already their greetings had become a competition of indifference, a test of who could feign the least care. For him the only thing was to make her wait, to turn around in his own time. For her he could see it was not left to chance, her movement had been planned ahead: it was swishing into his room with long wet limbs and sitting, as if in the library, on his armchair in nothing but a black towel.

'One second.' At last he turned, glanced up and saw the steam rising from her skin. Saw his defeat. 'Hello.'

'Hi.'

'What's up?'

'Nothing.' She smiled, gathering her treacled hair over her left cheek. 'I just came to say hello.'

'Let me just…' Ali turned back and flicked through his diary, pretending to search for some crucial demand on his time. A page here, a tut there. From behind came a click and a hiss, and the first cloud of cigarette smoke drifting through the room at cruise-liner pace. Then the click wheel of his iPod being scrolled. She put on a song for them. 'There,' he said, pretending to find something and make a note. 'Right.' He swivelled round.

Cece had the cigarette pack to her nose. 'Clove.' She closed her eyes. 'Do you know what they say about clove?' She released the smoke without inhaling, intact. The fruity aroma, with grains of pepper and camphor, settled under his desk light. 'Apparently it must always see the sea to thrive.'

'Where did you hear that?'

'On the Net.'

'Really?'

'I looked it up.'

'Why?'

She smiled. 'So I could have conversations like this. And be a big mystery.' Cece peered through a gap in the curtains. Outside, the shabby science block screened them from the road leading out of town. 'Can you thrive without seeing the sea, Ali?' she said at last.

'I live in London.'

'Easily then,' she concluded, looking outside once again, and he could not gauge her.

Was she joking, or did she really miss the sea, he wondered. He realized he couldn't remember what sort of place she lived in. A flat or a house? Or on her father's base? How little he knew about her, or clove, or anything that seemed to matter.

'And what couldn't you thrive without?' she said.

'Would you call this thriving?' he joked.

'That's true.' She was looking at his room.

'My camera, I suppose.' He considered it, annoyed by how seriously she had chosen to take his joke. Another pause, and surely she was now scrutinizing his belongings in a spree of judgement. He regretted each item in turn: the lava lamp, the Dalí, the cheap sheets. Without consultation or comment, she started to edit the room, removing things she clearly thought were gauche and moving to prominence those of which she approved. Ali had been waiting his whole life for someone to do this for him. The Virginia Woolf short stories were pulled out to face forwards alongside Zadie Smith and J.M. Coetzee, the lava lamp was unplugged and left outside in the corridor with a bollard someone had left in his room in week one.

When she was done she sat again and prodded out the half-smoked cigarette in a cup. He looked downwards to hide his disappointment – it was one of only three he had left, and they were expensive.

By way of recovery he approached for a kiss, but she, discovering a new interest in the hem of her towel, had already moved her head, allowing him to find only her brow. 'Mmm,' he improvised as his lips touched her hairline, breathing her in. 'I love the smell of your skin when you get out of the shower. The smell of afternoon sun.'

'Ha,' came the smirk, and then the laugh, the glimpse of white teeth between her lips. 'You're actually very cheesy, aren't you?'

He watched her loving this, wringing her hair between her fingers, a dripping metronome. She caught him.

'"The smell of afternoon sun". Are you synaesthetic or just trying to be?'

'Whatever.' He took – or gave – a kiss. Now he had admitted defeat, she allowed him to do so.

He kissed her again. But soon again she was silly with giggles. She began to gloat, impersonating the tone of his words in the kiss: 'I-love-m-mmm-smell-m-of-mmm your-skin –'

Ali stopped her. He had played the game, and he had lost it, and his defeat should at least earn him a truce – so he kissed harder, longer, stifling her consonants until they were a hum. He would not relinquish her lips, but she seemed to like this, surrendering little by little, and then she was content. And as she continued to hum, they both felt the sound. Her voice passed into his mouth without escaping. It was warm between them, it vibrated in their heads before burying itself, deep, somewhere in the recesses of his ribs.

This, he decided, he would remember. This kiss, forever.

And, in one way or another, he would.

Waking alone, Ali checked his phone. Three in the afternoon. Cece was gone again.

That she was gone was hardly a surprise. That she had risen and left so silently was a new development. She had bragged of her lightness of foot, her ability to move at full speed without disturbing the sleep of others. 'Boarding school dorms,' she had said in simple explanation, launching his imagination into an inaccurate depiction of kneeling prayers beside hospital beds, each accompanied with a white china basin and pitcher, the warm cinders of a fire and the cold feet of Cece tiptoeing across the moonlit parquet floor. He'd watched too many old British movies with his parents on Sunday nights.

In truth he had no idea when she had left and whether, for example, she had stayed and read his books, watched him sleep, read his internet history. This mattered to him.

He composed an emotional inventory of the day before he had fallen asleep. How many stinging jokes she had made, how many times she had brushed the hair on his neck as they kissed. And whether it was because he felt a release from the intensity of their habits, or it was simply the change of scenery, he felt strangely elated as he walked across the road to buy a sandwich from the newsagent.

Cece had been his all-consuming thought for so long, and he found it frighteningly difficult to build a safe distance from this obsession. To keep what she had left in his room, a fragrance, or a nod, or the wet footprints on his carpet, was impossible. There was no keeping them, only finding distraction from them.

Back at his desk, Ali ate his sandwich over a newspaper. He hovered over the photographs, noted down the names of the photographers he liked, ripping and pasting the cuttings into a scrapbook he kept in the cavity of his bass speaker, a place not even someone as casually intrusive as Cece would discover. The images coming out of Iraq – this month it was the Nisour Square massacre – were particularly arresting, the warpaint of black smoke across the sky, the stippled texture of the blasted buildings as rendered on the uncoated broadsheet paper, the curls of metal burning in their own brown oil, the bowed figures whose composure or terror was locked into an inevitability which, they were in the process of realizing, would come to define them.

He stopped eating around the edges of the sandwich. He stared at the horror in their faces and tried to imagine such loss, how the heart held so much pain at once. If you were narrowly escaping death every day and living only in the present, then what did this rupture feel like? What, in that second, did having your photograph taken mean? And what was it like to be the one taking a photograph of a person who had no guarantee of a future? What did it feel like to take this moment from someone, or to confirm it for them? And was it traumatic to do so? He looked again at their devastation and felt their sickening grief. But he also grasped a simple truth about himself – he liked photography because he could be somewhere yet also be removed from it. The camera was invisibility. He felt a little flash of self-admonishment for this immorality, but there it was again: the camera was invisibility, and that was what he wanted.

That's a woolly excuse for being a narcissist, Cece's voice in his head told him. He still imagined visits from Cece, even though he had seen her only hours ago. It was an old habit returned. But he would not engage with these visitations. He knew what madness became of that. He would love the real thing or not at all. He would do this for himself. And if he could not love the real thing then he would get away from it all, Cece, himself, this university.

Divorced from his thoughts, Ali watched the mouse on his laptop screen float towards the search bar, and with little conscious effort found himself looking at flights to Argentina. No, he thought, he did not want to follow Stov everywhere. So he typed in *Turkey*, and then *Georgia*, then *Pakistan*, to which, without a moment's doubt, he put a ticket in his basket. He didn't know why and wasn't sure what this meant, but he felt better for having done so. It reminded him of his agency beyond Cece: the special privilege of a life in which he could afford to go somewhere else. To enter other people's worlds. He may not have been as well-resourced as Simon and Cece, though he still had a little money from his summer job which, if added to his student loan, could get him there and back. Provided he didn't eat or need anywhere to sleep. Was he about to prove his independence to himself? Was he about to do something stupid? He dabbed at the crumbs in the box. Probably not. No, today was not one of those days his life would change.

'Did I leave a hairband in here?' Cece was back in the doorway.

'How did you open my door?' he asked.

She waved a credit card. 'Saw it in a movie.'

'I don't think you left anything.'

'No?' She tutted indifferently. 'What are you looking at?' She motioned to the screen. 'Going on your holibobs?'

Ali turned. 'Nothing. No. Just interested. Doesn't matter.' He shut the laptop. 'You can stay if you'd like?'

She seemed to consider this question more seriously than it merited. She was smiling. 'No.'

'Can we talk? I'd love to talk to you about something.'

Cece continued to beam affectionately at him, passing her hand over the stubble of his chin. And, as if in answer to the question he hadn't been allowed to ask, she shook her head, backing out of the room, and slowly closed the latch. He couldn't be sure, when the time came for him to piece it together, if she knew then how little they would see each other again.

12

Long, stately storks watched the market bustle beneath them. Their thin reaper bills gave a mechanical clatter, piercingly clear like a siren, when perturbed or charmed by each other, or perhaps to show their human subjects how sound should be made.

Under their nests in the battlements, scaffolds and disconnected pylons, the market had shrunk into a thin effigy of itself. Everywhere were signs of the life it had lost. Pavements were steeped in dirt where once people had gathered in number, blackened by marks where their pots would have cooked, and covered in feather-shaped indents where sellers had scraped their tools. A high wave of unease hit me as I saw the parade of empty inlets and arches, the minuscule collateral of our complacency. I'd seen it countless times, and it was never surprising but always a shock. Yet another place hollowed out, choked off.

Nadia bought some fruit and golden oils as we walked through. Sumptuous scarves, dyed wool, threads, drapes and rugs hung only in their tens, not their thousands, patching the walls where once they would have covered them. It had been so long since I'd bought things in person that I was disappointed no sellers approached me with trinkets, beseeching me to haggle and pulling me into that dance of empathy, pity, entitlement and regret. Even the tricks of the trade had died off.

Nadia led us through a courtyard that led to a series of steps crammed into the cleft of two narrow walls. Counting them, my heart gave the wrong kind of leap, and my knees ached in anticipation. This physical dread fully replacing my Western guilt, I made my way up the steps and followed her onto a ramparted roof.

Here it was open and bright, the air crisp. For the first time I saw the horizon and my body became placid, reassured. Roads were furled below us like dried bone cells. For that second, from this height, the details fell away, and it resembled the old world of thirty years ago when everything was easy and alive.

'There are nine thousand streets here.' In Nadia's voice was a pent-up pride in her city. With her tour, and her boasts about Fès, she was convincing us both.

'And how many' – I paused, pretending not to catch my breath – 'do you know?'

'I don't know. Perhaps nine hundred. You can walk it all your life and always find a new route.'

'I could get very lost here.' I considered the notion.

The air carried myrtle and the scent of orange trees, faint like a memory beyond full retrieval. Up here I felt free. Free for the first time in years, standing next to this strange woman, looking over a strange, infinite city which if I squinted could be from before the world fell in on itself. Before I did the same. I took another long breath and let my eyes linger on the roofs that once held a city I would never see, the one Nadia had been selling me all day.

She looked straight ahead, unaware that my body was flooding with air, and light, and the fragile high of nostalgia. 'This is where you will have the best flatbread of your life.' She pointed to a small inch of the honeycomb before running her finger north over the town. 'Then we will go to the Berber medicine shop. And I will show you the barrel makers. They sit in a bed of sawdust all day and make barrels from beech wood – the smell and the skill, it is perfect.' She smiled at my curiosity. 'Let us go.'

And so the day went. And it wasn't that I didn't want to see the wonders that she saw, but did I have the energy? From where I was standing, tourism felt like a kids' game. I was too exhausted for the barrel makers' sawdust, but I wanted to please Nadia and affirm her judgements. After all, we all wanted to like the place we were stuck in – because there was no getting out.

And so, under a pulverizing mid-morning sun, Nadia showed me this imperial city, occasionally explaining how, like her, it had some Tunisian, Jewish and French blood, how its districts of privilege and poverty had crissed and crossed until they finally separated into the wealthy Ville Nouvelle and the poorer innards. How, having been born in Marrakesh and raised in Paris, she herself had come to live here. She explained that, finally, the world had stopped coming to Fès, and that together they were a forgotten entity.

'I want to show you the sights. Because nobody sees them any more.' She looked down at the cobbles, mourning the lifeblood of her home.

I nodded, my hip throbbing, aware I couldn't disappoint her. My back ached, my feet were liquid, and I could feel the deficit of what I could offer compared to what she deserved. I wasn't enough, but I would try to be the audience she longed for.

She ran the back of her hand against the soft stone wall as we walked. 'We used to get money, protection, from big world funding, because Fès was dying – for a long time we had not enough water.' She motioned to the canteen in my hand. 'The tourists used a lot in hotels and swimming pools and the golf courses. They would use more in two weeks than one of us used in a year. And then from UNESCO, from Japan and China, we got millions, billions of dirham to buy water solutions in Fès and Meknès in the centre of Maroc because they said "Fès is too beautiful to die." They called it "The Miracle of Meknès", and the tourists kept coming.

But then, after Le Bouchon in France and the – what was it called in the UK?'

'Sanction 4.'

'Yes. Well, after that the money stopped, because the tourists stopped, because no one wants to pay for a city they cannot see. If you cannot see it, is it still there? Why would you give it any money? Do they know that in 2024 a heatwave killed a hundred and fifty thousand people here? In 2029 it happened again, and we lost eighty thousand this time. How have we been forgotten like this?'

As I listened, I felt the familiar sense of bewildered fatalism that rose and fell each day and had done so for the last couple of decades. I didn't answer.

'Sorry, am I boring you?'

'No. I agree, I get it. I just don't know what to say. It's not boring, it's paralysing.' How could I explain? 'The thing is, no one cares about anyone else any more.'

She nodded. 'We have all forgotten the rest of the world. We can only see what is in front of us. I do not think about India, or Sweden.' Tributaries of old smiles formed around her mouth as she looked to me, and I remembered how I should have come prepared to answer for the West. Whether I'd managed to redeem myself for Nadia I couldn't tell. Her falling estimation was as familiar as the passing slow, juddering traffic.

The tour sped up after that. A manic engine receded, a man whistled to a companion, the storks descended and at last it was over. The ungrateful tourist was exhausted. Whatever day she had emptied to show me round, I was not worth it. Nadia took me home, chased always by the sun. And there, beside their cat, I lay down.

The cutlery chandelier caught some unlikely light from the street, trapped it between the knife and spoon that hung from the ceiling. The travel exhaustion had arrived. In well-drilled, serried rows, my worries were now lining up for inspection, and an uncomfortable spring in the bed had somehow associated itself with the guilt of having left Kat the week before her twenty-first birthday. Had I even got her a gift? I could see her in the kitchen, buttering me some toast as I told her my plans.

'Disappointed but never surprised. Can't miss what I haven't had,' had been her conclusion as she handed me the plate. Her the parent, me the errant child.

I needed to get out.

The floor tiles were cool against the jealous heat. Even before sunrise it hung around like a ringing in the air. I could see Nadia's closed door. I took my water, my money and some keys she'd left on the desk.

In the hallway I realized my reader was not in my pocket. I stood stock-still, debating whether to return and risk waking Nadia. Instead I looked on the hall table for a pencil, finding one. I left, making a pencil mark on the walls at every turn to guide me back again. Like I thought I was in some old film. I wandered downhill away from the medina, past a woman who waited for me to go by before tapping on someone's shutters and calling to them. The further down I went, the more the town fell apart. Past a ruined riad encrusted with shards of glass, stone walls with felsic patches of baked paint, iron gates rusted into place and a hill of crates, I began to speed up, taking the cobbles six or seven at a time, until I found the kind of place I was looking for.

Through the pall of night was a cafe, still open, with a couple of figures sitting around their lamps sipping tea. I sat on a chair outside and asked for some. The man nodded so I waited, mopping the sweat around my neck.

Candlelight flickered until two figures, a man and his son, brought me some rosebud tea. At first they didn't try to speak, the man instead offering to share a shish pipe which was filled with a serrated, lung-clouding smoke that settled inside me like ash on snow. A golden, turpentine taste. I thanked him with poor French and an effort not to cough.

After a few minutes I paid, and marked the wall with the green pencil when they were out of sight.

So much seemed to happen after that. It had been so long, decades, since I had wandered in a strange place; the present was ingrained with fragments of the past, and strobed memories appeared in objects before me. A dumped metal birdcage became the iron bedstead Madison had bought after we'd married, and also the lead strips in the stained-glass image of St Michael that had looked down over Simon's funeral. Simon's cavernous funeral, memorable for the hailstones, big as berries, that had showered us on the way home. England. Madison. Kat. These things. All left in another galaxy.

I moved on, marking the walls, walking the dusty squares. The occasional smell of hot date oil preceded a night market in the arches and undercrofts – just tables of old clothes, crockery, tin pots, bicycle tyres, sandals and lanterns. Faces, cork in the firelight, eyed me until I moved on. Past a handful of soldiers playing cards beside the fan they had rigged to a pylon.

Further down, another alley was filled with the smell of kif, which faded as it grew darker. In the road, a long crack the width of my hand separated the cobbles for a few metres. A reminder of one of the heatwaves that had emptied the town. I sipped my water and told myself I'd take the next turning.

Echoes of footsteps spurred me on until I came to a man-made cave in the wall. I ducked under the enclosing curtain to see the owner, a stooped man with his back to me, weaving through his loom long fingers, plucking at a vast harp of colour. He hadn't heard me, his absorption in the hundred threads which were strung before him total – the yarn, each a different tone, blurred under his oil lamp. Somewhere, invisibly, the intersections became a rug, his long arms pausing to correct one of those minute gaps in the pattern where this was determined. A reader lit up in his robe pocket and glowed for a few seconds as he then moved to another machine, another new cloth, and all the potentials hung down to within a fingertip of the dirt.

I left before he noticed me and, feeling a little strange, made my marks on the walls with an intoxicated diligence. Ah yes, that was it. That pipe had been no shisha. Even if everything was a little different here, and my memory was a little rusty, it was still amazing how I'd missed the obvious flavour. Kif. What a simple old mind I had become. How easily I had fooled even myself. As streets thinned the old walls became new walls, the roads flattened, broadened and shrank behind the feral shrubs. Silhouettes became broken cars, my pulse delighting in the confusion. Normally my heart, knees and hips would ache after the day's exertions, but tonight all such sensations felt optional, like water channels that could be opened or shut.

The vista was of pitch-blue sentinels, large apartment blocks, watching a half-blasted moon with their backs to me like conspiring adults. Medium-sized hotel resorts all fully checked out. I remembered the travel adviser at the Ministry, his vague, pointless cautions – 'not war-torn like some of its neighbours, nor fully depopulated, the levels of overall danger in Fès vary considerably, but most describe a new wilderness developing in keeping with the generally abandoned riches of Morocco's imperial cities.'

The eyes of the dogs ignored me. One – was it the one from Nadia's house, with a chunk bitten clean away from the root of its tail? – cantered through the garden of a tower block and aimed a bark over its shoulder. I followed it over fallen parasols, ceiling fans, a collapsed table and a water cooler. I was no longer aware of the direction of my walk, only that the drug was at work in me.

I sat, dazed, and caught my breath, my age leaving my body. So this was falling off the wagon. It felt slower than I had remembered. Falling through honey. Good old dope, I had missed you.

XII

It was a week later, but one of those endless weeks. A week filled with all the seasons – cold and rain, still days, hours of perfect sun. It was a week filled with more that was new than familiar. And then, stranger than new things, came new routines. Waking in the same bed, the same shadows on the curtains, the same watery porridge, the same walk to lectures, the same seat with the split plastic upholstery, the same dodgy deals at the bars in the evening and the same warm, tasteless chips on the way home. Every day Ali woke up in his new bedroom it felt a little less weird and a little more normal.

As the week had progressed, he'd started running. He ran because all the students seemed to do something self-perfecting in the mornings, because he was no use in the gym and had never trusted himself to row in time with others. He ran because every night they all seemed to smoke more and drink harder and get higher, and every morning he woke up scared of the harm he had dared to inflict on himself.

His route took him across the parks, through an early surge along the paths that linked the maths, materials and humanities faculties, where so many familiar faces lined the playing fields, around the pond, and over the bridges that crossed the river. By the time he came over the cattle grids to the split meadow called Parson's Blest he had slowed, his hands were warming and the passers-by were no longer gown but town – parents with buggies and pensioners on bicycles. He was coming to the final part of his outward route now, a country road that left the new housing development behind its hedgerows and became suspended in blue quiet.

These past few days he had woken feeling both dejected and encouraged. Although Cece was still refusing to spend the nights with him, it was also true, he reasoned, that in as far as she belonged with anyone it was with him. In its own peculiar way his fantasy had become real: she had stepped out of his hopeless dreams and placed one foot in a relationship with him. But the other foot remained somewhere else – she wouldn't sleep beside him or save him from his thoughts. He sped up round the muddy bend, his legs like slopping buckets.

He had already enjoyed this arrangement for two weeks. Not that it was arranged. Cece and he were – what? Their relationship didn't seem to have a definition. They were sexual partners at the very least. After lunch, most days, she would find him in his room, lay on his bed or straddle him in his chair. A shared lust stalked them constantly. Once when she had sat on the windowsill, her naked back against the exposed pane between the curtains, he had wondered if his window would give way as Ravi's had, and he was terrified they would both tumble from the second floor to a fabled death. She came to him with an interrogative frequency and afterwards they lay and talked until evening, when they'd go out with everyone else as if they were nothing more than friends, perhaps because they weren't sure themselves, or perhaps because secrecy is the greatest aphrodisiac.

Possibly they would soon be boyfriend and girlfriend. He had broken up with Angie about three weeks ago, their online statuses now corroborating this. Angie's maturity was never more apparent than in her elegant parting ('I'm not ready to be friends any time soon,' she had said, 'but perhaps in a few years or so. I wish you well'), as ever older, worldlier than him.

Still Cece resisted commitment. She made speeches about how for every romantic notion there were countless realistic ones they failed to take into account. How romances didn't occur because of the options people took but because of the options they had. How single beds were the unacknowledged cause of so much student distress: without enough room to turn over onto their separate halves, these kids thus had to lie in each other's arms, making pillow talk unavoidable, leading to an emotional dependence and a confusion over the depth of the connection: 'At the one time in their lives when they should learn what sex is,' she had told him two nights ago, 'they're instead trapped in a lesson of what love isn't.'

She would have sex with him but not fall asleep with him, and that was that. For her, sleep would be an intimacy too far. As every evening approached, he hoped she wouldn't leave. He would imagine a Pompeiian ash suddenly petrifying their bodies, so entangled that archaeologists wouldn't be sure who was lying on whom. Then she would leave. And he would wonder if he would ever know the smell of her as he woke.

Yet there seemed no indication that she would stop their trysts. Their afternoon coupling wasn't so amazing as to warrant her persistence, he knew that. The sex wasn't bad, but Cece's capacity for methodical distrait didn't ever seem to fully leave her during what she had termed their 'erosis'. Occasionally it seemed she was locked away from him, the way she would pause or look away to the right as if recalling something, and it was all he could do to try to entice her back into the present.

Then there had been that time, on the eighth day, when she had wandered into his room in her towel. This was before morning lectures, when he had been going through the dozens of societies she'd signed him up to, pencilling into his diary The Assassins and then the one called Street Spirit because she'd said she'd be going too – whatever Street Spirit was. She positioned herself, still wearing her towel, a centimetre above him, and whenever he tried to close the gap she raised herself and asked another question,

'How badly do you want me?' and then 'What would you do to have me?' and then, finally, 'Tell me your darkest secret.'

And his answers seemed to disappoint.

'All right, what are you afraid of?' she implored at last, impatient.

'You won't stay,' he said.

Her oscillations worried him only insofar as they changed the odds of their being together. Once or twice he had wondered if she might be ill, not mentally, but not physically either. Cece had a joke for everything, a catch-all caveat of humour. And she had every right to keep him somewhere between encouragement and rejection. This itself did not make a person mad. But the deployment of her outbursts, if they were deployed, followed a trigger that was invisible to him.

By now he was on his fourth song. The lonely bullock which never explored its own pastureland, apart from the five metres behind its gate, stared out at him.

Around this point the mixture of music and hypnotic fatigue usually began to remove his problems and thoughts and hold them before him like someone else's: some pitiable subject whose film he was watching. Someone else's life was among these matted fields, these heavy-shouldered crows. The same synthesized chords swelled to their limits and just as fast seemed to recede from the world. It was a song Nell had given him that week because he had said he liked running to sad songs. It plotted this pain onto some other universal graph.

He thought about the little scenes of her divulgence. For perhaps the same reason she had decided to sleep with him, Cece often chose to disclose a little personal information afterwards. It seemed an act of largesse to herself as much as an answer to his obvious curiosity, and was evidently some effort, because she would smoke serially, or demand sweets, or immediately disappear for one of her listlessly described walks.

Other people in their year had begun asking him about her, as if he could explain. They weren't blind, and knew something was going on – they knew from Cece and Ali's 'propinquity', and from the distance at which they stood apart. It was the distance at which two people who have recently discovered each other's naked form stand together. And he was beginning to evade their questions because he knew Cece as little as they did. Over the weeks he had pieced together something of her early years. She had been to a series of boarding schools paid for by the army, near wherever her father had been based. Her education had been free in this respect.

'I'm not *rich* rich,' she had paused to say. 'Yes, I went to the best schools money can pay for, but the accent and the – what did you call it? – the *tiger*, these are just an impersonation of wealth. My mum was dumb enough to be educated rather than rich, my father was smart enough to be born rich and dumb enough to lose it. What I lack in houses in Provence, I make up for in honest, open ambition.'

Her father came from money, but had 'accidentally left it'. His own investments (property in Manchester and stocks in early video calling services) had never come in, and his inheritance had dwindled early. His short career in business, before the army, as a corporate conduit in Delhi, had been damaged by the mixture of Britain's post-colonial retreat and a single injudicious gesture – his pointing a finger towards a female client – perceived as an act of condescension. And thus he had found his reserves, prospects and, coincidentally, even his wife expired by the time he had returned to England with a five-year-old Cece and now two younger brothers (the products of a romantically parsimonious marriage to the pale sister of a junior asset manager from his firm). Cece's mother had suffered an embolism and died shortly after the birth of the youngest brother, Howard, and her father had grieved as much for his ignorance of her as for the woman herself.

Widowed, now earning an officer's salary in the middle ranks of a complacent army regiment and accompanied by three small children, Cece's father had brought her up by moving from school to school, dropping the children into new classes in Scotland, Bristol, Manchester, Hampshire and then just as abruptly pulling them out again as he pushed for a placement worthy of his talents.

She went on, describing how the year she had spent in Norwich had been one of her happiest, and how her father had moved them on once more following an argument with a lieutenant colonel of the Royal Anglian Regiment. With all the upheaval, her brother Cedric's schoolwork had begun to slide – homework was lost, tests failed, classes missed. Howard was a mystery to her in his easy existence; he'd never known their mother, never known what he was missing. Too many times the children had dealt with the mistrust of fellow students who would never fully accept these state-subsidized pupils, who didn't seem to possess the signs of acute wealth that drew rich little children to other rich little children. The parochialism of the wealthy sussed them out every time. Cedric could not bring himself to care about schoolwork any more. And Howard could not fail to.

Cece's father hit Cedric, she reasoned, because it was all he knew. And he let Howard be. This was simply how she claimed to understand it, and Ali believed her. Her father had been dispassionately beaten as a boy by their grandfather after he had absconded from his boarding school. It was the most memorable parental intervention their father could recall from his own childhood. In its absence, a child can mistake many things for interest, even love. Now a parent himself, he was uncertain for which things one should castigate a child and for which to offer tenderness, and so made arbitrary acts of discipline the moral structure of his parenthood. Guided by the sense that a child should be punished to give them a truer sense of consequences, he once slapped Cedric hard on the cheek when his school marks were low, and slapped Cece as hard when she dropped and shattered a bottle of milk. The punishment for Cece's tattoo, discreetly placed only to show her father what an untroublesome daughter she truly had been, was first a quiet lecture on taking responsibility, but a day later a palm across her face.

'That's appalling.' Ali had reached for her hand. 'Did you tell someone?'

She had smiled at his reaction.

'Cece, I'm so sorry.'

'Don't be. There are worse things.'

She didn't recall this with any great anger, nor self-pity. He wondered whether she realized how bad these facts were, or whether she simply no longer wanted to dwell on them now that she had escaped.

'After he'd let us go, we'd both run upstairs and cover the sound of his ranting with the radio. It's why we listen to the weather together every day, wherever we are.' She relinquished this explanation quietly. 'But it's not like my dad beats me and Ced all the time. He hit me, twice, but I never got the impression he wanted to. And he's never touched Howie. He's just not a very good officer.'

13

I'd mounted some steps and now looked from the balcony over the dried crater of an empty swimming pool. Pale satellite dishes caught the starlight like cherry blossom on water, and further out, beside the new town, lay the pocks and scabs of golf sand bunkers. From this spot, you could sense what the night had done to Fès: it had made a little reflection of itself in the landscape, in the odd clusters of rooms that flickered with candles or torches. Even after the European dust bowls had settled, the sky had never returned, leaving only a cloudy foam. But here night had come into its own again: it was an event to which few humans had access any more.

I looked for the inky dog around the walkway and spotted it across the road. Fear or caution would seem the appropriate responses to these ruins, but instead I slumped on a cracked sun-lounger and put my feet up.

Too many blackouts. Too many bloody noses. One or two police cells. Dope and I had had the kind of fractious relationship over which one must eventually make a choice. It wasn't the episodes, though – it was the risk. It was who you bought it from. Inevitably, like everything else, dope became a pretext for eviction. Those who synthesized it did so based on imported samples. That meant smugglers and dealers, which meant migrants. And the sentence for funding migrants was asset seizure and suspended exile. As the Ministry guide said, any drugs seized upon re-entry would be regarded as evidence for having funded 'terror'. But the Ministry said a lot of things. It warned too of the dangers of fake currency; the cons of other travellers; the types of weather of which to be wary: spectacular dry lightning over the mountains during the warmest evenings; pink afternoons; the departure of the lizards. But tonight only birds owned the sky, from signal towers to wind-sprained trees, darting across the night lines.

Minutes passed.

I wanted to fall asleep here but knew I shouldn't. Inevitably, I'd failed to mark some of the walls in the last few minutes and would be lost; sleep now and I could forget the way back to Nadia's entirely. Concentrate, I thought, stay awake. If life is revolt against death – who had said that? – then waking must be a revolt against sleep. Wake, I thought. Revolt against the night.

'Camus,' a voice said. Clear as the view. I turned around.

'Year Eleven. French.'

He was sitting on the balcony wall, looking over the city. It was his voice, coming from the short man-boy shape of a nineteen-year-old. Simon.

I blinked. He was still there, impatient for me to catch on.

'It was Year Eleven French, Ali, come on.'

'Are you sure?'

Simon turned and looked at me like I was an idiot. 'Of course I'm sure, Al. We read it at school. Mrs Revignon?'

'I can't really remember.'

'That's because you spent the class pining for Anitra. God, you never shut up about that girl.' He shook his head tolerantly. 'And yeah, we definitely did Camus. You got totally obsessed with reciting bits of the French under your breath before tests, remember? And I borrowed your notes and we all copied you for the exam. You never knew, did you?' He laughed.

'I knew you were hanging out with me for some reason.'

'No such thing as a free invite to a party, Ali. Come on, don't look at me like that – we got on OK. You knew it was a fair trade. Don't be lame.'

'I suppose so.'

'Man, I couldn't bear the Camus book.'

'You didn't like any books.'

'Yeah, but…' Simon scratched at his chin. 'That one was seriously pointless. *The Myth of Sisyphus*, remember? *Hissy-fuss. Syphilis.* Remember?' His laugh not a day over nineteen. He straddled the wall, unable to sit still. 'How was the funeral? What did you think?'

'It was OK.' What could I say? You can't criticize someone's funeral. 'What did you think?'

'It was pretty sucky. I thought the point of Catholics is that you get a bit of spice at your send-off. Drama. Tears. Not a dry thigh in the house.'

I allowed myself a long shudder.

Si went on. 'But I stopped watching soon after it started. Too depressing. No Dad, obviously. Just my old mum. My hot cousin was there but she looks like my grandma now, and she is one.' He began to lift himself up and down in tricep dips. 'But then I – suppose – I – looked – like – shit – in the end – too.' Simon stopped, panting. 'Couldn't stand it. I left the church for a while. I came back in later to see if it was done, and the Catholic priest was saying "Death is a part of life" and all that crap. So I just fucking left. For good.' He was admiring his arms in the moonlight. Then he looked at me with those winning eyes. 'Does anyone still believe it? "Death is a part of life"? Please.'

'I suppose. I never did.'

'Course not. It's mental. Like saying the sun moves round the earth, or your body is part of your hand, or a river is part of a stream. It's life that's the part and death the whole. Right?'

'Is this something you *know*? Because you're –' Before I could stop myself I had accidentally invented a gesture that meant 'dead'. It involved offering my left hand and quickly retracting it, as though the afterlife were accessible by key card.

It took this long for me to consider whether there was something in the dope. That I wasn't merely an old man who'd lost his tolerance, but that I was tripping hard. Because this conversation with dead Simon was a little strange.

'Death needs something to kill, it's given life by life.' Simon threw an arm out in the direction of his place of rest, the direction of England. 'Death is not a part of life, *life is a part of death*. I'm just saying: whatever the priest says – life is the food of death. Life is the petrol station sausage roll that death needs just to get through the day, you know?' Simon laughed at his own joke.

'Life is a part of death,' I repeated. 'Did you get that from Camus?'

He was doing tricep dips again on the wall, this Simon. This fit, young and self-delighting Simon. Unpausing. Flexing with promise and bullish energy. In his full unbearable glory, and so incomplete. Trying so hard it was exhausting.

'No, I'm just telling you it now. Open your eyes, Al.' He laughed and pulled at the stud in his ear, reminding me of the day we'd all first seen it, at fourteen years old, just before Mr Pullock's Friday maths test, and how he'd afterwards swaggered to his summons in the headmaster's office, reassuring him that piercings weren't contagious. 'How come you were there anyway – at the funeral? It's not like we've spoken since we were kids.'

'I got a message from school. I thought I should show my face. Felt like the right thing to do.' And then, because there seemed no other way of phrasing it, I said, 'Simon, what happened to you?'

'Same thing that happens to everyone else, mate.'

'What?'

'Life went from possibilities to probabilities.' Simon raised his arms akimbo as he tested his balance on the wall. 'If you're not careful, it just goes through you like a third pint.'

His act was irritating. I began to realize why almost no one had been at the funeral, what I had overlooked all those years:

this boy was deliberately unpleasant. 'Right. But what did you end up doing?' Why, I wanted to ask, why, when he'd owned the school, had he not owned the outside world? Why hadn't he become the unfaithful hedge funder, or frontman of a failed band, or global fraudster his youth had promised? And why had he seemed so enviable to me? He was all talk, I saw that now, all posture and attitude. But at fifteen, sixteen, seventeen, his gifts had been priceless.

'I drove a cab, basically as a stopgap,' he said. 'I liked it, time went by.' Then, louder, 'It was cancer, in the end. Can't say I didn't earn it.' He turned and winked at me. 'Refused to get that lump checked out, so I died like a man. None of that going to the doctor shit. Carry my folding umbrella and pull my wheelie suitcase into the hospital? I'm all right.' He chuckled to himself. 'Men don't go bitching to the doctor with every little complaint.'

And I could barely look at this boy.

What happened, he went on, was that he lived off those parents we had all so admired, and went nowhere. Filling the house with collectable figurines (not toys, of course) and build-at-home remote-controlled cars. Decade by decade, toy by toy, his mother and father indulged his impulses, treated him as a peer. Eventually, ill and in his later years, he moved back in with them again. Moved back into this emptied-out bedroom with his lava lamp, speakers and aftershave. There, he became just another older person in the house. When his father had died and his mother was bereaved, he'd faced independence for the first and last time. It didn't take long to fail.

For all his charisma, Simon cast a sad figure. In his fidgeting I saw everything, a slide show to the end of his life. And Simon, of all of us, dying in the place where he had grown up. *What's happened to Simon Penton?* we, his old school peers would have asked, and we'd have given him the benefit of the doubt. *Europe? Or stuck in Canada perhaps. Teaching guitar, busking, upwardly married or ageing disgracefully*, we'd have said. *He's landed on his feet.* But no. He'd lived so little, he'd loved no one, made no lasting friends, no life of note. Owned by death long before it had called in the loan, Simon's true existence had ended years ago, and his final possession had been that secret.

The clarity of a realization under the influence filled and emptied my mind, like strange hands fingering a ring, trying it for size. Death is the death of life. Life is the life of death. The words losing meaning, then form. Life is the life of death. But death is the death of life.

'What?' Simon asked.

'Nothing. Nothing. I'm just stoned.'

He then said, 'I'm not the mystery, you know.' And Dead Simon rolled his head, evenly clicking his thick, indignant sports neck. 'I'd love to be.'

'Well, I'm not.'

'Who said anything about you?'

This guy, all attitude and hair gel, was dismissing me. Something about him seemed to be moving away from me, shrinking on the balcony wall.

'Your parents still around?' he asked.

'No.'

'Too bad. Still, they died in time, eh? Before it really hit the fan.'

'My sense is my mother always felt guilty about that.'

'Sounds like a good mum,' he said, to himself. Then he asked, 'What colour are your memories then?' with his back to me, packed into a tight t-shirt, while he aimed an imaginary drive at the golf course. 'You know, when you think back. What's the colour of things?'

'Blue. Night blue.'

'Huh.'

'What about yourself?'

'Mmm? Oh, everything's kind of yellow for me, like faded or dried out. Sometimes when I can't think of a face, all I get is a colour.' He walked along the wall, his fascination with the precipice like a child's. 'Mrs Revignon teaching us about Camus, that's lemon-ish. You're orange. Cece is orange too. Funny, isn't it.'

Two birds chirped over one another.

'What about her, then?' Simon asked.

'I don't know.'

'Always thought you had something there.'

'I know.' He turned. I could feel him looking at me.

'Sorry,' I mumbled.

'Funny how things turn out.'

'Mmm.'

'Nadia's fit. Considering she's past it.' He tugged at his low-hanging trousers, hitching up the crotch as he always did when on the subject. A force of habit. 'You gonna?'

'She's not old. And no, Simon.'

'Cos you wouldn't do that to a friend, eh? Wouldn't do it to Stov. Your guy.' Simon sniggered to himself. 'Stov. What was his problem?' He ran a hand over the hairs on his neck. 'Gonna stay here or go back to England?'

'Don't know. I need to think. It's a nice place – I could cash in my return credit, live here cheaply.' An image of Kat came back to me, her face my home.

'Stinks,' he said. 'Even the dogs think it reeks.'

'I like it.'

'Al, do I detect an opinion? At last! A bit late, but better than never. Well, your funeral. But try and decide soon – it makes dying so much easier.'

'If you say so.'

He gave me his longest look. 'You don't like me, I can tell. Too crude, am I, for Mr Press Photographer of the Year 2021? Mr Family Man?'

'You don't know anything about my family –'

'Well, whatever. Thinking all the time doesn't make you better than everyone.' He walked past me now, turning into the main outer corridor, the darkness blotting him out. His voice was carrying up a stairwell. 'Nice seeing you, Al.'

I stared into the space he had vacated, and it held time still for a couple of minutes.

The fleshy moon now hung at half tilt above some vast casuarinas. The tinier muscles of my body seemed to relax with the sense that lay in feeling nothing more could possibly go wrong in a place as bereft as this. Insects were nudging and calling, telling me not to dream. Wake, they urged, leave this place.

Whatever I had smoked, it was not weed. It was not for people who wanted to keep even the vestiges of this reality. If weed was a gateway, this was a manhole into the slurry of my mind. And it made me realize there were things for which I wanted to climb out and return.

There were colours in the sky, separate little heavens divided by the clouds and kaleidoscoped by the glass of the desert wind. Like an old bar under the lights, port mauve and bottle green and whiskies of every kind.

A hint of pink signalled the sunrise. Cece always said that sunrises were more beautiful than sunsets. 'Any old chump can appreciate something ending,' she said. 'But it takes imagination to watch something begin.'

Following my marks back through the square, I passed policemen with long canes and spoke under my breath in flawless, fantasy Arabic. The contents of an old office block – stripped cabling, ripped hologram screens and blinds – flapped from its windows.

And then in a souk a young snake charmer, barely bearded, stopped me. He lifted the lid of his basket as he did so, and out came his snake, which wove itself around my arms. 'I feed her once,' said the man in English, 'and then sew her mouth shut. She never bites. She cannot.'

'How long will she live?'

'After a few weeks, she dies of hunger. Five weeks.' He scratched his chin in regret. 'So I will buy another snake, and sew the mouth of that snake.' He asked me for sachets and I gave what I had left, but now others approached with hands outstretched, begging and selling. Although I raised my empty palms high so they could see them, still they followed. I strode away in panic, lumbering and slow through the muggy slough of morning.

I wondered if the snake had felt the sweat between my shoulders, my fear on its ropy skin. I imagined its tense muscles wrapped around my loose neck. I wondered how long its rage would keep it alive.

XIII

Ali turned left up the unsurfaced road, the cattle grid reverberating through him. Then he accelerated towards the short oak tree that formed a little turning circle in the road, and, as he approached it, the leaves cast their shade across him. This was his favourite part, because no one else was ever around. The shadows felt cool as marble.

Three days ago, after she'd told him about her father, he had lain next to her, stroked her back and held her. He'd vowed to lighten things up, and so that afternoon suggested they played lecture roulette. Lots of people were doing it in the first term, mostly as dares.

He took the first go. Standing before the hall noticeboard, he closed his eyes and placed his finger on a timetable of lectures. And soon they were sitting in a history class, and nodding earnestly and prodding each other beneath the table while a nerveless young South African lecturer discussed how *mundus est immundus* meant not only that the world was unclean but that cleanliness was unworldly. When it became boring Cece whispered through the hair with which she curtained her mouth, and they walked out.

The next was her choice. After a little walk through the park on the way to the dingy English faculty, they sat through a talk about Galsworthy. 'What *The Forsyte Saga* demonstrates,' the old woman, whose face wasn't easy to focus on after the bottle of wine they had shared in the park, said, 'is that every life has a bigger backstory. Every peripheral figure in every narrative has their own history, which is of course the centre of another story, so there is no such thing as an extra here. No such thing simply as the protagonist or the father or grandson of a protagonist. Galsworthy offers a clear lens to apply to all other novels: every single person's life is given integrity by drama, of which they are the protagonist, even if in our own subjectivity we cannot see it.'

She means she's boffing her husband's best friend, Cece wrote in a notepad in front of him.

'No daughter can fully fathom their father's history, no mother their child's preoccupations. When they enter the narrative, they do so not simply as engines of plot, but as heroes and heroines of other unknowably massive dramas set in their own lives – and in the next room. In Galsworthy every entrance is an exit, every exit an entrance.'

Cece paused, and then wrote: *Shall we entrance/exit?*

These po-faced moments, where she was innocent, restive, devious, obtuse, questing, all this was her element, and the giggles escaping between them were like molten lava.

For their final spin, they caught the last ten minutes of a lecture in one of the larger theatres of the mathematics faculty, where they found only single seats on different rows. He crept to the back and Cece strode to the front. Having sat so far apart that any communication was impossible, Ali ended up trying to follow the lecture. He watched the back of her head as they listened to a man discuss the geometry of the asymptote. Cece even went as far as making notes, and when, a little subdued, they had left this last ride in their playground, she read them aloud in the pub.

'*The asymptote is a line which is tangent to a curve at infinity.*'

'Which means?' he asked.

'The word is derived from the Greek *asýmptotoi*, which means "not falling together". In some definitions the curve may not cross the line.'

'Meaning?'

'It means "two non-parallel lines that nevertheless do not ever intersect as they approach… infinity".'

'How is that? How can they not meet?'

'I guess they just run out of time. Or space or something.' She had flicked through the day's notes. They were meticulous. 'I think Galsworthy would like the asymptote. He's into loose ends.'

Ali looked at her notes. 'You can get an *oblique* asymptote.'

Cece had poured the final contents of Stov's baggie from the third night onto the table and with a menu carved the powder into two lines. 'They head towards each other for infinity but never touch. How very proper of them.' She had stood the menu in front of her hands. Now, ducking behind it, she put a straw to her nose and lowered it to the table. 'What's the point?'

By early evening Cece was full of impersonations of lecturers, freshers and the principal. She kept looking at the number of stamps they had on their hands from the club nights over the week, drawing on them, adding embellishments. Neither mentioned her father again, though Ali brought up the brothers.

It was odd, he thought, how all the ingredients which had made Cece could be mixed in a different way, how another two versions of her could exist. Were Cedric and the little one, Howie, like her? Would those features translate onto the male face? Did they have the look of private loss that her eyes could assume without warning? Did Cedric have a perfect up-at-dawn, team captain, drink-till-dusk physique? Did Howie do those same things to keep his companions guessing – taking off and putting on hats, starting and half-finishing cigarettes – as Cece did now?

'No, they're nothing like me and nothing like each other. Cedric finds the world very difficult. That's why I don't like being far from him. Listening to the forecast keeps us close.'

'Where's his school?'

'It's more like a home, really. Near my dad.'

'Oh.'

'It's OK. It has a quad too.' She laughed to herself, her nervous laugh, which he recognized now. 'Cedric started having fits, emotional ones, around two years ago. He cries and, well…' Her eyes – her entire face – flooded with a colour that she managed to suppress. 'Do you mind if we don't? I don't have to worry about Howie in the same way.'

'Of course.'

Later, Cece sat cross-legged, lighting another one of Ali's expensive foreign cigarettes.

'Are you going to finish it this time?'

'What's it worth?' She took a puff.

'About a quid actually. Hold still.' He took the camera out of his bag quickly, quietly, and photographed her floorward gaze, her eyes consumed, lost in thought.

'No photos, not now. It's been a long day.' She shielded her face.

He ignored her. 'Please. Just one.'

'Why does it have to be now?'

He turned the camera. 'Because I fall in love with you a little bit every time you smoke.'

He'd said the word lightly enough to test her, and so she tested him. 'Do you love cigarettes more than me?'

'You more.' He took one last photo.

She gave a sarcastic flutter of eyelashes. 'Why?'

He thought about it. 'Because you don't run out.'

'Oh, don't be so sure.'

As they left to attend their first Street Spirit Society, a girl named Petra wearing a large red cardboard box painted as a bus – complete with rotating black wheels and windows cut into the sides – ran into Cece and told her she was now dead and had been assassinated. 'You've been run over. Now you have to kill somebody else,' she said. 'Come to Assassins Soc. and they'll give you a target.'

The night ended in a cellar in the Caste Building, the one famous for the skins of animals that lined the walls. Ali remembered inspecting the trophies with Cece before it started: a lynx, a moose, an ermine. And then, in a circle, twenty or so artfully dishevelled post-rock fans sat and listened to a song on the CD player. When the singer's voice had dissolved they rose and embraced each other, held each other, some genuinely upset by the music, others laughing. The song – which was meant to be the sound of suffering, the saddest song in the world – was therapy by mutual despair. It was 'Street Spirit'. This was all the society was, sitting and listening to a stupid Radiohead song, hugging afterwards. And in three years it had never seen fewer than a dozen members in any week.

If it was funny at first, he quickly realized it would kill their high from the lecture roulette. Cece, instead of laughing at the pretensions, went blank. He knew he had lost her. This happy day had been entrusted to his hands, and he had dropped it. She remained in that hideous hall, quite still, staring at the animal skins as others got up and began to leave.

The organizers tidied and went. They left the lights on.

Eventually Ali left too. Cece just sat there.

She did say something, just before he went. 'We love this album.'

'We?' He had the horrible feeling she was about to say *Me and Simon*.

'Me and Ced,' she said, not moving.

Two days passed in which, like an infant, Ali's experience exceeded his comprehension. They saw each other but they didn't laugh.

Or spoke but didn't agree. The second day, she visited him in his room, but never sat down to stay. Just to check he was still pining, perhaps, or to practise the act of leaving him.

By the third day, he was running up to six miles before 7 a.m. He ran until his toes blistered, ran until he couldn't feel anything, even the last vestiges of hope.

'Hey,' he panted at Nell as he ran through the gate, the lactic burn already receding.

'Hey,' Nell replied. 'Oh hey, wait – Ali.'

He stopped and walked back to her, hands on hips, trying to catch his breath. 'Yeah?'

'You going back to the Games?'

'To my room, yeah.'

'OK. Well –' Nell opened her mouth and shut it again. She took off her alpaca hat and scratched her scalp. 'You know what's happened? Right?'

'Yeah?' he said. 'No. What?'

'Cece?'

He knew what Nell was going to say.

'She's gone.'

14

The next day I woke in Nadia's flat.

A second night on the sofa bed had left me rusty. Lifting my legs from the bed, there was a pause between command and movement. The refusal of my hip to hit its socket without strings of pain leading to my toes. The taste of deep sleep at the back of my mouth.

After Nadia knocked and entered the room, she looked frustrated and admitted, 'I don't know where he is.'

I was beginning to think this was all some awful ruse. A final joke, Stov's ultimate refusal to conform to expectation.

'He goes for days, maybe a week, and I do not know where.' Heat prickled her cheeks pink. As she unlocked the front door behind us, she wondered aloud, 'Sometimes I used to worry he is drunk, or maybe it is kif. But not now he is clean.' She shrugged.

'You're not his keeper.'

'No one is.' She ushered a dog through the front door. 'These animals are my family,' she said, scooping it up and dusting its ear. She dropped her flip-flops onto the cobbles in front of her and placed her feet in them with the care of a tightrope walker. 'Stov will come. Or' – she brightened – 'we can find him. We can try the usual places.'

We made our way down the street, following the mauve shadow of the riads' high walls.

'Nadia, I have a question.'

'Yes.'

'What is kif made out of?'

'Hashish from the Rif mountains. A lot of people smoke it, more since Le Bouchon. All the Crusoes – they smoked a lot.'

'Crusoes?'

'The foreigners who used to live here were famous for smoking it. Only Stov stayed. It helps you lose yourself. But then many people, they cannot return. Do not smoke it, Ali, it is legal, but it can be very – I do not know what you say – *moving*. Very bad. Stov can tell you.'

She directed us with swings of her canvas bag, and after a few minutes we came to a herbal medicine shop. It hummed with people gazing at everyday potions, tinctures and tonics, remedies for all complaints. Occasionally the shopkeeper's reader glowed through his pocket, sending the shelves upon shelves of glass jars into fiery rapture. Their contents – argan oil, twists of exotic branches, saffron, fingers of clove – gazed out in curiosity.

We looked round for a Western man; he wasn't there. 'This is where he comes first for his morning remedy,' Nadia said. 'Is there anything you need to buy?'

'I'd like some of the tea you gave me.'

'Ah! Green tea with orange leaves. And we will get you some mint for the tanneries. He might be there. Did you bring your camera?'

'Just this.' I held up my reader.

'Hard to be a photographer now?' Her brow wrinkled.

'Yup. The government made it impossible. Revoking press passes. Confiscating equipment, breaking it. My job became extinct.'

'So sad. Stov said you take beautiful photographs. The tanneries are stunning in their own way.' She gave his arm a squeeze. 'Let us try there anyway.' She bought tea, the mint and stuffed them in my pocket, saying, 'For later.' Then she led on again, back through the knotted streets, and I followed, half attending to the smells, the faces and stalls, and then I would not be able to see her, and she would call from some alley tucked in the arches, checking particular recesses and staircases for our friend. 'So, you photographed for newspapers?'

'Yes, mostly.'

'What kind of subjects?'

'Back then? Anything we could. Current affairs – witnesses, ordinary people. Everybody had cameras on their devices by then, so you had to be good, had to keep putting yourself in danger to make a career.'

'Like war?'

'Yes, once or twice war. Suddenly everyone needed evidence. Suddenly I was handed a career.'

'It must be strange – to have to watch these things and do nothing.'

'It was difficult not to get involved. It was important not to. Not to ask questions, just capture it.'

We passed in front of a table covered in washing products – old soap and toothpaste brands that had been preserved in some garage for the last fifteen years. My hand hovered above these objects like a hummingbird.

'Maybe you have questions about me and Stov,' Nadia said.

'I don't want to pry.'

'Pry?' She frowned. 'What is it, "pry"?'

'It means asking about things that are none of my business.'

'I think Stov is your business? You were kids together? And he is also my business, he lives with me – so I am your business, yes?'

I gave a nod.

'So it is OK to pry now?'

'OK.'

'You want to know everything, but you do what the Englishman does – you mention anything else.' She smiled at my false discretion. 'Stov is like this, so bad at lies. But I read him now.'

She was his match. And the piles of books stacked beneath an ashtray were as close to roots as Stov had ever laid. Just like the stacks in Cece's college room; both of them made furniture out of their copious reading. He was home.

'How did you meet?' I asked.

'Five years ago, on campus, after my fiancé broke up with me.' She looked at me incredulously, and then, seeing my face fall, implored me with a smile. 'Go on, ask me what you really want to know.'

I opened my mouth and hesitated.

She wasn't going to wait. 'Why are Stov and I here together like this?'

'Yes, that's the first question.'

'Wait,' she said. She held up a finger. Bangs rose from the metal workshops off the small square we had entered. 'This is where the vagabonds come,' Nadia said, uttering the unusual word slowly. Men and women passed us carrying plastic buckets, ghostlike in their silent ferry, and children splashed in the shallows where the fountain leaked its last brown water into little pools. 'If Stov has been in trouble it will be here. They gather against the water fountain.' She sighed. 'But he is not.'

A donkey cart crossed slowly in front of us. The cart driver stopped, his companion pointing to me and calling something out. He flicked an index finger in my direction once more and followed it with a rocket of spit.

We left briskly via a different exit hidden under starved, stringy palms. Nadia said, 'The people in this area do not like me.'

'I imagine having a Western partner is very difficult?'

'That is not the reason,' she said, adding, before I could ask what that meant, 'My parents were French aid workers, both married to other people, in Marrakech during the drought from Sanction

1. And they met here, in this district, and had me – illegitimate.' Nadia smiled. Her dignity was her strength. 'My father was a government worker. My mother was a delegate to France, and had to return to Paris immediately after the birth. So I was left here, growing up in a bathhouse. Later, when I was older, I worked in reception. Then my father, who knew me by email, he died very quickly. He was making a report on the new flu at the borders, and everyone exposed before the vaccine died fast. For a time a special proviso was arranged and I was sent to France for education, but when I was eighteen I had to choose.'

'Between France and Fès?'

'Yes. Between rejection and home. I was never accepted in France, they hated me more than if I had been pure Moroccan. I chose to return here. Mama could not accept it. Even my boyfriend then, Bernard, he would not leave France with me. But I preferred to be an outcast here, among equals. Bernard always said perhaps I could marry him and return to Paris if I changed my mind – but then everything changed with Le Bouchon, and now I can never go back, no matter who my boyfriend was, no matter who my mother is. And that day, Le Bouchon, is when I met Stov.'

'So without Stov you'd still be an – outcast?'

'Yes. Stov is not my problem. He is just another stray dog. They do not like a Western man here, but they fear more a mixed race. Everywhere.' She adjusted the bags on her shoulder. 'Even if Stov was my lover it could not be worse. We live together, that is all, and we are nothing more. The truth is we are both outcasts, Stov and me, we are a prison of two.'

'He's not your partner then?'

She remained quiet.

I moved on. 'And you can't go anywhere else?'

'I belong here. We belong here.'

'He was always very strong-willed.' I spoke like he was dead. It had crossed my mind that perhaps he was dead, or worse, irretrievably lost somewhere, and Nadia couldn't bear to admit it to herself, let alone tell me.

'So,' I said, 'second question: is he really coming back?'

'Yes,' she said at once, but then stopped and properly considered it. 'You have no idea, do you?'

'Of what?'

'Anything.'

The reek of the tanneries finally reached us – heavy air, thick with the whipping and baking of dried skin and what some instinct told me were bits of discarded rotting flesh.

'This is my last guess.' Nadia opened a door to an empty hammam and I followed as she felt her way up the dark, shallow steps, breaking two flights later onto a sunlit terrace. She turned and scanned. First the roof, then the streets, and finally the infinity of gravestones that spread out over the hillside. 'He loves the Jewish cemetery,' she murmured. 'And if he was there, we could see him.'

He wasn't, and neither of us needed to say it.

'At least you got to see the cemetery and the tanneries.' The palette of vats, like pores, shimmered hot colours through the stench, their sleek tops blinking towards the sky with every disturbance.

'It's spectacular.' And I meant it.

'Red.' She pointed. 'Made of poppies. Orange, from henna. Blue, of indigo. They use limestone and pigeon waste for stripping the hides of camels, goats, sheep, cows. And green, from mint.' She delved into my pocket and took out one of the sprigs of mint that she had bought at the medicine shop, tore the leaves and put them to her nose. 'For the smell.'

I copied her, masking the smell of chemical effluents and animal flesh, but nothing masked the acrid ammonia. Men and boys stood calf-deep in their blood-red or clay-brown vats agitating the skins in thick, hypnotic circles.

'You are a proper tourist now!' She laughed.

We stood watching them lay out the dyed skins and listening to the delayed scrapes of their knives as they cut up the finished ones. And I wondered if that was all I was. A sightseer from the future, come to gaze at this town lost in the past. If Stov was missing, or dead, or mad, then I was more lost.

'Let us go home,' Nadia said.

At street level she dropped the used mint leaves and tucked a strand of hair behind her ear, something Stov himself – back when he'd had long hair – used to do at awkward moments. Only with this gesture did I notice she was wearing no headscarf.

On the way, another stall was covered with old curiosities and junk, irons and cameras, cassettes that the children liked to unwind and twine around their wrists. Trash everywhere. Obsolete items sold like krill.

'What are we looking for?'

'Looking?' she asked. 'You cannot look for things here. You can only find things.'

'Does Stov ever mention me?' I said, handling an old plastic coat hanger.

She paused. 'He talks about four people. His friend from South America. Tom.'

The name meant nothing to me. I had missed Stov's life. 'Who else?'

'You, he says you were his brother. His dead mother, he says she was both his parents. And Cece.' Nadia considered the trash in front of her. 'Are there still big attacks in Europe?'

'Cece?'

'Yes. They are still close. He gets news from her. What is going on in different countries, where the wars are, where is safe. We have almost no news service now. Will it end this year?'

'We don't think so. In Spain there are a few attacks each year, but their war isn't over, the Plug Laws only paused it. Rumours are, the lowlands are quieter now though.'

'Rumours.'

'And Cece – have you met her?'

'Stov has seen her. I was working. Maybe a year ago?' Nadia picked up a junked laptop and weighed it in her hands. 'They left people to die, you know? First Le Bouchon in France, then the Plug across Europe, and they think that ending the fights in Spain makes it go away? Locking up these places – it was murder. I had friends who tried to get out. Where else were they meant to go?'

I made a nodding movement, aware it was inadequate. 'They had to do something.'

'They needed to do something *years* ago. When I was a little child. That was the only time. The things they did since – they give you only one return flight, or stop the immigration, or limit the number of babies – too late, no?' she asked me, as if I were responsible.

'They felt they had to anyway. Because otherwise they'd be just like their parents' generation.'

'Even if it makes no impact?'

'They had to show they were different. You don't know how much the older generation is mistrusted.' My voice thickened with the suffering of it all.

'I think I do. The young people here' – she dropped her voice – 'they hate the old. They are responsible for everything that went wrong. The young do not sit with them, talk to them. They don't want to know their past. They call them "abdicators".'

'In England they call us Babyburners. Guzzlers. Fairweathers. I don't even know who's right.'

'Everyone is wrong,' Nadia said. Then she looked at me with a tainted smile, the first sign of pity. 'They write to each other.'

'Cece?'

'Yes, he likes to hear about England. Even if he pretends not to.'

'Then why the hell did he leave?'

She nodded with satisfaction. 'You finally asked the real question. Well done.'

'And?'

'I do not know, Ali. When we find him you ask him. He has sold his credit, but you know that.' She put down the busted laptop and turned to him so he could see she wasn't trying to be evasive. 'I think he prefers living here.'

The storks were fading, line drawings in the sky. Evening was cooling over them. 'Did he ever miss me?'

'I think yes. One time he came home very sad, nearly blackout drunk, too drunk to get up, so he lay on the kilim and murmured about his mother. And then he said, "My oldest friend. I left my friend in the worst place on earth – in his own head."'

'His head?'

'That is what he said.'

'So he cut me off, but did talk to Cece.' I couldn't understand. 'Why?'

'This is everything I know.' Nadia saw my rising anger and softly took my hand in both of hers. 'You are here now,' she said, squeezing my hand. She looked at her watch. 'We should get back before the dark.'

We turned into an alley on a corner with a pencil mark on the wall. Almost home, we accelerated at the cafe and Nadia glided through the gateway, left the door open for me and entered the apartment. Following her, I stooped and cracked my head on the door frame and leaned against it in a grey pain, holding my forehead.

A hand gripped my shoulder. 'If you're going to hit your head,' a voice said as someone helped me up and embraced me, 'hit it harder than that.'

XIV

Ali had tried to explain it to himself. But it was no use. It was like trying to explain a face, a birthmark, an animal hide. No wonder Cece had laughed. There was no explaining. She wasn't perfect, simply unaware of her imperfections, the strange boldness of her markings. Sometimes she could even make him jealous, or angry. Sometimes her guessing of his thoughts had made him burn to hurt her in ways that, by her very nature, she would never suspect. In some ways, of course, she had already been punished for all her precociousness.

After she disappeared, these images often came to him. The days filled out into weeks.

In the autumnal weather he and Nell walked the six bridges of the town. Between the Maiden Field and the canal lock she told him that he looked ill. 'Like you've just woken from a bad dream.'

'Actually,' he replied, 'a really good one. I wish I'd never woken.'

Perhaps this was why one of his last times alone with Cece haunted him especially.

In it, he paused as he thought he heard the approach of a high voice. At last. How long can you listen for something before you begin to believe you hear it? Though perhaps it wasn't her; perhaps it was Kai instead, the Austrian guy so devoted to his refrigerated protein that his stomping up and down the stairs swinging his croissant-like arms in momentum had become as reliable as the whirring of the rowing machines in the attic.

All quiet. Nothing.

He listened again. Nothing.

'Hi.' Cece said from behind him. 'No need to jump, is there?' 'No.'

Yes, because someone had come through his door – a surprise normally, but more surprising because he'd stopped expecting it. 'What you up to?' she asked.

'Got lectures.' Ali listened for her response, and heard instead the sounds of the traffic outside. Still he hadn't turned. He couldn't picture her face. He knew she was beautiful, but that wasn't enough.

Then he looked at her. 'You look great.'

She gazed down to her bathrobe, pulled the cord tight until it ran through her fingers. 'I look awful.'

'Now you're lying.'

'I'm really not.'

'Liar. You look perfect.'

She frowned, tilted her towelled head in curiosity, laughed at his sincerity.

He unpicked a cigarette from the sticky pack in his jeans, plastered together by dancing sweat, and lit one. 'Did you know, *perfect* is a word taken straight from the Latin, *perfectus*. Completed.'

'Aha.' The smirk came. 'That's so lame.'

That weird atmosphere was there, the third resident who lived between her room and his and had chaperoned their visits since day four of term.

Ali leaned in for a kiss, found her collarbone, and searched upwards for her lips. He could feel the sound, the sensation of her voice, warm between them, vibrating in his nerves. Her voice became an external thing once more as she said, 'I can't. I'm not sure. I need time.' She released a sad smile as a show of goodwill. Evidence she was in a mood good enough to take things lightly.

'Seriously?' He stood and leaned forward again.

'Yes!' She walked towards the door. 'What are you doing in here all day anyway?'

He wasn't listening. He was gazing at the wall where his posters used to be. He had torn them down that week. Their corners floated on dry Blu-Tack. She had opened the door to leave. He didn't know what he was meant to say. How to save it.

Unsure where it had gone wrong, he was conscious that one specific future, the future he had privately imagined for them, was disintegrating. And now, in this exact moment, it was gone.

15

Early the next morning we left without waking Nadia. Stov smiled and gripped my arm a few times, to check my realness. He poured a handful of nuts into his mouth as I sipped from my water bottle and returned it to my bag. 'Don't fill up anywhere but where I tell you,' he ordered. Stov pointed to the moulded roofs, the pale green of the porous fringes. 'The watercolour palette.' He surveyed the town as we left it. 'That's what I love. Everyone loved it. The activity, the *bustle*. It was one of the things that at one time seemed important.' He looked back behind us, his eyes searching. 'I want to know everything.' He shook his head with happiness. 'First, home: how is it in the UK? What's really going on?'

'Well, they've cancelled the Border Review again.'

'And?'

'Someone drove into the Tyne Barrier.' I unfolded my reader to show him the story. 'We lost a week's worth.' As it charged in the sunlight it grew to its proper size.

'You want to take care of that device,' Stov said. 'People will grab it.'

'This? It's a dinosaur.'

'Dinosaurs are the future here.'

'It won't work unless it can scan my face and palm.'

'They'll take those too. If you're unlucky.' He gave me a serious look. 'How much is a homeward-bound ticket these days?'

'Cheaper to buy the plane. Flybuyers are all billionaires.'

'Do most people take their flight or sell it?'

'The vast majority sell it. They get an eight-year ration voucher for their ticket.'

'Most people never go abroad in their lives?'

'Why would they? They aren't told anything about the outside world. Only that others would – and do – kill to live in our country. They think it's all barbarians beyond the Channel.'

'I suppose it's effective policy,' Stov said. 'Racism is cheaper than border control, and just as effective. Does anyone at all get into Britain? Stowaways by sea, freight? Sailing boats?'

'No one sails any more, they get scuttled. The seas are a no go, with commandeers and navy patrols. They shoot on sight. Then a fourteen-year-old got through to Cornwall on a barrel raft, in April. It was a miracle.'

'And?'

'And they dumped her back in the Channel with fresh clothes. Published the footage.'

'So Sanction 4, Not One More and all the laws, you think they worked?'

'Maybe for a while, but they'll fail eventually, we just don't know when. The conflicts are getting closer. The opposition say it's a matter of time. There's a border conflict now in Nassau. They say the Belgian border might not hold much longer, but –'

'It could hold?'

'No, it's already gone. I know it for a fact. It went years ago. I watched from a press helicopter as the western coast fell into the sea. I took pictures of the grids of wind turbines sinking under the surface, waving like dandelions. It was desperate.'

We exited an arched gate.

'After that, UK border control took my cameras, phones and reader and wiped them all on my re-entry. The deleted my press ID. That was my last job.'

'Unbelievable.' He looked at me with concern. 'And what about you? Tell me all about Alastair. I seem to remember your family was a little risky too? Are you still married?'

'Not "married". Madison and I were always just friends, and she needed a way to stay in England.'

'But you were married in law?'

'Yeah. In a corridor, on the last day possible. All the council offices were full. Thousands did the same. There were three in my postcode alone, we all had a drink in the street. You could be quite brazen for a while, back then. Madison would introduce me to strangers as "my husband-in-law". But then Population Control began to come after the sham immigration marriages. Being registered at the same address as your spouse wasn't enough. Suddenly we were given spot interviews. And then there was Kat, of course.'

'Your girl.'

'A great kid.' I smiled. 'She's not mine biologically. Anatoliy was back in Mongolia. But he didn't make it. Easterners got *sanctioned* rather than sanctioned, you know. We thought because he was white it might make a difference. But it didn't, they said no. Anyway, he died later somewhere in the Lowlands, and so we said she was my daughter. It saved the kid and strengthened Madison's case. And I was always "Dad". She was too young to keep secrets. They were revoking the visa marriages by then and dumping people at Calais, at the mercy of bigots.'

Stov arched his back, stretching it. 'You have an accidental family.'

'I suppose.'

'And Kat, does she know where she comes from, who she really is?'

'We think so.'

Darling Kat. Kat who as a child was always pausing over words, or asking me the most difficult questions – 'When does a spider's web become a cobweb?' 'What is the name of the place where you are just out of the rain?' 'Why is your wound now called a scar?' A girl transfixed by the fog. Endangered by her bloodline. 'How many times have you looked at the clock and seen the minute change, just then?' Her impatient frown staring at the kitchen clock, waiting for it to change, holding it to account.

As I described her, Stov nodded. 'Sounds like your kid to me. You were always into people who had a sense of wonder.'

'I never thought of that.'

'And it sounds like you did the right thing.' Stov looked down at his feet. He was bulkier these days but somehow no less lanky. Where he once would have interjected, he angled his head as he listened carefully, nodding, to the odd facts of my life. 'At least to me. When I found out you'd taken on a compound family, I thought, that's the Alastair I knew.'

I considered the empty sky. The hot dirt rising. 'I'm not sure.'

'They owe their lives to you.'

'What kind of lives?' I shook my head. 'Thanks, but I didn't do much for Kat as a child. Her mother was right: I was only a husband-in-law. I'd travelled the world for decades, never staying long in the same place. And then' – I clicked my fingers – 'Britain had no place for photographers. We were disaccredited, our international Justifications deleted overnight. Every single one. I hadn't even covered the killings in Dover or the Canada borders. But I was suddenly gated with everyone else. I had no job, nowhere to travel. I was stuck in the UK with a strange baby and a strange wife in my home. My home, filled with things I didn't recognize.'

Stov's brown eyes were looking out onto the Jewish cemetery. Around it were long grasses, slicked by the wind. Days of white stubble on his cheeks protected his skin against the sun. 'If you honestly did your best, then you did your best.'

'I'm not making excuses. I just hadn't planned on being there much, for my friend's wife, and my wife's child. But then we had no choice. It all happened so quickly.' I rested my hands on my hips, breathing the cooked air with difficulty. 'For years Kat and Madison have been angry with me. Angry at my absence. Back in the day, when I returned from trips Kat used to listen to my stories of the world abroad like they were magic. But then, when I got gated just as she grew up, she realized I'd neglected her and her mother for years. And so she sees my past as some kind of theft. Sometimes I think she hates me.'

'That's not hate. That's just growing up.'

'Something like that.' I knew Kat knew. That her mother had fallen in love with me when that had never been the plan. All she had needed was a sham marriage. But she did learn to love me, and I didn't deserve it.

As friends Madison and I had mourned her husband, Anatoliy, together. As parents we had taught Kat side by side that the world was bigger than any relationship. A lesson she had apparently decided she would test by taking her flight this year, at only twenty-one. She had no idea where she was going, and might never come back. This she had said in the garden of the home where we had watched her run for the first time. Easily bruised but quick to disparage, she knew of the suspicion with which the world had accepted her birth.

We watched the road where the bus would appear.

'One day she'll understand what you've done for her,' Stov said. He still had the habit of gazing up at the sky to make grand, convincing statements.

I was drawing deep breaths. I wasn't as heavy as Stov, but he was used to walking in the sun. It gave him energy.

'Growing old,' he commented, slapping my arm. 'It's not for the faint of heart.'

Already the bus was making its way up the hill. It wavered in the heat faster than it grew towards us. 'Where are we going?'

Stov pointed to a sign to Ilfrahane. 'Work.'

'Your university?'

'Al Akhawayn, yes. I hear you went to the wrong university. Not the first time you've done that, eh?'

I sat on the pavement. 'I must be the joke of the town. Just another white man who thinks every Arabic word is the same.'

'We did have a laugh about it. Al Ak was built in the 1990s. I'm afraid you went to the one built in AD 859.'

The bus arrived, slow and sparkling orange. I followed him onto it; no tickets were bought. Stov simply gave the driver a squeeze of the shoulder and sat down in the middle. I sat beside him.

'The priest said you were hoping to convert? I thought he was joking.'

'He wasn't,' Stov replied.

'We have a lot of new Christians back home. They pray for the expats, for the wars.'

'There is only one prayer, Alastair.'

'For the world?'

'Every prayer – even yours – is a deference to a power beyond our understanding.'

Only a jolt from the engine marked the passing seconds, with Stov's eyes appealing to a credulity in me that he had no reason to find.

'So,' I said, 'now you. How did you find yourself drawn towards –'

'I haven't seen you in thirty years, can we not talk about religion? I'm not going to convert you. Some souls are better left unsaved.'

'OK, OK. I was just interested in the timing.'

'I can't do it. Timing is just another word for God.'

'Oh, come on.' I was smiling. I couldn't contain it.

'Listen: what do we call superstition that works?' Stov rotated the ring on his index finger with his other hand. 'Let's put it this way. I once asked the imam, the one you met, "What if you take a dog into a mosque?" And he replied that it would be improper to take dogs inside a mosque. Though, he said, if a dog happens to pass through it, the mosque is not thereby defiled.' He opened out his hands. 'It's the same with me. I wandered in.' He passed a hand over his shaved scalp. 'Of course: you wandered into that mosque too, Alastair, and got further than me. I always say that it's the atheists who teach us to pray.'

Stov still knew how to provoke me.

'We've got forty-eight minutes,' he said, looking at his reader and settling back, his head against the window with his eyes closed. The same arrogance. 'Can I read your Justification?'

I shook my head. 'It's private.'

'Not if some government shill has read it.'

'They just scan them – they don't care why this or that person decides to travel. Justifications never get declined.'

'Alastair. Why have you come?'

'No, you first. Why did you never go back?'

Stov tapped the time on his reader. 'Forty-seven minutes. You look mostly the same, you know? A little more grey hair for you, and less hair for me. Otherwise, just the same.'

'I don't think that's how age works.'

'I'm hoping it is.' With a laugh of resignation, he broke. 'OK, I'll go. I can tell you're up to speed on my little contract with Nadia. So what else: I'm not on the run. I never changed my identity. The UK government don't think I'm dead, to their annoyance. I haven't committed bigamy, forgery or seppuku. I have no children I'm aware of. I have both kidneys, I eat my greens, and my driver's licence is real.

'What else?' He looked hard at the ceiling. 'I lost two stone in South America, which made me perfect for certain kinds of work. They called me "The English Lord", and I could have been very happy there if I'd actually had the funds of an English lord. I then worked as a translator for a Bolivian army general. Did you know anyone can join the Bolivian army? Anyway, he trusted me because I had no interest in the politics, I just wanted to get my head straight.

'But as time passed I found myself liking the idea of money, you know? Lots of money. In Rio I befriended a guy called Tom, the wayward son of a major American statesman, who invited me to join him on Wall Street, where he planned on co-founding a company to export soy produce from Rio. He was a wild child but sweet at heart. Believe it or not, with no qualifications, after three years I was CFO at this Brazilian company – it sounds ridiculous, but there were only eight of us and I was the smartest and the sanest most of the time so they gave me the gig. Simple as that. OK, I quit not long afterwards, but I'd made quite a bit of money, which predictably by then was burning a hole in my conscience, so I made a large donation to a fledgling university back in Sucre, in Bolivia, where I'd left a good part of my heart. I thought that was that – I felt pretty good about myself.'

The town had sunk into the horizon behind us. A wing mirror rattled. He went on.

'But, completely unprovoked, five years later they gave me an honorary degree. I hadn't asked for it, but there it was. And then a few years later another one, because apparently they'd put some of my donated money into a fund and it had matured. Before long, hey presto – Dr Unwin of the Humanities. By then, ironically, I'd lost all my money half deliberately and half through vice, and now what I wanted was a soul. Again, predictable. So, thinking I might want to be a little closer to home, given the way things were going by then, I managed to get work on a tanker to North Africa, and Fès was a last shot at finding a hole in which to pour myself, find a riad and live out my days. I'd heard about the oldest university in the world. The cradle of knowledge. I thought I could always deal kif if that didn't work out. But it did, to everybody's surprise, because although they didn't want me the new place did, and I'm still here, more or less, after a decade. And to make things worse –'

'*Allons-y*, Stov!' He was interrupted by a shout from the front.

'Stov,' the bus driver called at the top of his voice.

'*Oui*, Amal.' Stov got to his feet. '*C'est quoi?*' Through the windscreen we saw vehicles blocking the road ahead, the dark lines of men waiting.

'What is it?' I asked.

'Mob,' Stov said.

'What?'

He pushed me from my seat. 'Get to the back. Keep your head down. It'll be fine.'

'What do they want?'

'Move!' He threw my bag after me as I clambered up the gangway and wedged myself behind the penultimate pair of seats on his side. It was only now that I wondered why we had been the only passengers, how odd it was.

After a swift exchange between Amal and Stov the bus came to a halt and the opening of doors was followed by a bounce of the suspension. They had stepped off the bus. I pulled my canteen from my bag and held it like a rock. Stov's voice was distinguishable between harsh passages of French and Arabic and the revving of a moped fed on dirty gas. Its misfires smelled like charred almonds.

You heard of bandits stealing Western readers and attempting to impersonate a route into Britain or Europe. You heard they would kill for a valid credit even though the odds of their using it successfully would be non-existent. I considered that I was worth less than my reader. Others would kill foreigners just for having a way out.

For minutes the voices grew and dimmed until the shoulders of the bus sagged with the weight of men getting on board. The doors closed and I held the canteen millimetres above my head, ready to deliver the first blow. The engine had already begun, the bus swinging blithely to the left, up the bank and around the barricade, as Stov's shoes came into view and now stood at my head as he threw a gesture out of the back window. His blue shirt was sweaty, his breathing hard. His right hand held a knife. 'We'd better keep you down there.'

'Who was it? Will they come after us?'

'No.' He walked away. 'But stay below the window.'

For another few seconds I lay, listening for the sound of other vehicles chasing behind us.

And then the crack of a shot, unmistakable.

I sat up, instantly forgetting my orders, to see three figures pointing weapons and one figure on the ground, prostrate and unmoving. A body. Another crack, this time followed by an immediate thud on the roof above us. Two more, one through the window.

I'd never visualized my own life before. Like the cliché, parts of it really did appear before me. Not everything, and not in order, but certain memories occurred to me, filled with the truest of details. I saw the unnamed bodies that sometimes washed up on the southern coast.

I saw images of Kat, a woman now and the measure of her parents.

Francesca, in the poem, asking Dante if there could be anything more painful than remembering the good times in misery.

Cece's sweat. Our skin touching at seven different points.

My father's final cup of tea on the bed tray after his operation, going cold at the same rate as him.

My mother's laugh as she witnessed the sham of my marriage.

The photo of Cece, the one I took at university. An image that defined my career, even if no one knew it. It became a very popular photo – famous, I suppose – and found itself reproduced thousands of times on postcards from city tourists, on the mouse mats and screen savers of foreign graduate students. The fluency of her after-movements, post-shot, occurred to me longest.

Terror can be beneficial. It makes instantly apparent what is most important, accelerates wisdom that can otherwise take years to evolve. Then, as the fear subsides, you realize you feel euphoric and entitled to be alive.

Stov appeared again. 'I need you to do something.'

I ignored him. Gazed back to the diminishing figures of the past, back at the face of Cece.

Cece's full name was being slowly enunciated by Principal
Faulk. In his hand Faulk held a Dictaphone as a conductor
holds a baton. Ali looked at Nell to interpret the silence. Faulk
was asking what he and Cece had been doing around the time
of her disappearance. Faulk already seemed to know the nature
of their relationship and had no interest in provoking defensive
answers about rights to privacy. He asked to have read aloud the
scrawled notes they had passed to one another during lectures.
Nell – who had helpfully fetched them from Ali's room – was a
silent pillar of support, though it struck him later he might have
more sensibly asked to be accompanied by a lawyer. How did you
get a lawyer anyway? Was this a legal situation?

Nell understood Ali's position better than anyone. She had
been the one who sat by his bed as he had retreated into silence
or swallowed sobs over Cece's sudden absence. Ali had confided
in Nell, told her of the seconds, minutes, hours, days, months and
years of a life, this vast mass of time he saw speed away from him
with imperceptible motion, like the spinning earth. She had politely
not mentioned, among other things, how broken he now seemed.

Faulk was looking at him, not Nell, asking him to explain con-
texts where the notes didn't make sense, asking him what Cece's
words meant, occasionally inflecting the lines in her voice to give
them possible meaning. Ali hated that. Does context always exist,
he wondered as he read their texts aloud, their Facebook messages,
their notes passed during lectures – complete with diagrams,
neologisms and so many uses of 'fuck'.

'Please repeat that,' the principal said, after another fifteen minutes.

'OK, it says:

'*Me: ?*

'*Cece: !*

'*Me: ??*

'*Me: Are you ignoring me?*

'*Cece: No. Listening.*'

(Here Ali remembered how she had raised her pencilled eyebrows to the heavens.)

'*Me: OK.*

'*Me again: You angry?*

'*Cece: Listening to lecture.*

'*Me: Don't lie. You hate Hemingway.*

'*Cece: A "lie" = the shortest distance between two points.*'

Here Faulk interjected, 'What was all this about?'

'It was, well, about me forgetting to wait for her. We were going to walk to class together.'

'Please continue, Ali,' said the principal.

'That's it.'

'Sir.' Nell spoke at last. 'I don't think it's fair to ask any more.'

'Thank you, Nell.'

'I'm speaking as a friend of Cece – as well as the student body rep.'

'I understand. I thought it might be helpful to see your communications. There is so much' – his voice trailed off – 'in between words.' The principal took off his glasses and folded them on the desk. 'But not here, alas.' He asked Nell to leave, and she did. 'And what do you remember of the night of August the ninth last year?' he asked.

'Last year?' Ali said. 'What was that?'

'The night you and Constance met.'

16

'Alastair.' Stov poked a foot at me. 'Are you awake?'
I flinched. 'What's going on?'

'It's OK. We're here.' He was wearing a new shirt. 'I'll explain.'

We descended from the bus into an immaculate college campus, a dial of timber buildings separated by an AstroTurf quad. Not one Nell could play frisbee on, nor Cece wander at midnight, but a plastic lawn, shining in the desert.

'Stov –'

'Say nothing.' At once he was gripping my arm so hard that the rouge of three days in North African sun disappeared from the skin. He let go.

'Let's get to the office first.'

In the office, Stov poured us both a glass of water over a sprig of mint. 'First, I'm going to tell you what I'm doing. And then – your turn.'

The leaves floated to the surface.

'I don't want anything to do with this.'

'Fine, then listen. I'm sure you'll think I've lost it, but try to listen to me.'

'You're in a gang now, is that it? You of all people have descended into violence? You're a fucking… knife-wielding geriatric? There's nothing more arrogant than a vigilante.'

'Vigilantes are self-appointed. I was –'

'Ordained? Oh fuck,' I said. 'What the fuck am I doing? Everyone's fucking gone.'

Stov exhaled with frustration. 'This isn't going to work,' he said, less to me than to the room in general. He got up and walked to the second door in the office, which adjoined the next room, and opened it. He spoke a few words in Arabic, and listened to the responses of the occupant. Back and forth it went. Finally he shook his head. Seconds later he stood to the side of the doorway and Nadia entered.

'How did you get here?'

'We have more than one vehicle in this town, Ali. And Stov says it's safer when I don't travel with him. Today he was right.' She sat on the desk before me, and, as though it were a perfectly obvious, asked, 'What do you think happened on the bus?'

'Alastair' – Stov closed the blinds, releasing pockets of dust – 'it's not what it looked like.'

'There was shooting,' I replied.

He motioned for me to drop my voice. 'OK.'

I whispered, 'Why were you being attacked?'

Nadia said, 'We had called out, publicly shamed, a man who was a murderer – of people like you and Stov.'

'Westerners.'

'No, no.'

'Brits?'

Stov chuckled and shook his head. 'Old people.'

'Here?'

'There are mobs, they're so angry,' Nadia responded. 'A month ago they murdered an elder playing dice in a market square. Four of them took a limb each and walked away with him, in front of his son. He was found strung to the roof of the old train station two days later.'

Stov took over. 'They're displaced. They don't have money, or hope. They blame people and they get violent. Major institutions, even the government can't handle it. You thought it was only in the UK? People here aren't just angry, they're thirsty. They think they're running out of time. And we're trying to prevent them.'

'So they're just murdering old people?' I felt for my reader. 'Are we in danger? Why haven't you left? We should go.' I got up, gave Stov a shove. 'We can maybe barter a passage for Nadia from the airport –'

'Sit down. Don't be ridiculous,' Nadia said.

'We can work something out.'

'Sit down,' Stov repeated. 'I sold my Justification ticket. I'm stuck here. I sold it, OK? There's no going home for me.'

'Are you in danger though?' I looked from Stov to Nadia, incredulous.

'Everyone's in danger,' he said.

'And you resist these people?'

Stov disagreed. 'We're trying to make amends. Trying to talk to these kids. Angry men mostly. To get them to stop. We try to initiate dialogue.'

'But then,' Nadia added, 'things like today happen, and they happen so quickly, and before you know it you have blood on your hands. That situation blew up because we were offering the boy amnesty for information.'

'You called him a man a second ago.'

'He became a man when he pulled a knife from his boot.'

'It wasn't your knife?'

'No.'

'Are we safe here? They'll come after you.'

'We're safe. No one stays long enough to hold a grudge.'

'So what is this place?' I was standing, or stooping. Or now I was not. It occurred to me that the door was either ajar or my vision must have been tilted. I was on the floor. 'Is this all a fucking joke?' I was certainly shouting now and Stov was leaning over me. 'What is a pristine bloody college doing in the middle of the desert? We have to tell Kat – we – we – I don't want her travelling, it's too dangerous, I was wrong –'

'Al, calm down. It's all right.' Stov put a jacket under my head. 'Just breathe now.' He sat at the foot of the desk, Nadia's legs dangling above me.

He sat with me until my vision came back.

They propped me up on the sofa while Nadia made calls on a number of devices kept in Stov's desk. The hospital, then the water station. Then the bus driver, Amal, came in and they held a conference over a reader. Stov pulled a book from his shelves, took a wad of meal sachets from its pages and with a nod gave them to Amal, who left.

Things were clearly calming down when Stov took a call, greeted 'Le Capitaine' and sighed slowly. He made several noises of solemn agreement before bursting into laughter as the two men rang off. 'It's looking OK,' he said.

He and Nadia sat, murmuring to avoid waking me.

By the evening, when I could sit up, Stov and I were alone. He spoke softly. 'We're fine here. But Nadia and I can't be responsible for you. Let's start again – tell me what's going on, and what you need.'

I finally told him why I had come. It was mad, I knew that, and a million years ago, when we were kids. But I started by showing him the photo of the four of us from the night out. He probably didn't even remember it. So I told the whole story of Cece. How we had met and how we parted. Of Simon's ghost. That I could remember it clearer than yesterday. That I wanted to find Cece. And that I thought Stov would know where she was.

'Why?' he asked.

'I know you're in touch.'

'Cece?'

'Yes. I need to know what happened to her. Why she disappeared. It must sound strange, but I have to know why she disappeared.'

'Why she disappeared?' Stov repeated.

'Yes.'

'OK.' Stov's eyes flicked to the blinds and back.

'I'm going to find her. Wherever she is.'

'And why would I still be in touch with her?'

'Nadia already told me. And so did Russell. You must know something.' I raised my hands to the high ceiling. 'I spent my credit coming here so I could at least make a start. You knew where she was more recently than me, that's for sure.'

'Ali, I'm not a mystic. Yes, we're in touch, we came to North Africa at the same time, around Sanction 3, when it became the last open gateway to Europe. But I don't know where she is.'

'I don't believe that. I know she trusted you. I don't think she'd let that go. People drift apart, sure. But for some reason you two didn't. And you know where she is.'

Stov paused. 'Look, if she doesn't want to talk to you, I'm not going to intervene.'

'Did you have a relationship with her?'

Stov tutted. 'No, Alastair. Get a grip. I was her friend. Someone she could talk to.'

'So you never got together. Did you want to?'

Stov simply looked at me.

'Then what did you have that I didn't? Why did she keep you and drop me? You know why she disappeared. Either you know, or you had something to do with it.' I gave him no time to respond. 'Do you remember what it did to me? You remember my desperate emails asking again and again if you knew anything after she vanished? And you were there right at the start, that night we all met. Do you remember?'

Stov stared. 'That night? Yeah.'

'We'd met her in the club, Plush.'

'Plush, then Simon's, yes. Why?'

'After she left university, our principal asked me about it.'

'Yeah, but you know why, don't you?'

'No.' That was why I was here. I could feel something rising in me, the frustration at being so near to whatever I had been missing my whole adult life. One piece of information that I needed in order to move on.

Stov breathed in slowly. 'She was raped that night.'

'What?' I sank, felt myself compact, curl like plastic in the heat. I had my hands on my knees. There was nowhere to look.

Stov took his hand off me.

'How do you know?' I asked.

'She told me. And that you were the only witness.'

'Me? I didn't witness –'

'You were there.'

'I must have been asleep.'

Stov said nothing.

'I didn't know. She seemed basically fine. Simon was – normal.'

'Normal.' Stov banged an open hand on a tray of papers on his desk. 'She was raped. And that boy-child friend of yours got away with it.'

Simon's funeral, I thought, empty. *Death is the death of life. Life is the life of death.* His bedroom. His bed. The lava lamp. It came back. My nausea at the wake.

Cece – just a teenager, just a child. My stomach turned. The most luminous, serious, funny, straightforward person. Raped, suffering, terrified. Lonely. Right next to me. How could I have missed it? How painful it must have been. How completely I had been blind to her. I wanted to be sick. How traumatizing it must have been for her to see me turn up at her college. What had she been doing even coming near me? How was she able to dance next to me, go to bed with me, bear me loving her?

Stov went on, 'I suppose Simon didn't say anything?'

'No, of course not. He wasn't crazy.'

'I thought maybe he was. And I was in South America by the time I heard.' Stov took a deep breath. 'By the time I heard, we'd lost touch. And I had my own problems then. That was my failing. So now you have it. The truth.' Stov drove a bead of sweat over his head with his hand. 'And what, you came all this way to find this out? One night sixty years ago.' He almost broke into a laugh and then didn't.

'You could have just told me over email.'

'No, I couldn't.' He looked at me like I was mad. And then his expression changed. 'At times I wanted to.'

'Why not, then?'

'I was the only person in the world Cece told, because it was me who had warned her about that shithead earlier in the night, I do remember that, and it wasn't my business to tell anyone else. And then there was the chance you knew, either because you were involved or were aware. I'm sorry, but that was a possibility.'

'Involved? You can't be serious.'

'It's not what I thought, but you can't be sure about anyone, can you? And then life went by. Perhaps you knew, perhaps not. Either way, I assumed you'd moved on. I had no idea you were still searching. Sitting on this for sixty-odd years.'

I stared glassily at his middle as he spoke.

'And besides, after a while I couldn't mention anything over email or phone. Immigration monitor everything, as you know. The reader is tapped, the phones are tapped. Nothing is personal any more. You were suspected as a "compound family", I knew there was a risk to you.'

'Immigration don't care about the reason my teen girlfriend ran off.'

'They care if it's criminal. They care about a good excuse to dump your family in the Nordics. I had to protect you.'

'OK,' I said, the words getting more distant from me. 'Thank you.'

'Alastair.' Decades hung in Stov's voice. 'How was I meant to believe that you didn't know about Simon and Cece? Eh? How do I know you didn't hear everything and do nothing?'

For a minute I failed to respond.

'I have no idea. I *had* no idea. I loved her. When we were together – and I couldn't understand why she left – if I'd known about it, I'd have reassured her that it wasn't me and I wasn't awake. I'd have done anything to mend it, I'd have lied if it would have helped. But I didn't even know about it. And then she disappeared.'

'And you didn't guess?'

'Not that. I thought maybe the stuff with her father. Something I didn't understand. Or maybe her brother Cedric was unwell and she needed to be with him. Something she couldn't handle at uni.'

'Well. I'm sorry it came to this.' He took up a pen and laid out the papers before him.

'Do you believe me?' I asked at last.

'You wouldn't still be here if I didn't.'

'But you cut me out for all those years because you suspected me?'

'I couldn't be sure. We fell out of touch. The world closed down. It happens.'

'Apparently it does.'

Stov shook his head at the whole mess. 'And you've been reacting to this thing ever since? Leaving uni, leaving England, leaving your family – all because you wanted to understand *this*? Living a haunted life and not knowing what's haunting you?' Stov smiled at my madness, but kindly. 'I don't know what to say. You've surpassed yourself.'

And then time simply went by.

'What are we going to do with you, Alastair?' he said at last. 'Mmm?'

'I don't know. I don't know what I'm going to do.'

'Yes you do. What did you write as the reason for travel in your Justification?'

'I said I was trying to find an old friend. I wrote that it was the last thing I wanted to get right.'

'Well then, let's do that. Let's see your Justification.' He got up and took my reader from my loose grip.

'Don't –'

'*I herewith justify my single return flight, as permitted by the Global Treaty for Comprehensive Extradition (2026). I have read and understand the terms of this agreement.* Have you, Alastair?'

'I have.'

'And the bit about their right to make any immigrants you help walk the plank didn't put you off? Let's see: *I understand that His Majesty's Government may deny authorization for travel and that due to border protection may not inform me of the reason for denial of Justification authorization. I understand that this is my only and last permitted international travel for which ticket authorization is free of charge. I understand that any future international travel must be at personal expense, and bought through the Department for International Travel Exchange and that the purchase of any credit bought elsewhere is void and will lead to criminal prosecution…*

'So,' Stov continued, 'your Justification says: *I wanted to know why I have lost a great friend. I'm travelling to Fès el-Bali to visit a former UK citizen, with whom I went to school.* Is this all?'

'There's more.'

Stov swiped the screen. 'Oh.' He swiped again. He read for a minute, two.

He looked up from the reader. He checked it again, shook his head, and said, 'I'm sorry for you.' He didn't read any more. He passed it back and touched my arm, held my shaking shoulders. 'And did you sign your personal guarantee of return?'

I nodded.

'And who was your guarantor? Not Kat.'

'My wife.'

'And what will become of her if you disappear among the bandits here?'

'She'll have to pay.'

'Jesus.' Again Stov delicately touched the stubble of his shining head.

'When you have had some rest at the flat Amal will get you to Tangier.'

'Tangier?'

'Yes,' he said. 'Cece's still there.'

XVI

One of the peculiar consequences of Ravi's broken window incident, and his loss of the use of the fourth finger on his left hand, was the source of his payout. St Julian's had never been rich, in fact, its grounds were only rented (at patrician rates) from a neighbouring college. Ravi's compensation, therefore, was siphoned from other funds. First among the sacrifices was a new opportunities scheme which had always seemed to some elders a watery social mobility effort and to higher college idealists a PR exercise. Aimed at talented students whose parents had had no university education, it was in fact the one that had brought Ravi from a background of greengrocery to a university in the first place.

When at last Faulk had explained that Ali's own place would be rescinded ('For academic reasons, you understand, Ali') his first feeling was happiness. He had comfortably failed all his second-year exams bar one. And so he didn't question Faulk's reasoning.

For the first time in his life Ali had just experienced a year exactly like the last. Little did he appreciate how this novelty would become normality, because at first it seemed so exotic. Every one of the previous twenty-one years had segued into the next: nursery had become primary school; Year Ten had become Year Eleven; school had led to university. But this twenty-second year saw no big change compared with the twenty-first – no new expectations, or friends, not even new essays or syllabuses (failing his second-year exams had seen to that). He had earned an insight normally reserved for a later stage: life would now contain static periods, and at some point we stop looking forwards to start looking back. And perhaps it was the principal's odd questions about that particular night, but the more he looked back, the more his memory circled the one time in Plush when they had all met.

('Who planned the evening? Did you feel pressured to go? Did Constance? Who else was with you that night?')

He left university after twenty-three months and six days. The same morning, surrounded once again by packed boxes in his college room, he emailed Stov, telling him what he planned to do. He withdrew all that remained of his student loan before it too was cancelled, bought a camera, shaved his face, deleted his Facebook account and, overdraft be damned, bought a one-way plane ticket. He flew to the Gulf. Indeed, he would go wherever chance sent him, now forever hiding the darkness that held his heart.

Four years later, outside a small town in Mongolia, in an international bar, Ali met a younger man named Anatoliy, a reporter, who offered to guide him to the banks of the new secret gas lines where vast pipes as tall as tower blocks sheltered new wildlife from the snow. They were also garlanded with mysterious memorials to smiling workers.

The photos he took there, and the story Anatoliy wrote, gave them work for another twelve months. As they chased the wars in Eastern Europe, Anatoliy became his close friend.

In the years that passed, they shared leads, tents, hotels and meals. With Anatoliy he found himself gradually able to tell of his experiences. Not one single outpouring – they were never stationary for long enough, nor able to speak above a whisper in many places – but a drip of hopes, fears and questions bled from him between the jobs they took together in this dissolving world. He didn't credit himself for having developed this openness, and instead credited Anatoliy with giving him the necessary perspective. 'We will probably die tomorrow,' Anatoliy would say with the resentment that made him so determined, 'so let's know whose guts we'll be covered in.'

Anatoliy himself would stir his powdered soup and speak of home in a monotone that didn't conceal his anger over its senseless obliteration. He saw no separation between his background and the stories he reported. The conflicts had removed all his discretion, privacy or self-censorship. Whenever Ali became shy or closed, Anatoliy would urge him on with a hearty 'Fuck you, finish the story!' or a 'No, no, rich boy, no time for meditation.' He would complain, a finger pointed at his own chest, 'I'm stuck with you, so you talk.'

Anatoliy and his girlfriend, a medic named Madison, became family. Madison was the optimist to Anatoliy's fatalist, the activist to Ali's pacifist. Of the three she was the radical, not because her politics were the most extreme but because they were the most hopeful. She even believed Ali would eventually attract a girlfriend, despite his insistence that he didn't do relationships.

In quarterly meetings, they would drink rough spirits, sing newly learned national anthems, loudly denounce the propaganda of their homelands, their presidents and television anchors. He and Anatoliy wrote scorn from anonymous accounts and made suicide pacts and laughed at the madness of it all.

Occasionally Ali would message Stov, who himself was never in one place. He wrote of the things he had seen, not with the objectivity of a reporter but with the honest terror of a boyhood friend. When he started to write about the disappearance of Cece, he did so with increasing fervour. And the replies stopped. The past seemed to have closed itself off from him in both geography and time. And so, during these years, he poured himself into his present.

One night in Sofia, when Ali and Anatoliy were celebrating Anatoliy's forty-sixth birthday, just the two of them, he was asked to make a promise.

Anatoliy smiled shyly. 'If someone kills me – and I hope I will be worth assassinating – you and Madison will look after each other. It's a horrible world, and you need help. Both of you.'

Ali raised his glass. 'Say no more. We've already decided to marry each other.'

'Don't take the piss.' Anatoliy's broad hand came down on the table. 'I have your promise. I will be watching.'

'You have it.'

The next day Anatoliy was called out before sunrise on a story. Ali flew to Greece. They never saw each other again.

17

Cece would be seventy-four now, a year younger than me but fifty-six years older than when I knew her. What had she seen? I'd been too self-obsessed to consider it, the life she must have led. I'd only given thought to our time together. As if she'd died when she'd left my sight. But she'd had traumas, joys, relationships, love. She'd have had jobs, discussed having children with partners, buried family, taken thousands of journeys, changed her linen hundreds of times.

She had been raped in a bed inches from my head.

Even now, Stov still had a few faded doubts about me and my involvement. I could feel it.

What did I remember?

The easiest question in the world.

But as I sifted my dreams, the answer eluded me. Asking my brain to rediscover old synapses. To run the hundred metres at seventy-five years old.

An old man, trying to remember something. Worse, trying to remember not knowing something. I could easily recall lying on Simon's floor. The whispering and the perfume. The texture of the carpet at my head. The rushing sounds when I moved.

But the order of events were shuffled by the huge bursts of adrenaline on the night, and the knowledge that lifelong memories were being formed. And yet where were those particular memories?

Round and round Simon's room my mind went. Desperate to slow down, to stop so I could start at a fixed point.

The problem was that my experience was made of what I was looking for. The exquisite tensions, the impossible staggering of my breath whenever Cece spoke or smiled at me. A night that, more than any other, had been happening to me.

I had never considered it might be happening to anybody else.

The screaming of thoughts in my head had drowned out any sounds more real. Dreams had made me blind. I searched and searched and found nothing.

My mind was in crisis. Looking for something it didn't want to find.

Could I truly now, at this age, recall the difference between dreams and reality that night? Drink and sobriety? Fantasy and fact? Had I known what Simon was doing in the bed above? Had I? Why hadn't I heard? Had she tried to wake me? Had I missed a call for help?

I asked this final question a thousand times and found nothing. Heard not a sound, saw not a flash.

I thought then of how Cece had made so many efforts to avoid sleeping alone with him that night, the constant refrain of the sleepover. Cece had been a girl. A child. And ever since, she had not once told me about the trauma which had affected her. Why not?

I hadn't done anything to harm Cece. I hadn't helped Simon in abusing her. I knew this.

Perhaps, though – and here the foundation of my self-defence began to crumble – perhaps I had been culpable of something. Her sexual consent with someone that night had been taken for granted; it had only seemed a matter of whom she chose. There was a piece of her to be taken. A yield to be claimed. My assumption of this had enabled something. Her sexual availability, which I had never doubted, was Simon's alibi. At the time my only regret was that it had not been me who had seized it.

This was the realization that I had in some way let her come to harm. The person who I lived for. The person I had loved.

I had let my need for Simon's friendship, my fear of his charisma, my desperation for his validation, blunt my awareness of his casual predation in that room. Regardless of whether, indeed, I had fallen in love with Cece that night, I had let the primacy of another man's respect prevent me from deterring him. The greatest offence of my life had been made by another, sure of my blessing. What kind of love was that?

Again, I asked what noises I had heard. And though the answer was none, what were my chances of proving this now? Who would trust what I remembered? Had I made these mistakes or had they made me?

I was culpable of having endorsed Simon when his reputation deserved worse. I was culpable of lending him my presence as an introvert, a nerd, a virgin, which made him all the less threatening. In this we thought we both benefited. In this we both enabled the other.

The beats of this logic passed through my brain like a tune, impossible to forget.

All this time sucked into something but facing away from it. Trusting the pull. Trusting the worth of my own obsessions, giving in to them because they had outlasted all the other parts of my life, mistaking longevity for worth. I had now made this error twice. Once at the age of eighteen, after we had met, for three months. And then again at the age of twenty, after she had disappeared for the rest of my life. All for someone who had never asked for these actions to be made in her name. She had never asked anything of me.

The centre of my life, everything I had responded to and formed around, was weakening. The stories we remember and tell – when these stories break, so does the teller.

And now the hardest questions poured in.

How did the living Cece judge me now, if she ever thought of me? Surely I had been filed away, somewhere deep and forgotten. How should I be judged? By my behaviour? Towards her it was petulant, indulgent and selfish, the attitude of a child.

Or did she judge me by my actions? The kindest thing she might say of my actions is that, at the decisive moment, there had been none. I had not been awake. By all I held dear, I hoped she knew that.

I didn't think myself superior to that callow boy, but I thought that boy better than his mistakes. He was a fool and a coward; a narcissist. He was not aware enough of himself to have borne any further malice than that.

Why had I come here at all?

I brought up the Justification on my reader.

I finally understood it. Cece's alternating – between companion and combatant, certainty and loss, humour and gravity, presence and absence – now made sense as symptoms rather than stratagems. Likewise, my own choices now began to connect into a single thread I had never previously seen.

I read the end of my Justification:

I'm old now, the age of my mother when she died. I don't want to die like this.

I have not been stupid – I have known and I have understood – but I have become aware of my inability to grasp the wholeness of things and people.

I haven't much time.

I feel myself disintegrate.

I cannot 'Justify' my travel in a world where we have spent our chances. I have nothing to lose.

If I must, then it is because of this: I need to know something first. I want to know what happened to the woman I loved. I think the man who used to be my best friend will be able to tell me. I want to know them, to love them again. I just want my past to connect to my present. Even if that's not possible, I am trying to recover an experience by which I can connect myself to what I am, to the world which I will soon leave.

Ali Turner

No answer ever failed a question more. I didn't have any worthwhile reason for arriving like this, in the midst of a humanitarian crisis. Crashing back into her life. And I realized I should never have made this journey. It was selfish and moribund. And the feeling of this recognition was a weight falling through me.

But also I wanted to see her more than ever, now that I knew. Now I had the answer – the key – to what I'd never understood. Everything had changed. Finding her meant something now. It was still true that I didn't have a good enough reason to have made the journey, but it was also true that the reason I did had never been clearer.

I could apologize in person, perhaps I could say I understood now. We could acknowledge the errors and the facts of our past. There could be forgiveness of those freshers' arguments. We would put into perspective the loss of a time when such dramas could exist, when their trivialities could seem so significant, their significance so trivial.

If I could see her, just for a minute, there might be hope for us beyond that. I would know immediately.

18

A week later I was in a Tangier town square, a crossroads between the medina, the old museum, the fish market, the port and the boulevard. I had the morning sun on my face, an orange juice in hand. Oranges were somehow less orange than in Fès, and tasted of water. Birds picked over the piles of trash that rose like teeth from the flat building tops. Teenagers with kitchen knives slung loose from their shorts pointed towards me. They shouted the names of football clubs as questions, until I gave them a thumbs up or a thumbs down. Triangulating this with the names of politicians and monarchs, they identified my nationality within a few seconds.

'English! Old King!' they laughed, especially when I shrugged and toasted their declarations.

I paced the edges of the inner town, walking the time away as though against the weight of a treadmill, for three more hours. The only colour not pasted over by the grey dust of exploded breeze blocks seemed to come from the graffiti. The yellow of the soldiers' faces, the pink of their victims' blood, the green of their dollars. Some carried stains, others bullet marks, to prove their accuracy. The teens watched in mute disinterest as I turned around and headed to find Cece.

On a courtyard mosaic I saw her at a plastic table. My hands, my entire body, shook in syncopation. A straw hat described paths of shadow and sun across her face. It was abundantly freckled, far more than before. The same fleck of brown varied itself a hundred times, her forehead and cheeks a thesaurus of one mark. But it was her, all so her. She was looking at a reader – a newer one than mine but marked with sombre scars across its keyboard screen – and with her other hand took a bite of flatbread. And she seemed taller, or I had shrunk.

When she laid her reader on the table, she said, 'I've read your message three or four times.'

'I wrote it more than that.'

'I'm not sure what you're doing here.' We both paused as the acrid rotting of something breezed through the air, I looked round for its source; Cece didn't. 'How far have you come?'

'Not far,' I lied. And then admitted, 'A long way.'

She looked at me quizzically. 'Perhaps Stov was right.'

I looked at her.

'Never mind.' She hovered her bread above a dish of oil and flicked her eyes to me. 'You don't look so well.'

'Thank you. I know.'

'Are you sick?'

'No.'

'You have family?'

'Yes.'

I explained my life in terms that seemed appallingly simple. And as our water turned warm, she asked me about the UK with an air less disconnected than Stov's, presumably because her brothers were still there.

I tried to sum up the mood. 'It's like we're all waiting for something to happen.'

She waited for me to elaborate, and at last said, 'I should mention that I don't have much time today.' She pointed to the doorway to indicate that she would need to leave soon.

'I understand.'

'No, I'm afraid I mean it: I'm on four repatriation tribunals. There are three shipments of ammunition for every shipment of food until something changes. We have no money – which is fine, because most of the kids here have never seen money – but soon I will be here only for my own conscience. And when that happens, I'll know it's time to go back. You know how it is.'

I shook my head.

'You're not here as aid?'

'No.'

'Why then? A credit burned just to see me and that renegade in Fès?'

I couldn't find my words quickly enough.

Cece got up. 'I'm afraid I'm out of time. Can we talk later?'

'I wanted you to know...' I interrupted, my chest throbbing so hard I had to speak louder to hear myself. 'I wanted you to know I know what happened at Simon's. That night.' I tried to fix her eyes again. 'When, when we were kids. Stov just told me. I'm so sorry.'

She sat immediately. Her grey fringe moved in the wind. An empty plastic bottle on the next table caught in the breeze and fell.

I continued, my voice rasping. 'And I wanted you to know I was asleep, and I wish I'd woken up and stopped it. But it wasn't me, Cece, and I didn't know about it. *I. Did. Not. Know.*' The tourists turned around and looked at us.

'I know that,' she said quietly, and put the bottle in her bag.

'Cece, wait, please. You did?'

She nodded.

'When? How come?'

'I always knew.'

'I don't get it.'

'I was ninety-nine per cent sure. I wouldn't have had sex with you otherwise. But without ever asking you, I'd never have that final one per cent.'

'But you never did ask me. How was I meant to convince you? You could even have thought it was me.'

'For a millisecond, I wondered.'

'What did I say?'

'Nothing you said, just – I knew. I knew the boy who did it wasn't you. And there was only one other person it could have been.'

'But. But.' I closed my eyes to focus on the words, I ignored the heat, the smell, the bruising condescension in her face. 'So why didn't you talk to me, trust me? I would have taken your side.'

'How gracious, Ali.' Her voice was cold.

'No, no, I mean, I could have helped.'

'Could you?' She spoke slowly, 'How?'

'Cece, I was asleep.' My pulse had become my whole body. I stayed a trembling hand under the table.

She nodded. 'You were the only one there that night: if you weren't a witness you were complicit and if you weren't complicit you were too oblivious. There was a tiny voice at the back of my mind asking – did he know? Was he awake? And aware? Did he pretend to be asleep? Did Simon silence him? Could anyone have slept soundly while that was going on?'

'So, what – was it all a test? Us? To see if I had let it happen or something?'

'It's actually a bit simpler than that.'

'What?'

'I saw you on the first night at university and felt so excited and relieved that I'd be there in this big scary place with you. I liked you, believe it or not, despite all of that: I liked you. And I was sure.' Her face relaxed. 'Then we happened.'

She rested one hand under another. She was done.

'What's left of the presidential gardens is beautiful. Enjoy your visit, Ali.'

I could feel the rancid breeze tugging at my last strands of hair, clinging together like survivors. Wind is the great separator between youth and age – something you learn as a photographer. Windswept becomes weather-beaten.

'It's a shame it happened, like this,' she said.

You will never know how deeply I remember every second of this, I thought. *How much I interpret your every movement.*

My hand on the table opened and closed involuntarily. Still for a moment, her hands imitated it and moved to her lap. 'Give me a second. So why didn't you tell anyone else about that night?' I asked. 'The police? Me? Your father?'

'I did, eventually, I told the principal,' she answered. 'He and I were having our termly one-on-one meeting. And he mentioned he'd lost a son, and would never want any of his students to feel alone. And for some reason that set me off. I don't know why I chose to tell him of all people. On one hand it felt monumental, but on the other I also believed he was too eccentric and senile to remember. Like I was telling a tree. Even as I told him he had that same faraway look as always. So I didn't expect him to do anything about it, let alone go interrogating you. I look back on it now, and he should have gone to the police. That was his job. I had taken the leap of finally reporting, and he failed miserably. Until recently it used to make me incandescent. But he was just another guy protecting his institution, his interests. Didn't want any fuss, so conducted a half-arsed rogue interrogation.' She paused as we both considered the principal, long dead. 'Look, I do have to go.'

'Cece, I promise I was asleep.'

She sighed. 'And I promise it's what I told myself. And, when I got to know you, it's what I believed to be true.'

'If Stov had stayed that night too – if he had just stayed – maybe he would have woken.'

'Let's not blame other witnesses for failing to exist. Simon would never have dared if it were Stov in that room. What does that say?'

'I get it. But I mean, I don't even know when it happened in the night.'

'You can guess.'

'Tell me. Please?'

'If you must know: do you remember us chatting in the middle of the night? Mucking around with Simon's aftershave bottles? I got under your sleeping bag and we whispered about Simon. And books and school and things.'

'Yes, yes, I do remember that.'

'Do you remember what happened next?'

'No.'

'Sure?'

'I don't remember.'

'OK. I watched you fall asleep,' Cece's steady eyes averred. 'I was so excited to have met this great boy. I couldn't sleep. I lay awake for another hour, eventually poured myself another tequila downstairs, and went back in with Simon.'

'And then?'

'I blacked out. I don't remember anything until I woke up four hours later.'

'It happened then?'

'I'll never know why I had that last drink.' She shook her head. 'I didn't even like alcohol. I was just a girl, just acting up. In the big city, escaping the pressure, the exams. Escaping my family. Playing a version of myself. And while I was passed out, that's when it happened.'

For a minute or so, neither of us spoke. Her fingers drummed on the table as she shook her head in the denial of some internal question. Finally, I asked, 'Why did you go? Why did you disappear?'

Cece put on her sunglasses. 'What do you mean, why? I didn't have good enough reason? Did I need to behave normally?'

I shook my head. 'I don't know.'

'There was an accumulation, Ali. You can't refund me a year of my life, or my twenties. Or the nights it comes back to me, even now, a hundred years later.' She checked her reader. 'Look, I'm leaving now, Ali. This isn't worth missing five minutes of someone's tribunal for, is it?'

I had no idea. 'Why are you on a tribunal?'

'Who are you to ask? I don't have to answer your questions. This is just a holiday for you. I mean, the penny's dropped, we're all taking flights only in the most careful way possible. And here you are, taking up international stalking in your seventies. Do you think that might be the worst fuel ever burned?'

I said nothing.

'Sorry, but it's almost funny, isn't it?' Cece folded a leg over her knee, revealing the little round ankle tattoo of her first rebellion, which hadn't faded at all. An everlasting full stop. She continued. 'You know the coast is a war zone? People still die in the Alboran. The Spanish have gunboats there permanently. Are you not interested in all these other people whose lives we're in?'

'I came here for you. And for me.'

'And yet you don't seem worried about getting caught. The UK will tear up your Justification, you know? If you don't have the right to be here. You'll be marooned. A Crusoe.'

'I know that.'

'What about your family? Do they know you're here? If you abscond or go missing, what happens to them? There are no transports you can trust.'

'I wanted to see you.'

'Look, let's talk tomorrow. Here or the station?' She gathered her scarf over the skin of her face and neck.

'Station.'

As she walked us back to the foyer, she asked, 'Do you still take pictures?'

'No, it's too hard. They cleansed the press pool. The last time I travelled they broke my camera.'

'Accidentally, of course.'

'A very thorough accident.'

'Well, find another one,' she said. 'Take images. Publish them. Besides, they were the only way you ever could emote.' She put on her sunglasses. 'See you tomorrow.'

19

It was night at the airport, and before our bus arrived the gales were already surrounding it. I recognized one couple as the only faces I knew from the journey out. About eighty years old, awake and bright-eyed.

There were a few loners at the airport, like me, but most of the travellers seemed to have gathered into one group or another. *What type is he*, I could see others wondering, *rich, important or dying?* A few younger ones, almost all families, were in the front of the airport. One or two Flybuyers, the wealthiest, their faces conspicuous by their calm, sat alone anywhere they could find enough space to guard their large suitcases. The majority, the older travellers, were spread across our seats. In their fragile excitement they knew the magnitude of their trip, the preciousness of every escaping second. They were lucky like that, we all were, knowing the significance of their journey, knowing absolutely that they would never do the like again.

The pity of so many of life's major events is that we don't recognize them at the time. They are too well camouflaged in the everyday. And only after they have passed can we see those significant things for what they are. But not here. To know this was the last flight we would take was to gain a kind of clarity. And this final journey offered a grandeur to our last age.

Taking a flight worth eight years of rations is to put a value on your own fulfilment. It is to say *I have lived through these times of suffering and decline, I have measured the worth of resources against life, survival against stimulation, and I am worthy of this one, extra pinprick in the firmament. My life is a worthwhile expense of energy; it is not mere existence. We do not intend harm, but we need this. We are sorry.*

I am sorry.

As we waited, I wrote a message to Cece, explaining why I had decided to go home. I apologized for not meeting her at the station, and for having already begun my return journey. She had been so busy, I said, so useful, and my presence benefited no one.

I had bought a very expensive antique camera under the old pier and used up its memory card taking photographs from our bus. The piles of luggage bursting from the clearing house, the funeral pits among the suburban maize fields, and the splashes of colour where the ashes had fertilized the crops, faulty weapons abandoned at the harbour where the gulls and children sit, the sinks of green water that once were bomb craters. I clicked the button until it was finished. My last photos were of the junction between the dried canal rivet and the receding gravel pits of the sea, where many decades earlier the reservoir had decanted its last litre into the ocean. As a man called Anatoliy had once taught me, I then removed the memory card, neatly broke the shutter plane of the camera between my fingers and used a coin to scratch away the serial number printed in the diaphragm of the casing.

With my reader I uploaded and sent the photos to an old colleague of Anatoliy who would be able to tell me how to publish them. I also sent them to Cece, apologized one last time and thanked her. Before folding my reader away I added that I had spent my adult life using her as a focus for regret and unmade choices. *We might have been something more,* I wrote, *and my obsession let everything else pour through my fingers. Yet the fact remains: I loved you then, and even though I don't know you now, I love you still.*

Someone had lit a fire in the base of an old drum. Its colourful logos peeled off and floated into the air like lit cigarette papers. A few people, including policemen, gathered round and warmed their hands. I moved towards it as everyone eventually did, out of the cold, its intensity scalding our faces when the flames lapped in our direction.

Another gleeful passenger had folded their reader into a paper plane. They threw it around the fire from passenger to passenger, daring it to catch the flames.

On way home, I wrote to Kat.

As dawn broke, I sat and watched the taxiing aircraft, the convoys of aid workers and researchers, the security guards stop-searching bags, frisking even the children.

Then I wondered. I could go back and explain to Madison, but I wondered if she needed it. She was still running her campaign, still fighting the Not One More laws and having her office raided every year. She had given up on me, moved on.

And Kat would always be angry with me, not because I had failed as a father, but because I had been too distracted to try. I could have been a parent and a partner. I did in fact have a family in my life, I had simply failed to notice it. This is life, I thought: it goes from having what you want to wanting what you have.

I used to think that my memories and I breathed life into each other. But now I know. I gave the memories my real life, and they sucked the years out of me.

Little did I guess, as a young man, that Cece would be my only experience of romantic love. This glimpse, and the shock of its evaporation, was the love of my life. I hadn't tried to have a real life afterwards; I'd merely skated over existence. I would experience other kinds of love, but not romantic. Why else would I keep these memories so obsessively?

What would have happened if we'd got married straight out of uni? How many kids would we have had? Where would we have lived? Would she still have become a lawyer? Would I have been enough for her? And did she ever think like this?

Meanwhile, I had ignored my real-life luck. Spurning Madison. Above all spurning Kat, who could have been mine; she always knew when I was thinking about her. I had been enough for Kat, but at the time hadn't wanted to be. And now I saw she was everything I'd never have again.

Headwinds picked litter off the runway and dropped it as abruptly. Why was I going home, I wondered. Another journey away from something rather than towards it. That was never the point. Travel, flights, living. And would I be going back into Madison and Kat's lives for their benefit or mine? They were each moving on – Madison had found another man, and Kat – well, Kat was throwing herself as far into the world as she could. Neither wanted me back. My family had been the opportunity of my lifetime, but I had snubbed it.

If those leaked photos of Tangier were traced back to me, it would draw danger to anyone I lived with. I could bring nothing for them but trouble. It occurred to me there were fewer and fewer reasons to stay, but none to return.

I stood and then sat again. Perhaps, like Stov, I would never go home. My mind seemed to be in retreat, deserting my body when it needed instruction. Was I about to do something stupid?

Instead, my body decided for me and simply got up. I didn't belong anywhere, it somehow knew, which was oddly freeing. I left the terminal, and at last my mind caught up. I emailed Stov and asked if I could stay with them. I knew he would say yes. Maybe, just maybe, Cece and I would cross paths again. Perhaps I would actually get to know the person I'd always loved. She was my surpassing hope.

Floating on the unrealness of this act, I went to the car park and looked for a bus.

In an old payphone booth beside the bus stop I called the Department for International Travel and keyed in the codes for cashing in my return flight.

'Thank you, Mr Turner, today's value of your flight will be seven hundred thousand and ninety-seven pounds. This will be transferred to your account at 3 p.m. our time. Can you confirm that you understand this and wish to proceed? You understand this means you cannot come home?'

'OK.'

'Sir, before confirming your refund, the Department for International Travel Exchange will need a Justification for your choice today.'

'Another one?'

'Yes, sir.'

'I didn't know that.'

'Sir, if you do not have a reader to hand, you can simply say your Justification down the line to me now and it will be transcribed onto your record. Would that be easier?'

'What if it's the same as the one I gave you when I took my outgoing flight?'

'We can duplicate your first Justification, sir. Would you like me to do that?'

'No, it's OK. I'll give you a new one now.'

'Very good, Mr Turner.' The woman paused. 'Sir, while your outgoing Justification is simply held on record, I should tell you that all second Justifications are monitored and assessed accordingly.'

'You mean someone will actually judge this one?'

'Yes, that is correct.'

'OK. Why?'

'Sir, this is part of a wider screening process monitoring the motives and activities of non-returning citizens. This screening is designed to ensure you will not be affiliating or involved with any parties hostile to His Majesty's Government of the United Kingdom and Northern Ireland. It will be completed prior to the release of payment for your inbound flight.'

'And how will I know if my Justification is good enough?'

'If there are any issues the payment will be reasonably withheld.'

'So I can't resell my ticket if I fail?'

'You have already agreed to return your ticket. The screening is simply to confirm the approval of your payment.'

'What? What do you mean?'

'Mr Turner?'

'You've taken my ticket but might not pay for it?'

'Those are the conditions, yes, sir.'

'So I could be abandoned here with nothing? Why wasn't I told this before?'

'Sir, this is designed to ensure that non-returning citizens can neither use British funds for purposes hostile to the United Kingdom and Northern Ireland nor return here. We reserve the right not to disclose this process in advance.'

'That's fucking crazy.'

'Sir, would you like to say your Justification down the line now?'

I would have liked to have told her to drown in the sea, but she seemed to have my future in her hands. 'It can still be just personal?'

Her voice softened, briefly characterized by a Yorkshire accent. 'Sounds like you will be fine. If you want to amend at any point, please just say "cut" to go back five seconds, and say "stop" to begin again. But please note –'

'You'll keep the whole thing.'

'That is correct. Are you ready to begin?'

I ran a finger along some Arabic in the scratched Perspex of the booth. Four ragged dogs were sitting outside, intrigued by the leather of my bag. Above us the final contrails of a flight could be seen evaporating – solid parallel lines farthest away and then one soft sinking whisk. 'Yes, let's go,' I said.

For all the boredom, the days and years, most lives are settled in a few decisive moments.

Afterwards, on the bus to Fès, I sent another message to Cece.

> Cece,
>
> *I don't expect you to reply to this, but I thought I should let you know.*
>
> *I planned to return to England, but I've changed my mind. Left the airport and cashed in my flight and I'm instead going back to stay with Stov and Nadia in the town. Not sure what I'll do but I'll find something there. There's a university there, Al Akhawayn, where Stov teaches. It's an elite school, mostly for government children. But it's safe and it's quiet. I'll try to get a job. Until you hear from me again, that's where I'll be.*
>
> *There was very little waiting for me back home. My friends, family are better off without me. Stronger without me. If I belong nowhere, then I prefer to belong nowhere here.*
>
> *I'm 200 miles from you in Tangier. If that ever feels like a short distance, please make it. If your work ends soon, please visit me on the way back to the UK.*
>
> *Yours,*
>
> > *Ali*

I didn't sleep on the bus. Checking my reader every five minutes or so for her reply. I listened to music from the old days, returning a dozen or so times to one particular point of high euphoric fix earned through three minutes of build. I wanted it again and again. I wanted it to be playing when Cece replied. I refreshed my reader. I wrote to Kat and Madison repeatedly, deleting draft after draft. I wasn't coming home. I'd never been home, had I? It was the right thing to do, but impossible to put into words.

The sun was falling into the horizon. This day had already slipped away. There were still days when I supposed I must have made all of this up, that this life could not possibly be the same one I had started. Not simply here, but the whole world seemed so brutal – it would send a person mad to contemplate it for too long. What if a person lives for one hundred and fifty years? How, at this rate, could their imagination sustain the pace of change it encountered? They would desperately cling to the last state they understood and live in denial of anything beyond it. Or the elastic of their mind would simply wither and no single, fixed point of understanding would hold. We would all go mad eventually, and the point of our dementia would get earlier and earlier, relatively speaking. Perhaps that explained me. Perhaps we had all lost the plot somewhere in the middle.

It was easy to forget that there are free, happy, hopeful days. I, we, all needed something, some figure of hope, no matter how illusory, to give meaning to our existence, to justify ourselves. Love is dreaming, after all. This is what I had told the woman at the Department for International Travel.

I refreshed my reader. Perhaps Cece had read my messages. Perhaps she never would.

The spreading desert gilded the bus windows. Hope in the desert is the purest form of hope. Hope for wide, blanketing palms, lemon and orange trees. Hope for signs of life, for oases thick as green marble. I refreshed my reader.

It said, *1 New Message: Cece.*

20

Ali,

Thank you for your note. It is a shame you couldn't meet again after all. While I can't say I fully know your reasons, I believe I understand them.

Ali, I wanted to tell you what happened to me when we were teenagers. I can't count how many times I have planned to tell you all this but failed. The feeling of having the words ready and yet hiding them at the last minute – that feeling became almost normal for me in my late teens. It returned to me today when you cancelled our meeting – just when I was prepared to tell you everything. One moment I was planning what to say, the next I was explaining to myself that I couldn't – saying to myself that this story could still not be shared with the one person I wanted to tell it to.

I'm not sure why you travelled to our little war zone, or what you wanted to hear when you arrived – perhaps you realized when we met at the hostel that you weren't going to get it. In any case, I can't change what I have carried with me this last half-century, not even for the benefit of a weary traveller or an old friend. What follows is the truth. I've told it so few times that it hasn't gathered any elaborations. Neither has it deteriorated as a long-forgotten memory. It is fresh. It has been important to me that, if in no other aspect, this element of the event remains uncompromised.

What you do with this story is your choice. I hope it gives you more clarity to read than it gives me relief to write. But do not think that my telling you this unburdens me in any way; you have not done me a favour by travelling to Tangier as my paratherapist. Whatever your motives, don't think healing me is one. This story cannot be fixed, it can only be told.

I can still remember every detail of that night. I haul it with me everywhere; every seat I buy, it has bought one beside me. It doesn't grow old and die, it won't vanish if someone says the right combination of words, it has no half-life. It sleeps with me, wakes with me, is me. It is in my posture and speech, it is in my choices, my successes and my mistakes. What happened denied me knowledge of myself, my true self, because I was forced to fake something significant for the rest of my life. For the faking to work, there could be no private cell of myself exempt from this act. And the cost was measured in time and effort and integrity and my truest, most private privacy – in other words, my entire self.

I changed my every fibre to survive. To move past it. And, eventually, I did. I've grown up, Ali. Years ago I stopped being totally haunted by this story, by those pathetic teenage boys. I'm a woman in my seventies now. I've been more than that experience for decades.

I don't believe I owe you – someone I hooked up with for a few weeks at university – anything, not my time, not an explanation. It's more than you deserve and more than I need to give. But I will do it for your sake, not mine. Yesterday – can it only have been yesterday? – I accused you of being emotionally disconnected, and I apologize for it. In return I hope you will prove me wrong; here is the story you should hear.

The walls of Simon's bedroom were covered in bumps. I still remember the sensation of being able to see them and then losing them again in the background, and then finding them again and drawing faces between them. I drew an old woman and her dog as I lay there the morning after, unable to move, waiting for you to wake. The old woman smoked a pipe.

What I remember first of all, and most of all, is the touch of my skin where I shouldn't have found it. The skin between my vulva and the inside of my thigh – I could feel it, and I didn't know why. And meanwhile I couldn't feel the skin of my left foot, where had that gone? As I opened my eyes I looked under the covers and saw that my jeans were off and my pants were missing – not lingerie, not underwear, but pants: pants I had worn since I was fifteen, and they were comfortable, covered with little French flags which made me happy every morning I put them on – and their overworn, overwashed cotton should have been the thing preventing contact between my vulva and my leg, or indeed, it occurred to me in that second, between my vulva and anything else. I can still feel the embarrassment of that thought. Where were they? At first the idea of anything untoward didn't even occur to me, I was just bemused. My brain was cloudy and my memory was blank. How had this odd thing happened?

I had gone to sleep drunk, you see. I had had more to drink than I was used to, perhaps than ever before, with the exception of my school friend Sarah's 18th birthday, when we drank flavoured vodkas and accidentally put a fork in the microwave at the end of the night.

But going out with you and Simon wasn't like that. You London boys drank in a different way. There was a 'seize the day' spirit to the way my friends drank, enjoying any opportunity for excitement beyond the clutches of boarding school or countryside boredom, while you city kids drank suspiciously, strategically. You couldn't only hold your booze, you could suppress it. I saw that night for the first time the act of drinking to stay sober – where the effort is the diversion.

So, that night I had failed to abide by my own rules, but I didn't think it would matter. Because I was with two good, smart, proudly alcohol-tolerant guys who would be there if anything happened. In the club we met the other one, Stov, and while you and Simon were counting each other's worth in units, Stov pulled me aside and gave me a word of advice. 'Take the couch,' he said. 'Or at least don't sleep alone with that one.' He motioned to Simon and I wondered what he'd meant. 'Not safe in cabs?' I asked. 'Something like that,' he said.

His words returned to me in the morning. Now the penny dropped, now I calmed myself, whispered to my pulse 'Shhhhh', and '1-2-3-4', and I told myself perhaps the underwear had in some way come off in my sleep. Naked from the waist down, I felt for the thing that was irritating my groin. Running my hands between my legs I encountered, again, strangely, only its absence. Beneath my t-shirt (Simon's, borrowed) I looked at my breasts as if to see handprints of gropes, but again nothing. Sitting up quietly – Simon was still asleep beside me, straddling his half of the duvet like a bronco – I found the pants wrapped around my left foot. With your body, Ali, curled on the floor in front of me and Simon spread out on the bed behind me I found myself considering two options, a pair of hypotheses that couldn't possibly apply to real life, or at least my real life:

a) I had taken off my own pants unconsciously in a man's bed. Or somehow they had come off in the night. I couldn't remember taking them off, or my jeans, but then I couldn't remember anything after my last shot before sleep. How easy is it to unconsciously writhe your way out of a pair of M&S knickers, I wondered, mostly to avoid facing the alternative option, which was:

b) Someone had removed my pants and, as the tender skin on my vulva indicated, sexually assaulted me.

And then all I could think was: this isn't me, this is not me, this is impossible. I'm a sensible girl, I'm not someone who gets molested or raped. I simply failed to countenance the possibility. I thought at once of my father finding out, or knowing every time he looked at me, or even my father not knowing and my having to look him in the eye and lie, and in an instant I refused to accept this hypothesis.

Perhaps someone had only humped my half-naked body. Yet even that couldn't have happened to me, I thought. I considered again my exposed skin, and thought of my legs being shoved out of the way as this humping might have occurred.

If someone had done this to me, then who? There were three possibilities:

i) Simon, the person on the bed beside me, with whom I had, as you knew, had some sexual relations in the past – namely we had given each other 'friendjobs': the kind of adequate, mercenary handjobs that were natural to kids from institutions like boarding school (me), or Roman Catholicism (him). However, it had all stopped some weeks before. I had told him I preferred his friendship, something he took rather well at the time, and our adventure to Plush was just that: friends on a night out. It could most easily and obviously have been Simon, which was exactly why the possibility of ii), you, was worth assessing.

ii) After all, whoever had done this had been extremely bold. They had known the high risk and had the confidence either that they would evade suspicion or that their action would evade discovery altogether. In other words, they were gambling on my never even realizing it had happened, or on my accusations being aimed at someone else. And least suspicious was the boy on the floor, not the boy in the bed.

iii) The third possibility was that it was some combination of Simon and you. Perhaps one did the restraining and the other had the fun, perhaps in turns. The case for this theory, of course, rests on why, otherwise, the other boy wasn't woken by the assault mere inches away.

In any case, there was no way the room did not contain someone who hadn't hurt me.

By now my mind was begging my voice not to cry out. My body felt like it was shrinking, caving. Grabbing my phone from my clothes on the chair, I stole out of the room and closed myself in the bathroom before the first sob left my mouth. I dialled my friend Sarah's number first, but she didn't pick up. So I tried my father's number and then pressed cancel before dialling the police. I pressed cancel, dialled my father again and pressed the call button.

But I pressed cancel again.

I had realized how he would react, what he would do, how angry he would be with everyone involved. How humiliating he would find this and how hard he would fight for my justice to dispel his humiliation. What could I say to explain why I had slept in a room with two strange drunken boys? I did wonder then if I had invited what happened to me, even deserved it. I was more afraid of his reaction than the idea of what had happened. I thought of everything that would follow. Every television court drama I had seen flooded my mind. Every news story about sexual harassment, libel, consent, drugs, age, alcohol, something called statutory rape – all this language entered my brain and I guessed what I would have to endure if I told anyone, especially my father.

I didn't know, or remember, what had happened before I woke, so how would I prove it? How would I prove I hadn't wanted it? What if it went to court and the defendants employed cunning lawyers and trained witnesses? Would they investigate my background, looking for flaws to use against me? My sexual history, my previous relationships? My every use of alcohol or drugs? My part in Sarah's 18th birthday when the broken microwave set off the alarm and the fire brigade was called? My every indiscretion dredged up and reframed to discredit my voice, to show publicly and on the record that the assault had been consensual. And I was a vindictive or confused little girl.

I didn't know all of the procedures at the time – I was 17. But instinctively I knew how girls like me would be treated. They would first probe and test my body, not to corroborate my version as true but to test it for lies. They would slowly penetrate me with cold plastic brushes and speculums to make my body talk. They would paint my groin with orange disinfectant iodine and interrogate my abrasions. My vagina would be an unreliable witness, too close to me to be trusted. I would be picked up by my father from the hospital or police station completely broken and twice violated.

My body would prove nothing for me. And because I couldn't remember, I would again be told it was consensual. My voice would be strangled, my mouth covered for a second time. They would twist me, mute me and do everything to destroy me. I would be besieged by questions. A disorientating mixture of general and specific demands, a deliberately blunt act of surgery designed to expose and damage my image, sanity and reputation. A judgement of my moral worth. Long loaded requests for mundane information designed to expose cracks in my story and add legitimacy to my treatment.

Why had I chosen not to eat? How tall was I? How much had I drunk? And how much water had I drunk? Ah, but in my first statement I said I'd only drunk 2 glasses. Couldn't I remember? Who had I got the bus down to London with? Where was my phone? Had it been deliberately off? When had I last charged it? When had I planned to see Simon? When had I planned to get drunk? Had anyone else touched my drinks? How could I be sure? Who had bought my drinks? Did I usually travel to London to get drunk? Had I vomited? Where had I vomited? Had I ever vomited due to excessive drinking before? Had I ever drunk alcohol at school? Had I ever given my younger brother alcohol? What had been my plans to get home? When had I intended to leave? What had I packed in my bag for the night? Why had I stayed at Simon's? What had I been wearing? Did I normally wear that? What time had I fallen asleep? Had I woken at all during the night? Had I interacted with anyone else during the night? What colour had my underwear been? How many sexual partners had I had? When had I started having sex? How did I define 'sex'? Did I know the legal definition of 'sex'? Did I remember what time I had woken up? Why did I think I couldn't remember the period between going to sleep and waking up? Wasn't there anything I could remember of that time? Wasn't that strange? Shall we let the jury decide?

I would be forced to listen to them characterize me as promiscuous, a slut, a waster. I'd been asking for it – and I would have to bite my tongue as they wove this narrative again and again. A portal returning to that night would be torn into the fabric of my life and I would be dragged into it day after day after day. My family would have to listen to it without being able to reply. They would have to sit in silence as I was caricatured and slandered, and a version of that night would be told in which my stupidity would shame and bewilder them, and my loose morals would potentially ruin the life of a promising young man or men.

All of this occurred to me in a matter of ten or twenty seconds. If you don't believe that a person can envisage so much so quickly then you don't understand the imagination in a state of fear. The imagination in danger is the most rapidly creative force in the world. The sobs began to rise again and I turned on the shower to mask the noise. And then, without thinking about it, I stripped and got in.

I stood under the water and waited for the heat to restore the sensation in the tips of my body. I inspected myself but failed to recognize these things, these arms, these legs, this torso and vulva. My buttocks and my feet. I didn't trust my physical self, I blamed it for not waking me up, for concealing from me the secret of what had happened in the night. It was remote from me, keeping things from me, it had been entered by something in some way that it wouldn't tell me. I didn't know who had touched it, hurt it, or what indeed I was losing forever by washing it.

As I poured more and more of Simon's soap over it, I realized that the only real evidence was draining down the plughole. Perhaps my case would have rested on DNA or something else, now gone. The absence of evidence would become the evidence of absence. And this was the final factor, I decided; it would be impossible to tell anyone now. Worse things than this are concealed for less compelling reasons.

I got out and dried myself. I remember seeing Simon's hair on a comb sitting on the shelf and thinking of the things that had been inside me. The body in the mirror was still mine, even if fingers or dicks had been forced inside it, along with the sticky dirt which accumulates on the skin of everyone who has been inside any club on any night. Possibly granules of salt from the tequila, I thought, or biscuit crumbs. I vomited. I vomited as silently as I could, which – when you absolutely have to – is dead silence. Again I vomited, and when I rose, I swelled with a tearful rage and whispered to the mirror to call the police. But then I thought again how it would go, how I might end up reading about myself in the paper, anonymized, an 'alleged victim'. My moniker would be the doubt that hung over me, my body and my memory. 'Alleged', which always sounds more natural in teenaged, ironic scare quotes, perfect for this trivial spat between promiscuous youngsters. This 'victim' had, it would be claimed, in reality rather liked it, been game for it, and more. I would read it over and over again: that I was a slut who simply hadn't handled my booze. And one day I would have to cry to a different mirror: that's not me, this can't be happening, that's not the sum of me.

Odd as it may sound, I didn't wonder at this point which of the two boys had done it. It made no difference. I would be that drunk girl, while whoever the accused was would be the well-liked, well-set, fresh-faced young man with an awful lot to lose – all because he'd been one of those 'boys will be boys' boys.

I put on my clothes. The elastic of my pants was slightly torn and I fiddled manically trying to repair it before giving up, putting on my jeans and tying my jumper round my waist so that the sleeves covered my groin. The shame began there.

When I went downstairs you and Simon were there, joking about your hangovers – 'So hung. Overhung. Excessively hung', etc. The two of you treated me like I'd been in the kitchen since you'd got up. Simon made me a coffee and did his pull-ups on the kitchen door frame as you two talked.

'You hungover?' you'd asked me.

'Hangovers are a waste of time.' Simon interrupted. 'Bit of exercise, black coffee – sorted.'

'Black coffee dehydrates you, actually,' you replied, and the next line I remember exactly.

Simon said, 'There are two types of men in this world. Men who drink black coffee, and women.'

And then I said: 'You're half right, Simon. There are two types of men. There are men who divide the world into types of men, and men who don't.'

Afterwards we walked to the station together.

You tried to talk to me a couple of times, and I wondered if you knew that under my clothes I was marked, my groin red and unfamiliar, foreign. I barely said a word, for fear my mouth would open and the agony would pour out of me. All I knew was that I was afraid, that part of the fear was not knowing who I was scared of, and that I had to get away. I wanted to see Cedric and hold him. I felt like I could barely stand up, but it was OK – because my brother would be there to hug me soon.

On the train I watched the blackened walls of the tunnels. It occurred to me how difficult it would be with Cedric – if I told him and if I didn't. How, if I told him, I would immediately want to ease his distress, to show that I was OK, not broken, no one had died. I didn't want to put him in a position where he felt obliged to stand up to another man and find himself a coward. He'd had enough of that in life with my father. I didn't want my trauma to become his humiliation. A humiliation different from how my father's would be – humiliation based not on pride but tenderness, yet equally damaging. I would have to smile for him, protect him, tell him I was still there for him.

But if I didn't tell him, then that meant telling no one. I would never tell Howie or Sarah. It meant having no one to walk beside me in a crowd, or watch me as I fell asleep, or guard me in my dreams. No one would be there to reassure me when I felt ashamed of my anxiety, or paranoid, furious, self-doubting, bitter and hurt. Before that night I had known myself to be a strong individual, yet suddenly the idea of being alone at home or in a bar made my head spin.

And this was the reality I went home to. I tried to bury it and focus on my life, things that made me happy and so on. But it wouldn't let me. It lived like a worm in my stomach, feeding invisibly off me. I was alone even – and especially – in the company of others. Neither food nor sleep nor conversation seemed relevant. I turned off my phone and computer and didn't touch them for weeks. I slept in front of the television, using it as a night light to fend off nightmares in which I was drugged, or had my arms pinned to the floor by the elbows. On weekends I would become nocturnal to avoid sleeping in the night. I spoke to no one unless spoken to, attended my classes and went to the library, where no one was there to hear me swearing until I went hoarse in the Girls'. I found the best waterproof mascaras on the market, the surest ways of concealing my nightly weeping – by chilling face cream in the fridge, or laying used teabags over my eyelids to reduce the puffed pillows they had become. My work began to slip, I would skip class to be alone in the empty changing rooms. My grades began to suffer. Some days I couldn't shower, some days I couldn't stop. I changed schools. Fortunately I was still smart enough to pass my exams, but soon I was no longer destined for a top college, only a fairly good one. I would have gone travelling instead, if I had felt this was something that could be run away from.

When Howie asked what was wrong, I would say 'boy trouble'; when Ced asked I said 'revision stress' or 'hormones'. I once even lied that I had irritable bowel syndrome to explain my actions. I thought the darkest, most destructive thoughts. Death is wasted on the dead, I thought. At night I would take my French flag pants from their hiding place beneath the bottom of my chest of drawers and inspect the little strands of broken elastic in the waistband – the only surviving evidence of the event – to remind myself of my own sanity.

I became so angered by this, like it was a disease – a disease of lying every day. It was tripping me and trapping me in almost every scenario. My finest qualities – humour, kindness, forthrightness, self-belief – were robbed from me. My quick wit became skewed and fragile. Whatever someone had done to me had left me insular, jaded, insecure and unpredictable even to myself. I had been imprisoned in my own mind. For his, or their, few minutes of fumbled, chaffed delights – my jailer or jailers had thrown away the key.

And mostly because I didn't know who it was who had done this to me, but also partly because I was afraid it would have been you getting accused, I kept my secret. I liked you. I had real affection for you, Ali. Which, for someone who failed to defend me while his friend held me down and violated me, was a big deal.

Slowly, and no one will ever know how slowly, I learned to live and function again. I didn't heal, mind you, I merely reconstructed my behaviour from salvaged parts of my old self. I resembled the old me – that was the idea – but these were simply running repairs. Despite the trauma I carried with me, I was too smart to fail at school and so, in a new school, with some intense weeks of revision – a haven from darker thoughts – I easily qualified for a college like St Julian's. Not that I applied somewhere so unremarkable; I was pooled. There I planned to socialize again. I had left school with almost no friends, and siblings who hardly knew me. It was a fresh start. Life began to resemble life.

I'd had no idea you would be there. And when I spent a little time with you it felt right, against my every waking instinct. You were closer to what I was than any other person at that campus – an orphan of your own confidence. An outsider. I slept with you immediately, partly because of this and partly because it was what I wanted. But then as those weeks passed, a doubt occurred. And though I knew the answer, I found myself over the next month occasionally wondering about your predilections, afraid just for a millisecond that you would show me the sexual character of the man who had popped off my jeans like a beer top and violated me. But you never did. I wasn't a masochist, or caught in a Stockholm cycle of abuse fantasies. I was just determined to know that you were not the boy who had violated my humanity, leaving me reeling from the rupture again and again. I was falling in love with you, Ali, you see. All I wanted was permission from myself to enjoy that.

In the end I believe it was strangeness, not the strangeness that had drawn us together in the first place, but my strangeness as I searched and tested my memories, that drove us apart. It was only then that I truly knew that Simon was the perpetrator, and that we were the victims.

And in the end I wasn't sure I could be with someone who, even if they were not complicit, had been in thrall to someone like Simon. Permitting him. Allowing your weakness to give him power, the power to take something from me. And because of him you lost something too.

I am glad he is dead. I never wanted my victimhood or the identity he gave me. He owes me years of sleep, a million moments of happiness I couldn't enjoy. His one decision meant a thousand seconds of total, terrifying isolation per day for me.

He made me learn the hard way that I was more than my anger. I could be tough, virtuous, and sexually strong. But full recovery is impossible, and I'm not fixed now because he has died. No one from that night has not paid to some degree. We have all paid. And what good – and if not good, then wisdom – has come from all our anguish? I wonder, some days, what would have happened had I not gone to London that night. Would another girl have been raped in Simon's bed, beyond the cares of your sleeping eyes? Perhaps. In any case, you boys' power games would have led to the suffering of someone, eventually.

And I know you thought you were different, Ali. I know for you some things were called 'love' and 'beauty'. But let me tell you, from the backwater of the dying world, from the ruins of civilization: there is no beauty in subjugation. I learned this over and over again.

Simon should not have abused me. And you should not have waited so long to ask so few questions. It is too little, and far too late. Years ago Stov used to forward me your emails asking where I was, what had happened to me. But I asked him not to say. It was too painful, too big, to express. And yes, I had told Stov my secret some weeks after the assault, and not you – but only because I remember that he had expected the danger. And he never judged, he just listened. For years he was my only support – and at times I owed him my life.

Ali, I now come to the hardest part of this message. I believe you have stayed in Morocco in the hope we will meet again, perhaps strike up a relationship again, of some sort. The truth, though, is that I write this from the Terminal. I am going home, Ali, back to England. Our work here will never be done, we cannot unbreak what is broken, and we have little capacity to do any further good. The presence of the Europeans here now only sells a false promise – of funds, organization or a plan – to fix what we have excelled in showing the world how to wreck. If I believed I could change lives for the better I would stay in Tangier. My impact these days however is too dubious to justify the interruptions it causes. Whatever the new conditions of life are, I am resigned to allowing people to enjoy them without the pity and meddling of strangers. I will go home and make my protest there. We'll see how long it lasts.

I considered coming to Fès, to see you. You would not deserve it, but that isn't why I won't. We are old enough to know better than to live in the past. We will not see each other again, but

I believe I know now for sure that you never intended me any harm, that you loved me, and in these shrinking days that is the most precious loss of our lives. Too valuable to bet on twice.

Trust, once broken, is impossible to repair, Ali. Like elastic. We would never recover a decades-old connection, such as it was. As close as we have ever been, time will never bring us together.

It's not that I am so desperate to see my siblings. It's not even that I think we're too old for this – I have been practising migration law for ten hours a day for the past thirty years, I have fought governments whose mandates abandon people to die. I am still fighting. I have earned the right to act on impulse. No, it's that I don't want to join you in retreating from all this. Your life is not over, the world hasn't ended. You have a family; we both have made our lives, now we must live those choices. If you don't see them again, then you have many years to do more. Take your pictures again, write down your story and send it to your daughter. And then go and start treating the future like it might exist. Do something – it is vast.

Ali, at least we have been spared the pains of growing old together – the ageing and fears of jobs and money and watching the scales fall from one another's eyes. What we lost in fulfilment, we kept in potential. That is the best I can say.

You are decent and thoughtful. You are lucky, too. To have funds, a reader, a camera, a voice and freedom. Many don't. To have a friend in Stov who cares about you enough to tell you the truth. Use these for good.

If we have failed to make the most of us, this thing which once we called love, then we must make the most of our selves. After years, this is what I achieved. I became more than my rape. But you, you've lived an obsession with a girl who you were too self-absorbed to actually know. You loved an idea of me, whatever that was.

You are the tragedy of this.

Please enjoy the world now, and do something in it that makes me proud. Make me love you. Love is a mortgage, not a gift, so pay it every day. The rest of our lives is a chance given, not a chance taken away. Ask yourself questions again, Ali: What are you reaching for? How much of what you say do you mean? Does the satisfaction of getting life right outweigh the embarrassment of getting it wrong? Don't sell kif, don't simply teach at rich universities. Do something good. Join the living. If you don't do anything then you don't care. Loving is doing.

And remember Galsworthy, remember what they said at that lecture – every entrance is an exit, but every exit is an entrance.

Good luck, Ali. I will think of you.

Constance x

Clove. Someone's food smelled of rich, fruity clove. I looked around, but the smoke was sourceless. Clove, like Cece, had to see the sea to thrive. Always drawn to the coast. It was the fragrance of my hammering, breaking heart. No one had ever told me grief felt so like fear.

Staying still, closing my eyes, I said a prayer. It is atheists who are always the most saved by prayer.

And in this prayer it occurred to me that going back to Stov, even if I would never see Cece again, was still like going home to family.

When it was over, I wrote a letter of my own.

Dear Kat,

When you left me at the train station, your last word was 'Write'. And that's what I've done.

I couldn't write you messages – I didn't know where to start. Messages seemed so broken up, so small. I wanted you to have the whole story.

When I began this, I had planned to give you only one story – the one in the past. I had thought giving a description of who I had been, and what I had done, would make sense alone and bridge the gap between us. I had hoped, when I started this, that it would form a skeleton key for all the things about me which made no sense.

But, darling Kat, it quickly became something else. I couldn't keep it separate, you see. Couldn't separate it from the day. It became a story about things I hadn't done. It became this story, the present, which is now yours.

I was not the leading actor in my own life. A lot of this life is a reaction to someone else's actions. It's not my story, but it's the only one I have. And the one I deserved.

The woman in this, Cece – she asked me to remember and to explain. To understand what I had. This is what I have tried to do here. Please read it, Kat. Please remember it, remind me of it every day when the mind fails, when the will gives in.

I have not been a father to you. But I have loved you.

Dad.

x

21

Kat's gaze followed the line of the hills. A confluence of waters formed a purple bulb at their base where silence gathered around four small islands. She breathed in. Sunlight and the permanent dew made everything magnificent. It was her birthday.

Above her were the altitudes she had just reached. She had flown in an aircraft and it was everything she had imagined. Everything, indeed, that her credit was meant to be. Her mouth was still filled with the taste of winds coming off the steppe plains, and behind them the semi-deserts. Every thing was aware of every other thing. The coniferous woods, the Caspian Sea, the larks overhead. The late-afternoon moon floated on the water.

'No stars out yet,' Jose informed her.

'Not looking for stars,' she replied.

'What are you looking for? Or are you listening to something?'

Kat ignored him.

'I'll see you back at the car then.' He motioned to it.

She turned and looked. 'Of course. It's right there.'

'OK, OK,' he said.

She closed her eyes until he had gone. 'I hate the whole of him,' she whispered as he trundled from the car to urinate in the vegetation.

'Alright, shhh.' Mel giggled through her wine. 'We're tolerant people, remember?'

'That's a different kind of tolerance.'

'Please don't pick a fight with him.' Mel unfolded her reader across the ground, loading up a map and checking it. 'We need him till we've settled.'

Jose had only come along with them because Mel wanted someone who had been abroad before. Not that Jose wasn't useful – his understanding of the tipping system had got them out of at least two near-confrontations and he had stopped Mel from taking photographs of parliament buildings just as a couple of policemen had approached. But he was one of those deeply condescending people who are also somehow deeply stupid. He was patrician without being older, patronizing without being wise. Kat had experienced from the second day onwards one of those complete dislikes of a person that cannot be understood through intellectual analysis.

Kat took a deep breath. 'OK.'

The two women held hands as they watched insects pour down the valley.

Mel said, 'Are you scared?'

'Of what?'

'Everything. This place, no people.'

Kat frowned. 'Not really.'

'Me neither.'

Kat was twenty-one today.

That night they drew the tent from the back of the jeep. They ate their tinned food and, over the campfire, launched the tins into the air like rockets. They listened to Jose play his ukulele and drank the cognac they'd bought by knocking on the door of the little corner *astanovka* to wake the woman sleeping behind her till.

After leaving the townships they had hardly seen a soul for weeks. They camped every night in the burned beauty of the open plains, and met a nomadic tribesman who welcomed them as guests with smiles. In the townships they had been told it was rude to smile in public at someone you didn't know.

Towards the border they encountered lines of women beside the road near the stations, shaking large key rings. They stayed in the apartment of one, and in the morning Jose's wallet was stolen in the square by a man looking for a lost reader, who demanded that Jose show his bag to prove he hadn't mistakenly taken it as his own. The man then grabbed his wallet and disappeared into the local museum, where no one understood Jose's desperate pleas. Jose left on the next flight, he'd had no choice, and soon they missed him guiltily, not simply for his knowledge but for the simplicity of his comments, which seemed to dispel the jeopardy of travel. Jose – and they, by extension – had benefited from his sheer lack of fear, the dissonant ease of his bearing, his stupidity.

Four days later the two women met a Lithuanian named Ana, who travelled with them as far as the lakes. Still and quiet, she was a closed woman, speaking only when spoken to – unless it was on the subject of literature, when she came alive with knowledge of old classics: Flaubert, Proust, Dickens, Henry James, Toni Morrison, Virginia Woolf. At her urging all three women swapped readers for hours at a time and compared their favourites as they drove the crumbled roads. For the next three weeks, books finally began to impact upon Kat as strongly as she had always expected. Akhmatova was the first poet she had ever read of her own volition. Jane Austen became the first author whose works she completed. Suddenly she understood books and became convinced they understood her. Her affinity with them became impossible to separate from the wind-stirred clouds behind the mountains, Mel, the service stations and motorways at daybreak, the sound of the rains on the car bonnet, smoking and trying to find an English speaker on the radio.

Ana left them after three months to make a dash for the Chinese border. She stole a little money, but not everything, leaving a note saying she would send them what she owed later. Mel spent the next day in silence in the passenger seat, occasionally looking down at the necklace she had bought on Ana's advice – a silver fern. They argued over the driving for the rest of the week, even broke their rule of never separating in a new town, as Kat stormed out and wandered the torchlit streets in search of a vintner, wondering whether she liked Mel at all or whether she had only enjoyed her company these last weeks because she had been beside Ana, like the song just after the best one on an album.

Her reader lit up. *1 New Message: Dad.*

Two weeks later Kat was standing alone at the top of a Burabay outcrop. She watched two of the nomad children running around the entrance to their camp. She recalled, as a child, her mother chasing her around Ali's garden. How her mother would slow down and speed up, turn suddenly and chase her in their laps of the endless lawn. She remembered running terribly fast, delighting in it, and remembered their explosions of twisting and giggling, creating their love and declaring it all at once. Running, travelling, moving – climbing trellises, diving into water, kicking through rock pools – is where life is lived, she thought. It is what makes memories.

She thought, as the children tumbled to the ground with resounding shrieks, how memory always rubbed out its workings, so you couldn't see how you had got it. But movement, she came to think, was the creation of memory, some new nexus between time and space. Today Kat felt her sense of self more than ever before. It wasn't about growing up, but about the creation of memories independent from her parents and their home. It was because she had moved, cashed in her credit, *travelled.* The sense of who she was, the identity she was forming, needed to be stimulated by the simple act of moving. The further she went, the faster and more lost she became, the more she remembered. And the more I have to remember, Kat thought, the more I become myself.

Until now she had merely existed, as a toddler does, forever in the present. But abroad she was capable of making sense of life. She turned and left the children prodding at the dirt with sticks, rapt in seriousness. She got in the car and read five pages of her book, *To the Lighthouse*, before turning on the ignition. Old people read history, she thought, and young people read books about how hard it is to be young. Was this why her father never read? Because he was never the right age at the right time? No wonder her mother drank. She opened her window and drove as far as she could without turning the wheel more than forty-five degrees to the left. Maturation, she considered, is the slow process of realizing how unimportant you are.

After about fifty minutes she finally arrived at a junction, and, as she waited obediently before the empty traffic lights, caught sight of something dark in the overgrowth a few metres up on the opposite bank. A heavy, deep body with long legs and almost no tail, the elk's bony antlers rustled in the branches like wind over sand. Spanning two metres, the pink branches of antler bone met a coat of blackish red velvet at the head, lighter beneath the legs where crusts of mud hung in long hairs.

By now it was dusk. Kat carefully got out of the car. The animal's neck moved with massive ease, pausing only to give Kat sidelong gazes as she made reverential steps. Now two spotted calves and a larger mother appeared from the hillside and considered whether to interrupt. They did not approach either the male or the human. Kat wondered at the ages of the younglings, and slowly reached for her reader, but at once all three elks raised their heads high, opened their eyes wide and stiffly rotated their ears, curling back their upper lips and hissing softly. They began to step away.

'Wait.' Kat moved her hands away from her reader, but it was no use. The younger animals gathered behind the male and disappeared with the sound of snapping twigs. The mother held her vigil an extra second or two before galloping into their trail.

Calves grow quickly and lose their spots by summer's end, her reader said afterwards, shrinking in her hand to save battery, making the ones she had just seen under a year old. She read on, learning that most elk are physically declining by age sixteen, and that a twenty-year-old elk is very old. The bulls generally do not live as long as the cows. If summer ever ended, they would be gone from the steppes.

ACKNOWLEDGEMENTS

In one of my favourite Acknowledgements, the author thanks 'everyone I have ever met'. This is tempting, but actually some people deserve very special gratitude.

I'm grateful to Anna Webber, my agent, who believed in the book regardless of its authorship. A figure of publishing inspiration and profound principles, her instincts and guidance mean that this book exists.

I'm grateful to Susie Nicklin, my editor, for taking a gamble on it. Her editing was so constructive, so psychologically immersed I occasionally felt she knew my characters better than me. Her vision has made it feel like a novel meaningfully responding to the world – which is the faith any writer dreams of. Also at Indigo, I'm grateful to Honor Scott for her skilled marshalling of this often overdue author, to Luke Bird for his bold jacket, and to Sarah Terry and Maddie Rogers for their work on the text.

I'm grateful to Laura Bates, who generously and brilliantly advised me on the realities behind some of the book's themes, in particular regarding sexual violence, trauma and reporting of sexual violence. It has been an education, and humbling, to have her feedback.

I'm grateful to Tobi Wilson and Brydie Lee-Kennedy for their respective editorial notes. They are the best of friends and it transpires also excellent book editors. Damn them. To Chris Foxon, whose annotations grew angrier as they got better, and redeemed much of the book's unconscious privilege. Sadly not all.

Whilst I'm technically indebted to every text I have ever read, I owe particular inspiration to writers including Julian Barnes, Emily St John Mandel, Alan Hollinghurst, Jennifer Egan and Michel Faber. No single book occupies my thinking all the time, but equally none of these authors' works ever feel very far away.

I'm particularly indebted to the writings and witness accounts of victims of sexual violence. The work of Chanel Miller and Lucia Osborne-Crowley were both viscerally powerful, astonishingly measured accounts of mental and emotional processing of sexual trauma by victims. I found their remarkably crafted writings eye-opening as a man and instructive as a writer.

In researching the book, I was also able to draw on the horrifying but not wholly surprising 170 testimonies (as there were then) of sexual assault, rape, and systemic and casual sexism within my former school, published by Everyone's Invited. I'm a man who has benefitted from every available privilege in terms of gender, sexuality, race, religion, class and background – and here again I have benefitted from the work and honesty of others.

I'm grateful to my parents, David and Chrissy, who have always encouraged me to write, even when I already was. I'm sorry not to have shown you this work sooner – but your opinions matter to me almost too much, because you have loved and supported me so far beyond deserving. Thank you.

Finally I'm grateful to my wife Charlotte, to whom this book is dedicated. If it's allowed, she deserves both acknowledgement and dedication for having made me write, finish, submit, cut, publish and promote this book against the headwind of my doubts. She has read it, edited it, interrogated it and refined it. Evidence of her ear for storytelling and emotional literacy is on every page. I cannot give her back the hours or repay her energy. But having her faith has meant the world. She is a great editor and a tremendous person. Thank you.

While all of these generous people have helped the book, no amount of advice can fix its many shortcomings, and I am responsible for any insensitivities and errors.

Finally, I would like to thank everyone else I have ever met. If they have read this far, they deserve it.

Transforming a manuscript into the book
you hold in your hands is a group project.

Joseph would like to thank everyone
who helped to publish *Constance*.

The Indigo Press Team

Susie Nicklin
Phoebe Barker
Honor Scott

Jacket Design

Luke Bird

Foreign Rights

The Marsh Agency

Editorial Production

Tetragon
Sarah Terry
Maddie Rogers